Pippin

A Wandering Flame

Laura E. Richards

PIPPIN A WANDERING FLAME

CHAPTER I

PIPPIN SAYS GOOD-BY

THE chaplain seemed to be waiting for someone. He was sitting in his office, as usual at this hour of the morning the little bare office in a corner of Shoreham State Prison, with its worn desk and stool, its chair facing the window (what tales that chair could tell, if it had power of speech!), its piles of reports and pamphlets, its bookshelf within arm's reach of the desk. (Bible, Concordance, Shakespeare, the "Life of John Howard," Pickwick, the "Golden Treasury"; these, thumbed and shabby, jostled the latest works on prison reform and criminology. An expressive bookshelf, as all bookshelves are.)

One would not have picked out Lawrence Hadley for a prison chaplain; if chaplain at all, he surely belonged in the army. Look, bearing, voice—that clear ringing voice we remember so well—all bespoke the soldier; and a soldier he was, not only because of his service in the Philippines—he was in the army till his health broke down—but because he was born one.

As I said, he seemed to be waiting for someone. His eyes were watching the yard, taking note of each figure that came and went, seeing that old Pete was walking lame, that French Bill was drooping and poking his head forward, a bad sign with him; that Mike was whistling, a good sign always; but while his eyes looked, his ears listened; and now, when it seemed that he had been listening a long time, came the familiar knock.

"Ah!" The chaplain's chair, which had been tilted back on two legs for meditation, came down on four for action. "Come in!"

"Pippin, sir!"

"Come in, Pippin! I was looking for you."

A young man entered and closed the door behind him, making no sound. He moved with an extraordinary grace and swiftness, like some wild creature, yet there was no haste or hurry about him. At first glance, the two men were of something the same build, both tall and square shouldered, holding their chins well up and looking straight forward; but there the resemblance ceased. The chaplain was sandy fair, with blue eyes as kindly as they were piercing; the other was all brown: brown, crisp, curling hair, brown skin, brown flashing eyes. The eyes were not flashing now, though; they were as nearly dim as they could be, for Pippin had been saying good-by, and now was come the hardest parting of all.

"Well, here I be, Elder!" he said. "I s'pose it's time I was off."

"Yes!" said Mr. Hadley. "Yes, I suppose it is. Well, Pippin, we're going to miss you here. The place won't be the same without you."

Pippin made as if to speak, but the words did not come.

"I just want you to know," the chaplain went on slowly, "what a help you've been to me this past year, especially the past six months. I don't know—I really do not know—how I shall get on without you, Pippin!"

Pippin cleared his throat and spoke huskily.

"Elder," he said, "say the word and I'll stay! Honest I will. I'd be proud, sir, if I could help you, any way, shape, or manner. I would so!"

The chaplain laughed rather ruefully, and rose from his chair. "That would never do!" he said. "No, no, Pippin, you mustn't think I'm not just as glad to have you go as I am sorry to lose you. You'll be helping outside instead of inside, that's all. We shall not let go of you altogether. How about Sandy Colt, Pippin?" he asked with an abrupt change of voice. "You've been with him a good deal this past month, I've noticed. How about him?"

Pippin considered a moment.

"Sandy," he said, "is all right; or I think so, Elder. I've been round with him, as you say. I kind o' thought mebbe you got him put on bindin' with me?"

The chaplain nodded.

"I kind o' thought it squinted that way. Well, sir, that boy is about ready to go on the straight; leastways he's sick to death of crooks and their games, and that's the first step. I—kind o'—think—" the words came more and more slowly—"it's about time to leave Sandy alone with the money box, Elder."

"What do you mean?" The chaplain looked up sharply; met a glance full of meaning, and smiled. "So you knew, eh?" he said musingly. "I wondered if you did, Pippin."

"Know!" Pippin's eyes were shining now, and he spoke with suppressed energy. "What would you think of it? Lemme tell you, Elder! I've wanted to tell you ever since. I'd ben tryin'—tryin' hard. I'd found the Lord—found Him for keeps, and I knowed it; but yet, along that summer, after—that day, you know, sir—I couldn't seem to keep holt of Him *stiddy*. Now wouldn't that give you a pain, sir? Honest, wasn't it awful? But 'twas so!"

"Not awful in the least, Pippin! Did you ever see a baby learning to walk? He'll tumble down twice for every new step he takes. You were learning to walk, Pippin."

"Well, I got the tumbles all right!" Pippin shook his head. "Here was the Lord helpin' me, helpin' me good, and you too, Elder, and Warden, and Pete: and yet with all that—gorry to 'Liza!—with all that, if the devil didn't get in his licks too, call me pudd'n head! He'd wait till I was dog-tired, mebbe, or some one had spoke ugly to me. 'Huh!' he'd say, 'you're no good; what makes you think you are? You're spoilin' a first-rate crook,' he'd say, 'and you'll never make anything else, 'cause that's where your gifts lie,' he'd say. 'Nobody'll ever trust you, either!' he'd say. 'Sweat all you like, and pray all you're a mind to, and sing your insides out,' he'd say; ''twon't make any difference. A crook you are, and a crook folks'll think you!' he'd say."

"But you knew better!"

"Course I knew better; but there's times when knowin' don't seem to help; and them times he'd get me down, Satan would, and kneel on my chist, and lam into me—Green grass! he *would* lam in!"

Pippin was silent a moment; the chaplain watched him, silent too.

"Come one day," Pippin went on, "he got me bad. I tried singin', but that wouldn't do; I tried prayin', and all I could make out was the Lord was real sorry for me, but I'd got to play this hand alone. When you come round I tried to speak up and answer pleasant and cheerful, but I guess I made a poor fist of it. I see you look me over; then you went off kind o' thinkin', whistlin' that tune—what is it, that tune you give us when you're thinkin' somethin' up, Elder?"

The chaplain laughed outright.

"'Am I a Soldier of the Cross?'" he said. "You know too much, Pippin."

"I know this much!" cried Pippin. "I know you sent for me half an hour later, and I come. Here were you, and there was I, and on the table was a box full of money, and you were counting it over; might have been a hundred dollars."

"Just!" said Mr. Hadley. "My quarter's salary!"

"Looked to be! Well, sir, I don't need to tell you. You began to ask me about my cell, and was I careful about this, that or the other; all of a sudden you pulls up and looks at your watch. 'Hello!' you says. 'Ten o'clock! I've got to go and speak to the Warden about something. Just watch this money till I come back, will you, Pippin?' And off you go full chisel, and leave me—"

Pippin's voice broke, and he brushed his hand across his eyes. The chaplain laid a quiet hand on his shoulder; his own eyes were dim for a moment.

"And you think Sandy is ready for that?" he said quietly.

"I do, sir!" Pippin straightened his shoulders and threw up his chin again. "I know for myself that was the devil's last kick. I've never had no more trouble with him since that day; and I think Sandy's time has come to find there's somebody trusts him and looks to him to be a decent chap from now on. Then there's Tom Kidd—but I'm keepin' you, Elder! Mebbe you was goin' out, sir? Pleasant day like this—"

"I'm keeping you!" The kind hand still on his shoulder, Pippin was gently propelled toward the door. "Time you were starting, Pippin, since you are determined to go in this way, without help or company. I'm coming down with you, and you can tell me about Tom as we go."

Down the stone stairs, talking earnestly as he went, pausing now and then for the unlocking of an iron door which clanged "good-by" as it shut behind him; through the narrow corridors whose brick walls shone with the rubbing of generations of shoulders; through the guard room, pausing here to shake the friendly hands of a dozen turnkeys, clerks, attendants, all wishing him good luck, all bidding him not forget them for they would sure miss him; down the final stairs at last went Pippin, the chaplain still at his shoulder, through the door behind which he had left hope three years ago, to find her again on the other side—out into the air and sunlight, a free man.

Now came the last handclasp—long and firm, saying many things; the last clear glance of love and trust between blue eyes and brown; the last word.

"And remember, my son, that wherever you look for the grace of God, there you will be pretty sure to find it!"

"That's right, Elder!" said Pippin. "Amen! I'll look for it, sure! And I'll never forget all you've done for me. So long, Elder!"

"Good-by, my son! Good-by, Pippin! The Lord be with you!"

The chaplain stood on the steps, watching the lithe, alert figure as it strode along the highway; coming to the corner, it turned, waved a salute and vanished.

The chaplain sighed; he was glad, heartily glad, that Pippin was "out," but he would miss him sadly; everybody would miss him. He had been the sunshine of the place, these six months past. He looked up at the gray walls, the frowning windows, and gave a little shiver; sighed and smiled, squared his shoulders, and went back into the prison.

Pippin, too, as he waved his farewell at the corner, smiled and sighed and squared his shoulders, then he thrust out his jaw in a way the parson knew well.

"Now, bo," said Pippin, "it's up to you! Green grass! I'll miss that man, I sure will. I'll miss him, and the Warden, and them little tads of his, and Pete, and—gee! I'll miss the whole darned show. Now wouldn't that give you a pain? Let's look it over a spell!"

He looked carefully about, and, finding a large stone, flicked the dust from it with a clean pocket handkerchief (which he then inspected anxiously, shaking every speck of dust from it before repocketing it) and, after laying down the bundle he carried, sat down.

"It is up to you, son!" he repeated. "The Lord will see to His end, you needn't worry about that any; you'll find your own enough to heft. The Elder knows a lot!" he added meditatively. "He doesn't give you no easy talk about blessin's an' golden crowns an' that: no, sir! 'You've got to behave,' he says, 'or you'll be back here again. And the way for you to behave is to hold fast to the grace that God has given you and to get hold of what He has given to others.' Yes, sir! Straight talk is what Elder Hadley gives. An' I'm goin' to do them things; just watch me! And to begin with, I'm goin' to do some forgettin', a heap of it. I'm goin' to forget the crib, an' the gang, and the— the *en*tire b'ilin'! Yes, sir! I'll say good-by to 'em." He stopped, and taking off his cap, turned it slowly round and round in his hands. "Say good-by to 'em!" he repeated under his breath.

He stared before him, as one seeing visions at once strange and familiar. A cellar, dark and noisome, under a city street: an old woman in a long blue cloak and a white cap, crouching over a spark of fire: a half-naked child playing on the naked floor: in a corner a man sprawling half-drunk, smoking a clay pipe. The child stumbles over the man's feet, is clutched and held fast in one hand while the other shakes the burning dottle from the pipe on the little bare back.

"To larn ye manners!" growls the man.

The woman rises painfully, totters across the cellar and brings down her staff with astonishing force on the man's head—"She must have been a hundred!" Pippin thinks—bidding him get out for the drunken brute he is. Whack! Whack! The second blow brings the man staggering to his feet and out of the door, protesting thickly, "I was only larnin' him manners! He'll remember that, see if he don't."

The child shrieked when the fire touched him; he is now whimpering piteously. The old woman finds a rag and rubs something cooling on his back, muttering some words—what were they? Pippin racks corners of his memory.

"White—white—patter, was it?" And then, "St. Peter's brother," and—no, it is gone. But he knows the other! He sees her now take the child's two hands in hers, hears her croon the unforgettable words to the unforgettable tune:

There was an old man,And he was mad,And he ran up the steeple.He took offHis great big hat,And waved it over the people!

"I won't forget that!" said Pippin. "No, nor I won't forget the whole of Granny Faa: some parts I'll keep. She was good to me many a time, and give me snuff out of her box. But I'll forget Dod Bashford all right. Just watch me—"

He paused, for the vision came again. A dark night, a dark house, shrubbery gleaming wet about it. A match flickers, carefully sheltered by brawny hands, and shows a small window, as of a pantry, standing partly open. Somebody is bidden with an oath to "boost the kid up!" A boy of ten is seized by other hands and raised to the window. "Get in!" says a rough whisper. "Round to your left and open the first door. If you make a noise, I'll cut your heart out!" For some reason—it is not clear what— the boy is unwilling, hangs back, struggling in air, pushing away from the window-sill toward which he is thrust. "Will you?" growls the rough voice, and the lighted match is held to his leg. Still the child struggles dumbly for a little; at last, with a smothered shriek, he gives up and climbs in at the window.

"Green grass!" mutters Pippin. "I'll forget *that*: watch me!"

He blinked twice or thrice, then straightened himself. "There!" said Pippin. "There ain't no such folks in the world. I don't know as there ever was—except old Granny! I'll keep her in it, 'long of them things she done for me. And anyhow Granny was out of it before we begun to do auto sneakin', country houses, and like that. She was dead by that time. Now, son, you think of all the *good* folks you know. Count 'em over, what say? Take the other taste out of your mouth, see? There's Elder Hadley first and foremost: keep your eyes on him right straight along: he's like—like a window that's open, and no bars to it, and you see the Lord through it, some way. Then there's the Warden, and Mis' Warden—gee! remember that dinner she sent me in one day I pulled her little tad out the water? There was—" Pippin's eyes kindled—"roast beef, mashed potatoes—" he was checking the items off on his fingers—"fried parsnips, pickles, apple pie—green grass! that was a dinner! And she sent it to me by name, and her thanks, Elder Hadley said, all because I see that kid fall into the cistern and hauled him out. Well! and the kid—some kid that!—and he follerin' me round after that, every chanst he got; and the others, too, and nothin' doin' but I must sing to 'em. And then old Pete! gee! Pete'll miss me, and me him. You make brooms 'longside of a guy for a year and you know what each other thinks; and Pete is *all right!*"

He paused once more, seeing things. No distant vision this time, but the familiar scene on which he had just turned his back—forever, he and the Elder hoped. A long vaulted room, bare and bright; forty or fifty men at work making brooms; the clean, sweet smell of the broom corn almost driving out the prison smell—almost!—near the door, under the watchful eye of an official, two men working together, binding and clipping, himself and Pete. Pete was talking, as he had talked that last day they worked together. He knew Pippin was going out, and he, Pete, was in for life. Seemed an awful waste, Pippin thought. Just because his mad got away with him once—Hear Pete telling his story in a husky rumble, cheerfully, as a matter of course, this fourteen years now.

"I was cuttin' and rollin' my tobarker on the palm of my hand, and the old woman come along and give me a slap in the face. I shoved her off with my elbow and went on rollin' my tobarker. She come up again and hit me over the head with a stove lifter. I forgot I had my knife in my hand, and I just hit out and jabbed it into her. I hadn't oughter done it, but yet it oughter *been* done, 'pears like."

"Old Pete! And him, you might say, the Warden's right hand now, after ten years in solitary under the old management. Warden Merrow had him out of that in good shape, now I tell you! Takes care of the cows and pigs, sleeps with 'em, or so handy by he could hear if a shoat had the teethache, or like that. Warden sends him off to buy cows, order in his pocket, proud as a peacock; back in three days and he *is* back, on the dot. I tell ye! That's the way!"

Pippin lifts his chin, squares his shoulders once more. "Look at here!" he says. "If I'm goin' to set here all day belly-achin' over the folks back there, I mought as well *go* back there and stay back! It's bein' on my own, you see, after bein' a bunch of corn in a broom, as you might say. Green grass! I wish't I had some folks of my own!"

A silence followed. Pippin studied the road before him, drawing patterns in the dust with his stick. Mike Hooligan give him that stick: it come from Ireland, and was the pride of Mike's heart; he wouldn't take gold for it. Now wouldn't that—He examined the stick carefully. It was an excellent blackthorn with an anchor carved on the head. Mike had been a sailor, and was "in" for making too free with a marlinspike on a shipmate's head. Finally, holding it up before him, he addressed it as if it were a living creature.

"Well! I ain't got no folks, see? But supposin' I had—what I would say—I'd have 'em dandy, that's what! And—what's to prevent my kind o' keepin' in the back of my head that if I *had* folks, and they *was* dandy—and they would be, for the reason I wouldn't have the other kind—why, I would act accordin' *to*. See? Well, you would! Now lemme tell you about the folks I'd have. Kind o' get 'em set up, see, and then I can carry 'em along, some kind of way, in the back of my head, and they'll do me good and keep out—other things."

Whistling softly, he took off his cap and turned it slowly round and round, considering.

"I'll have me a ma first!" he said. "She'll have a blue dress and a white apron, and—sort o' pink cheeks, and when she speaks, she'll sort o' smile all over her face. 'Sonny,' she'll say, 'sonny, come here and I'll give you a piece of pie!' No! I'm goin' too fast. 'Sonny,' she'll say, 'have you washed your hands? Go wash them good, and *then* come here and I'll give you a piece of pie.' That's the talk. Golly!—think of her carin' whether my hands was clean or not. She would, though; you bet she would! I've seen fellers as had that kind of ma. We'd have real good times together, Ma and me! I'll have me a pa, too. Lemme see what kind I'll have!" Again he paused, considering, his head on one side, his face grave and earnest. "Tall, I guess, and big; big enough to lick me if he wanted to, but he wouldn't want to, and I wouldn't make him want to, neither. Smoke a pipe, and talk kind o' slow. Fought in the Civil War, I expect Pa would have, and no end of stories to tell. When he came in from—from—I expect he'd be a farmer: that's it! that's it! Nice white farmhouse with green blinds and a garding and white ducks and all the rest of it—Green grass! I wish't I was feedin' the ducks this minute!—Well, when Pa came in, he'd set down and smoke his pipe and then's my time. 'Tell me about Shiloh!' I'll say, or Gettysburg, or some place else. And pa'll take me between his knees—I see the Warden take his boy so, and it stays by me yet—and smoke, and talk, and gee! I'll hear the bullets zip and see the flag—old Pa! he'd be a good one, surely! Then—I wouldn't have no grandmother, because there's Granny Faa; no kin to me, but she give me snuff—but—there's brothers and sisters. How about them?"

Pippin whistled "There was an old man" carefully through three times, weighing, sifting, comparing. At last, "My brother ought to be a baby!" he announced. "That's the best way. See? That way I can watch him grow, and see him cut his teeth, and learn him manners—" he frowned, and drew his breath in sharply; then he shook himself and squared his shoulders. "Didn't I tell you I'd forgot that?" he said. "But my sister'd be in between. Call her about four; pretty little gal—pretty little gal—"

Once more the vision! An alley, or narrow court, where clothes are drying. A mite of a girl trying to take the clothes down. She cannot reach high enough; she stamps her little foot and cries. A boy comes and takes them down for her.

"Thank you, boy!" she says prettily.

"Say Pippin!" says the boy.

"Pip-*pin*!" cries the child in a clear, high little voice.

Pippin runs his fingers through his close-curling hair with a puzzled look.

"Now—now—" he said; "when was that? 'Twas after the first things I've forgot, and before the second. Pretty little gal! What was her name now? Polly? No! Dolly? No! Well, anyhow, I guess I'll have my sister like that little gal. Say her name was Dolly—and *that* ain't right somehow, but 'twill do. Now! you understand? Them's the folks I'd have—if I had 'em! See?"

He nodded to the stick, rose from his stone, and stretched his arms with a cheerful gesture; then he took up his bundle, a large bandanna neatly tied (it held a change of linen; the chaplain had offered him a small trunk and a second suit of clothes, but he liked to travel light, and could wash as he went along, he said) and swinging it over his shoulder on the end of his stick, Pippin took the road.

CHAPTER II
PIPPIN MAKES A FRIEND

ELDER HADLEY had tried hard to persuade Pippin to commit himself to some definite plan when his time was up. He wanted to give him letters to this friend or that, who would help him to this or that position.

"Give you a leg up!" said the good man. "Why not? I'll guarantee your conduct, Pippin, and they'll be glad to help you, and give you a good start. It may make all the difference in the world to you."

"No offense, Elder," replied Pippin, "but I'd ruther not. I'd ruther walk on my own feet than other folkses', even yours. Long as I've ben here, I've took all you gave, and thankful; but now it's up to me and the Lord, and we'll go on our own. No offense in the world, and thanking you kindly, sir!"

"But what are you going to do?" asked Mr. Hadley.

"Haven't the first *i*dea!" replied Pippin cheerfully. "But I'll find the right thing, just watch me! You see, Elder, this is the way I look at it. I was fetched up to a trade, and it was the devil's, wasn't it? Well! So I got a wrong start, you see. Now I've got to find the Lord's trade, the one He meant for me to find, and you can't find unless you look. That's the way I see it. I'm going to take the road and find my own trade that I was meant for: I'll know it when I see it, don't you have no fear!"

Pippin fared merrily onward, walking briskly. As he went, he talked aloud, now addressing the stick, which he called his pal, now an imaginary comrade, now the beloved figure of the chaplain. This habit of talking aloud had been formed in his prison days. A wholly social creature, he loved the kindly sound of the human voice, and when there was no other to hear he must listen to his own. He even called up the family that his fancy had fashioned, and pictured them walking the road with him, "Ma" in her blue dress, with her pink cheeks and bright eyes, "Pa" brown and stalwart as himself ("only he'd wear a beard, kind of ancient-like and respectable"), the little girl, even the baby. A fanciful Pippin; but "I like to have things inter*est*in'," he would say, "and they can't be real interestin' unless you have somebody to chin with. See?"

He was deep in an imaginary argument with the chaplain concerning the merits and demerits of Chiney Pottle, who had occupied the next cell to his.

"I don't say he's lively company, Elder, nor I don't say he's han'some. Take a guy like that, color of last week's lemon, and he's got somethin' wrong with his liver, most likely, and Chiney sure has. He has pains something fierce; I hear him groanin' nights. I see a yarn in a book about a bird interferin' with some guy's liver: well, Chiney sounded like that. But what I would say, you start anybody else groanin' or belly-achin', any way, shape, or manner, and Chiney's *all there*! Shuts up on his own, and is orful sorry you—"

"Hi!" said a voice close beside him. Pippin started violently. He had been so absorbed in talk that he had not heard the sound of wheels in the soft dust of the road.

The driver of the wagon pulled up his horse and surveyed him curiously. "Who were you talkin' to?" he asked.

Pippin blushed, but met his questioner's look cheerfully. A thickset, grizzled man with an honest face, now screwed up in a puzzled expression, bent forward over the dasher.

"Who were you talkin' to?" he repeated.

"I was just talkin'!" said Pippin. "I admire to talk, don't you?"

The man looked about, to see if any one else were near: then again at Pippin. "You don't look like a drinkin' man!" he said.

"That's because I ain't!" Pippin smiled.

"Nor yet you don't look loony! Yet there you was, footin' it along, and talkin' nineteen to the dozen. Looks queer, to me!"

"Does it? Now I maintain that it's more natural for a man to talk than to keep still."

The man studied Pippin with shrewd, observant eyes. At last, "Like a lift?" he said.

"Thank'ee!" said Pippin, and in another minute they were jogging along the road.

"Nice day!" said the stranger.

"Dandy! Havin' elegant weather right along. Don't know as ever I see better. As I was sayin'," Pippin turned toward his companion, "talkin' is the way of natur', or so I view it. When a man keeps still—well, it may mean one thing and it may mean another. He may be gettin' religion: I never spoke for three days when the Lord was havin' it out with me: but then again it may mean that he's plannin' to get out, or that he's goin' home. Why, I've known men that never stopped talkin', mornin' till night, fear they'd lose their minds if they did; in solitary, they was."

The man looked at him sharply. "What are you talkin' about?" he asked in a different tone.

Pippin's eyes met his squarely. "When a thing is so," he said, "it's so. I found the grace of God, and there's no lyin' in mine from now on. I've ben doin' time, sir! I'm just out of State Prison."

"Is that so?" The man was silent, his kindly face grave. "What were you in for?" the question came at last.

"Breakin' and enterin'!"

"Whew!" The gray-haired man drew in his breath with a long, slow whistle. Again he studied Pippin's face intently. "You foolin'?" he asked at length.

Pippin shook his head. "Poor kind o' foolin' I'd call that, wouldn't you? I'm tellin' you the truth."

"Whoa up!" the man checked his horse, and looked about him. A lonely road, no house in sight, no sound in the air save the distant barking of an invisible dog. After scanning the landscape, he took a careful survey of his horse, leaning forward to scrutinize every buckle of the harness; at last his eyes came back to Pippin with a very grave look. "I guess we'd better go into this a mite!" he said. "I ain't accustomed to— no, you needn't get down! I don't mean that. I want to understand where I am, that's all. Out on parole, are you, or—"

Pippin stared at him; then broke into a laugh. "Or run away? That what you was thinkin', sir? Why, if I'd run away, would I be tellin'? I guess nix! No parole, neither. I'm out for good; served my turn—and had my lesson!" he added in a different tone.

"Breakin' and enterin', too!" the gray-haired man repeated. "How come you to be breakin' and enterin'? Weren't you sayin' something about religion just now? That don't go along with burglary, young chap!"

"Brought up to it!" Pippin replied briefly. "My trade, from a baby as you may say. I've give it up now, and lookin' for another."

"How long were you there? In prison, I mean!"

"Three years. It'll sound queer to you, sir, but I count them three years the best I've had yet in my life."

Glancing at Pippin, and seeing the bright eagerness of his face, the stern look of the elder man softened. "How's that?" he said, not unkindly. "Git up, Nelson!" he

13

clucked to the horse, which started obediently on a jog trot. Pippin drew a long breath, and threw his head back with a little upward glance. One would have thought he was giving thanks for something. Then he looked at his companion, timidly yet eagerly.

"I don't know as you'd care to hear about it, sir," he said, "but perhaps if you had a boy of your own—"

"I had! I'd like to hear, son!"

Pippin breathed deeply again, and squared his shoulders, settling himself in his seat. "I thank you, sir. I'll make it as short as I can. Well! I hadn't no parents, to know them, and I growed up anyhow, as you might say, kickin' round the streets. Come about ten years old, a man bought my time of the old woman who had a kind of an eye to me—she was no kin, but she was good to me sometimes—and I went with him, and learned sneakin'."

"Sneaking?"

"Sneak-thievin'! Hallways, overcoats, umbrellas, like that! I hated it, but I learned it good. Shopliftin', too, and pocket-pickin'! I could pick your pocket, sir, and you'd never know I'd moved my hands. Your pocket-book is in your inside breast pocket—" the man recoiled involuntarily—"and I'd advise you to change it, for you see, sir, in a crowd, any one in that line that knew his business would slit your coat and pinch it just as easy—Well! So I learned that, and at the same time I was taken on breakin's. I was small up to about twelve, and I did the openin' and gettin' in part. I always hated that. You may not believe me, but I didn't really like any of it much, but it was my trade, and I wanted to do my best; and anyhow—anyhow I had to or I'd been killed."

"What do you mean?"

"Just that! He was that kind of man, the boss who bought my time. I saw him kill a boy—I guess I won't go into that! Well, sir, I grew up big, as you see, and I cut loose from Bashford's gang. I'd learned all he had to teach—all that was worth learnin'—and I was counted a master hand for a young un. Pippin the Kid—I had other names, too, but no need to go into that. I was as proud of 'em as I am ashamed now, and I guess that's enough. He tried to keep me, but I was fed up with him and his kind, so I licked him in good shape and went over to Blankton, 'crost the river. Along about then I got in with some fellers of my own age, who thought breakin' was the only trade in the world. They were keen on it, and they meant to be gentleman burglars, and get rich, and own the earth, or as much of it as they could cover. They'd been readin' a book about a feller named Snaffles; I called him a mean skunk, but they thought he was all creation; well, they were good fellers, and we chummed up together, and pretty soon I got my pride up and wanted to show 'em that I knew all they did ten times over. *I did*! They had growed up in homes, nice clean homes, with mothers—green grass! mothers that took care of 'em, taught 'em to say prayers, kept their clothes mended; wouldn't that give you a pain? If I saw them boys now, wouldn't I put the grace of God into them with a jimmy—not that I carry a jimmy now!" he added hastily. "I wouldn't, not if it was handier than it is, and it's dreadful handy! Now a file's different!"

"Why is it different?" asked his companion, half smiling at his earnest look.

Pippin's hair curled thick and close all over his head, like an elastic cushion. He ran his fingers through it and produced a small file.

"Anybody needs a file, you see!" he explained. "There's your nails, for one thing; a crook has to keep his nails and hands just so, or he'd lose his touch—and yet an honest man takes care of 'em too, or ought so to do! This file is a good friend to me!" He replaced it carefully, the other following his motions with wondering eyes. "But a jimmy, you see, sir," turning an animated face toward his companion, "is a crook's tool, and no one else's. Well! Where was I? Oh, yes, I had joined them fellers. Well, we made up a gang, and we got us a name; the Honey Boys we were. Crooks are real childish, or apt to be; I expect most folks are, one way or another, but there's lots of crooks that ain't all there, or maybe they wouldn't be crooks. Elder Hadley would say—but I haven't come to him yet. So we was the Honey Boys, and we was goin' to steal di'monds and jool'ry, and the kings of the earth wouldn't be in it with us."

"My! My!" said the stranger. "An' you lookin' like an honest feller! I'm real sorry—"

"I *am* an honest feller!" cried Pippin. He leaned forward and laid his hand on the other's knee. "Just look me in the eye! I couldn't pinch the Kimberley di'mond, not if it was stickin' out in your shirt front this minute. There's no pinch in me! Just you wait! Now was the time when the Lord began to take a hand. That is, of course He was playin' the game right along, but you couldn't see the cards; now they was on the table, so to say. He'd give me just so much rope, and that was all I was goin' to have. The first big job we undertook I got pinched and run in. Green grass! how mad I was! You see, it wasn't my fault. One of our gang had a hunch against me—I'd licked him one day when he robbed a kid. Brought home a little gal's bracelet he'd took off her at the movies; wouldn't that make your nose bleed? Well, I made his, I tell you, and he laid it up; kind of Dago he was, with an ugly streak in him. There was four of us on the job—country house job, and him and me was the two to go in while the others kep' watch. So we went through the rooms, did it in good shape too, got quite a lot of swag and didn't wake a soul till just as we was gettin' out the window. He got out first and I give him the bag; just then a door opened into the pantry where we was. He caught me on the sill, give me a shove with all his strength and knocked me back into the room, then he slammed the window and run off. I was too mad to move for a minute, and then before I could get the window open, there was a woman standin' by me—a tall woman she was, in a white gown. She just looked at me and says she, 'Why, it's a boy! Oh, your poor mother!' That took me kind of sudden, because I hadn't no mother, so to say—and I guess she see the way I felt. I believe she would have let me off, but just then her husband came in, and—well, it wasn't to be expected he would look at it any such way. So I was run in, and I got three years."

"In Shoreham?"

"In Shoreham! P'raps you know the place, sir?" Pippin's eyes lightened inquiringly.

The stranger shook his head. "I never was in it, but I've seen some that have been—and more that ought to be. Pretty hard place, I'm told!"

"It used to be!" said Pippin. "They tell tales—and there's things still that don't seem to belong, someway, to the Lord's world. Left-over barber—barberries—no! barbarisms, Elder Hadley calls 'em. That's it, barbarisms! Him and the Old Man— that's the Warden, sir—are doin' of 'em away as fast as they can, but you can't clean a ward with one pail of water. And there's old crooks that wouldn't understand; they—I dono—" Pippin shook his curly head, and was silent, seeing visions. His companion jogged him with his elbow. The story was proving interesting.

"You say you found the Lord there; or the Lord found you! How was that?"

"I found Him!" Pippin laughed joyously. "He didn't find me, and reason good: He never lost me. He knowed where I was all the time. I'll cut it as short as I can. The first year I was no good. I was mad, and I stayed mad: there was nobody I inclined to chum up with. There was some kind o' made up to me, but I didn't take to 'em someway. They was dirty, too. One thing I'll always lay kind to the Honey Boys, they was clean. Brought up clean, you see; learned to wash, and brush their hair, and that; mothers learned 'em. Green grass! and think o' their—Well, anyhow, I took to that like a cat to cream; I've never been dirty since, nor I can't abide dirty folks. I just grouched off by myself, and planned what I'd do when my time was up; nobody thought I was any good, and I wasn't. All I thought of was how to get out, and then get back at Chunky—he was the Dago guy I was tellin' about. I'd study over it all day long. I wouldn't kill him, I thought, just smash his face (good-lookin' guy, great on the girls, an' they on him), or break his back so he'd never walk again, or—*I'm tellin' you this because I am ashamed to tell it*, and because I want you should know what the Lord raised me up out of. I tell you I'd sit there after workin' hours, hunched up in my cheer, never speakin' to a soul, just feelin' him under my hands, feelin' his flesh go soft and his bones crunch—"

Pippin stopped abruptly, flushing scarlet. "Lord, forgive me!" he said simply.

"Amen!—Well?" The gray-haired man was looking expectantly at him. "Go on, young feller! You can't stop there." Pippin gave a gulp and went on.

"The chaplain used to come and see me once or twice a week, and he give me papers to read—nice papers they was, too; I liked 'em—and said I was in a bad way and didn't I repent, and I said no, I didn't, and he'd shake his head and say, 'Hardened! hardened!' kind of sad, and go away. He'd ben there a long time, and it had soaked into him, as you may say. He'd lost his spring, if ever he had any. Well! come one day—I'll never forget that day! bright, sunshiny day it was, just like this—I went to chapel as usual. I liked to go to chapel, 'count of the singin'. I'd rather sing than eat, any day. I never noticed the words, you understand, but I liked the tunes, and I sang out good whenever I got a chance. So I went in with the rest, like a sheep, and sat down, never lookin' up. I'd got a piece of string, and a feller had showed me a new knot, and I sat tyin' it, waitin' for the singin'. I never took no notice of anything else. Then a voice spoke, and I jumped, and looked up. It was a strange voice, and a strange man. Tall and well set up, he was, kind o' sandy hair and beard, and eyes that looked right through you and counted the buttons on the back of your shirt. Yes, and his voice went through you, too; it wasn't loud nor yet sharp, but you couldn't help but listen. '*The Lord is here!*' he said. He let that sink in a minute; then, 'Right here,' he said, 'in this chapel. And what's more, you left Him behind you in your cell. And what's more, you'll find Him there when you go back. *You can't get away from Him!*' I can't tell you all he said, but every word come straight as a rifle bullet. I wasn't the only one that sat up, I tell ye! 'Twas different talk from what we was used to. He spoke about ten minutes, and it didn't seem three; then he stops short and says, 'That's enough. Now let's sing! Hymn !' Well, there was some sung, like me, because they liked it, and there was a few here and there was professors, but half of 'em didn't pay no attention special, just sat there. After the first verse he held up his hand. 'I said *sing!*' says he. 'And when I say sing I mean *sing!* Never mind whether you know how or not; *make a noise!* I ain't goin' to sing alone!'

"Gorry! I can see him now, standin' there with his head up, clappin' two hymn books together to beat the time and singin' away for all he was worth. In two minutes every man in the place was singin', or crowin', or gruntin', or makin' what kind of noise was give him to make. Yes, sir! that was Elder Hadley all over. I let out my voice to the last hole; I expect I bellered like a bull, for he looked at me kind o' quick; then in another minute he looked again, and that time he saw all there was to see. I felt it crinkle down to my toes, so to say. Bimeby, as we were goin' out, after service, he

17

come down and shook hands with us all, every man Jack, and said somethin' pleasant. Come to me, he looks me right through again, and says he, 'Well, boy, what are *you* doin' here?' I choked up, and couldn't say a word. It wasn't so much what he said, mind you, as the way he said it. Why, you was a real person, and he *cared*; you bet he cared! Well, sir, 'twould take the day to tell what that man did for me. He told me that 'twas true, the Lord *was* there. And that—that *He* cared too. It took a long time to get that into my head. I'd been kicked about from one gutter to another; nobody ever had cared—except old Granny Faa; she give me snuff sometimes, when she was sober, and she kep' Bashford off me as much as she could—but still—

"Well! I'll bile it down. Come one day, somethin' started me wrong; I don't know what it was. My head ached, and the mush was burnt, and I didn't give a tinker's damn for anything or anybody. I did what I had to, and then I sat down and just grouched, the way I told you. Crooks is childish, as I said; maybe other folks is too, I dono. Well! So Elder Hadley come along, and he says, 'Hello, Pippin! What's the matter? You look like you'd been frostbit!' he says. I tried to fetch a grin, but it wouldn't come. 'Nothin' doin', Elder!' I says.

"'What's the matter?' he says again, his kind way.

"'Hell's the matter!' I says. I used language, them days; never have since, but I did then.

"He sits down and looks me over careful. 'What's "hell"?' he says.

"'Everything's hell!' I says: and then I biled over, and I guess that mush was burnt all right. He listened quiet, his head kind o' bent down. At last he says, 'How about takin' the Lord into this, and askin' Him to help?'

"'Nothin' doin'!' I says. 'There's no Lord in mine!'

"'*Stop that!*' says he. I looked up; and his eyes was like on fire, but yet they was lovin' too, and—I dono—somethin' in his look made me straighten up and hold up my head. 'None of that talk!' he said. 'That's no talk for God's boy. Now, hark to me! You like me, don't you, Pippin?'

"'You bet I like you, Elder!' I says. 'There's nothin' doin' in your line here, but you bet I like you. You've treated me white, and you're a gentleman besides.'

"'Now,' he says, slow and careful, 'what you like in me is just the little bit of God that's in me. The little bit that's in you finds the little bit that's in me, do you see? And *likes* it, because they belong together. There's another bit in the Warden, and another in Tom Clapp there, though I'll own he doesn't look it (and he didn't); and there's a bit in everybody here and elsewhere. And that's not all! Go you out into that field yonder and sit there for an hour, and you'll find other little bits, see if you don't! And see if they don't fit together.'

"He pointed out of the window to a field a little ways off: I could see the buttercups shinin' in it from where I sat. I stared at him. 'Go along!' says he. 'What do you mean?' I says. 'I mean *go!*' he says. 'I've the Warden's leave for you whenever I see fit, and I see fit now.' I looked at him, and I see 'twas true. I got up kind o' staggerin', like, and he tucked his arm into mine, and he opened the door and we went out. Out! I'd been in there a year, sir. I don't believe you could guess what 'twas like. He marched me over to that field—we clum over the fence, and *that* done me a sight of good—and told me to set down. Then he give me his watch—gold watch and chain, handsome as they make 'em—and said, 'Come back in an hour. Good-by, boy!' and he went off and left me there. Green grass! do you understand? He never turned round even. He left *me*—a crook, a guttersnipe, a jailbird—out there alone in the sunshine, with the buttercups all round me."

Pippin's voice broke. Mr. Bailey produced a voluminous bandanna handkerchief and blew his nose loudly. There was silence for a few moments. Pippin went on.

"Then, after a while, I found the Lord, like the Elder said. He come all round me, like the air; I couldn't get away from Him. A little bird come and tilted on a bush by where I was sittin', and he sang, and there was a bit of the Lord in him, and he said so, over and over, plain, and I heard him. And the sun shined on the buttercups, and they had a bit too, and appeared like they knowed it, and kind o' nodded and was pleased; and the leaves on the trees rustled, and they appeared pleased, too. And like a voice said inside me, 'It all belongs, and you belong too!' and all at once I was down on my knees. 'It's the Lord!' I says. 'I've found Him, and He's the Whole Show!'"

CHAPTER III
PIPPIN FINDS A TRADE, "TEMP'RY"

THERE was a silence when Pippin finished his story. He had no more to say. He sat erect, looking straight before him, with parted lips and shining eyes. Jacob Bailey glanced at him once or twice, and cleared his throat as if to speak, but no words came. Again he looked his horse over, slowly and critically, as if he rather expected to see something out of place.

"That strap's worked a mite loose!" he muttered. "He crabs along so, you can't keep the straps in place."

Finally he blew his nose with much deliberation, and turned toward his companion. "Young man," he said, "I'd like to shake hands with you!" He held out a brown, knotty hand, and Pippin grasped it eagerly. "I believe every word you say, and I thank the Lord for you. I—I'd ought to have trusted you from the beginning, same as your face told me to, but—"

Pippin shook his head emphatically. "I couldn't ask no more than what you've done. I thank you, sir! I thank you much!" he cried. "You've listened real kind and patient, and it sure has done me good, gettin' this off my chest, like; a heap of good! It has so! And how could you tell? I've seen crooks looked like—well, real holy and pious, different from me as a dove from a crow, and they wasn't, but the reverse. Behooved you be careful, is what I say."

"Especially being guardian of the poor!" said Jacob Bailey. "Yes, son, I run the Poor Farm, up to Cyrus. It's as pretty a piece of farm land as there is in the state, and a pleasant place whatever way you take it. Now—you say you are lookin' for a trade? How about farmin'? Ever think of that?"

Pippin pondered. "I never had any experience farmin'," he said, "but I love to see things grow, and I love the smell of the earth, and like that. I should think 'twould be a dandy trade all right."

"Well!" Jacob Bailey's eyes began to shine too. "Now, young feller, I tell you what! I—I take to you, some way of it. I don't take to everybody right away like this; I'm some slow as a rule; but—what I would say is this: I'm kinder short-handed just now at the Farm, and unless you find something you like better, why, you might come and have a try at that."

"You're awful good!" cried Pippin. "Say, you are, Mr. Bailey, no mistake. I feel to thank you, sir. As if you hadn't done me good enough, lettin' me blow off steam, without this!"

"Nuff said about that!" Bailey spoke with the gruffness of a shy man. "You done me good too, so call it square. Well, you think it over, that's all. No hurry! I'm there right along, and so's the Farm; and farmin' is as good, clean, pleasant a trade as a man can find—or so I hold, and I've farmed thirty years."

"I'll bet it is!" Pippin climbed down from the wagon, and the two men shook hands again, looking each other in the face with friendly eyes. "I'll bet it is, and I wouldn't wonder a mite but I might take you up some day, Mr. Bailey. I only want to make sure what it's meant I should do, and if it is farmin' I'd be real pleased, I wouldn't wonder. And anyway, I'll look you up some day, sir. I will, sure."

"So do! So do, son! Good luck to you, Pippin, if that's your name. Git up, Nelson!"

Pippin returned the greetings with enthusiasm, and Jacob Bailey drove off with many a backward wave and glance.

"Real nice man!" said Pippin. "Ain't it great meetin' up with folks like that? Now behooves me hasten just a mite, if I'm goin' to get to Kingdom before sundown! He said 'twas about a mile further. Hello! What's goin' on here?"

Pippin was not to get to Kingdom before sundown. He stopped short. A man was lying beside the road, motionless, his feet in the ditch, his head on a tuft of grass: asleep, it seemed. An elderly man, gray and wizened, his face seamed with wrinkles of greed and cunning. Near him on the dusty grass lay a scissor-grinder's wheel. Pippin bent over him, looked, looked again, then knelt down in the dust.

"It's Nipper Crewe!" he said. "He's—no, he isn't! Hi, there! Crewe! Hold up! What's the matter?"

"Some kind of fit!" said Pippin. "There's no liquor in him. Here, Crewe, wake up!"

He shook the man gently: the lids quivered, opened; the bleared eyes wandered, then fixed, and recognition crept into them.

"Pippin!" he said faintly.

"That's right! It's Pippin, all right. How you feelin', Nipper?"

"What's the matter?"

"Search me!" said Pippin cheerfully. "You appear to have had a fit, or something. You'll come out all right."

"Where is it?"

"Where's what? Your wheel? Right handy by; I expect it dropped when you did, but it looks to be all O.K. Took up grindin', eh? Good trade, is it?"

A cunning look crept into the dim eyes.

"Good enough. Gets you into the house, and then—" his breath failed; he lay back, gasping, in Pippin's arms.

"Now wouldn't that give you a pain?" muttered Pippin. "Nipper," he said aloud, "you're feelin' bad, ain't you? Now here we be on a good road leadin' to a town only a mile off. There's three things to do: I can carry you a little ways at a time till we get to a house; or we can set right here and wait till somebody comes along; or I can lay you so you'll rest easy—as easy as you can—and go and fetch somebody. Now—"

"Don't go!" It was only a whisper, but the groping fingers caught Pippin's sleeve and held it convulsively.

"Go! Not likely, if you feel that way!" Pippin sat down cheerfully. "It's nice to sit down, anyway. Say we put your head on my knee—so! That's easier? Good enough! Why, we've been—not to say pals, Nipper, but we sat side by each for a matter of a year. It's not likely I'd leave you, is it?"

The man shook his head feebly.

"I ain't comin' out!" he whispered. "I'm goin'! I'm used up, Pip!"

"Sho! What a way to talk!" Pippin glanced round him uneasily. "Somebody'll be comin' along in a minute, and we'll get you into the city, into a nice hospital—"

The man shook his head feebly, but vehemently.

"No you don't!" he said. "No more hospital in mine! They had me in one, and I shammed well till they let me out. No more of that for me! I'll die on the road."

No one came; it was a lonely road at best, and at this twilight hour the Kingdom folk were at their suppers. Impossible to leave the man, who was evidently dying! Pippin rolled up his coat and put it under the sufferer's head. Still looking about him with keen anxious glance, he spied a tiny runnel near by, wet in it one of the two new handkerchiefs the Warden's wife had given him, and bathed the gray face which seemed to sharpen as he watched it. He bent lower.

"Crewe! Nipper! Have you got any folks? Can I take any message?"

"No! All gone!"

"Nipper!" Pippin's voice grew eager, his face glowed. "You have got some one! You've got the Lord, and He's got you. You're goin' to Him. Ain't that great? Listen!"

The sick man raised himself suddenly.

"The wheel!" he said. "Take the wheel, Pippin! You was always white—I bought it; I leave it to you—"

He was gone. Pippin laid him down gently, and covered his face with the hankerchief.

"Poor old Nipper!" he said. "But there! He's better so. He hadn't hit it off, as you may say, Nipper hadn't. I never knew much about him, but I knew that much. Give him a new start, some place where there's no rum, and he might do great things. Now what comes next? I expect we've just got to wait here till somebody comes along. I couldn't leave him this way, what say?"

Pippin sat down by the roadside. He made no pretense of regret for the departure of Nipper; seeing that he hadn't hit it off here, what object in his remaining, bein' he was let to go?

"Nipper's ma, now, may have thought he was a nice kid, and no doubt done her best by him, but if she'd had any idea how he was goin' to look an' act when he growed up, why that lady would have been discouraged, she sure would. Hark! there's somebody comin' at last!"

The disposal of poor Nipper's earthly part was a tedious business, but it was accomplished finally. Pippin followed the coffin to its resting place as in duty bound. The authorities questioned him pretty sharply, but finally let him go with an admonition not to go sittin' round the ro'ds, but get to work at something. There had been one doubtful moment by the roadside, when the man who picked them up (he chanced to be a selectman of Kingdom) asked who owned the wheel. Pippin looked at him with puzzled eyes, and fingered his file. Why not? he was saying to himself. He knew scissor-grinding, knew it from A to Z. Why not take hold, now, since it had dropped right into his hand, so to say? Yes, but how did he know—he, Pippin, was on the straight now, forever-and-ever-give-glory-amen, and Nipper was a crook from 'way back. How did he know—but then again, *did* he know? 'Twas all right to stand straight, but no need to straighten so far you fall over backwards! See? Mebbe this was what the Lord had in view, he wouldn't wonder!

"I expect it's mine!" he said.

The man looked him over sharply. "You expect it's yours?" he repeated. "What do you mean by that?"

"It's mine, then!" said Pippin, decidedly, and laid his hand on the wheel. It was a leading, he decided. The man stood irresolute a moment, but Pippin smiled at him, and nodded assurance. "It's all right, boss!" he said. "It's mine right enough, see? And I'll see to it. What we've got to do now is to get this poor old guy buried, what?"

Finally, here was Pippin with a trade ready to his hand.

"Temp'ry!" he assured himself. "I don't feel that the Lord picked out scissor-grindin' for me, but while I'm lookin' about, 'twill keep the pot a-b'ilin', and while I'm grindin', I'll grind good, just watch me!"

Pippin had spent for supper and lodging one of the dollars Elder Hadley had given him, but he had no idea of spending the other. Sharp-set for breakfast, he carried his wheel through the main street of Kingdom, his quick eyes glancing from side to side, and stopped before a door bearing the legend, "Bakery and Lunch." The window beside the door was polished to the last point of brilliance; the loaves, rolls, pies and cakes displayed within were tempting enough. "This for mine!" said Pippin, and stepped in.

"Mornin'!" he said to the crisp, fresh, rosy-cheeked woman behind the counter. "Nice mornin', ain't it?"

"It sure is!" was the reply. "What can I serve you?"

"Well! I was wonderin' if we could do a little business, you an' me. Say I sharpen your knives and you give me a mite of breakfast; how would that suit?"

The woman looked him over carefully. "You a knife-grinder?" she asked.

"*And* scissors! Wheel right outside here. I'll grind while you get the coffee. That's straight, isn't it?"

"'Pears to be! What do you ask for a bread knife?"

"You tell me what you're in the habit of payin', and I'll ask that. I'm new to the trade, and I aim to please. Here, sonny!" as a black-eyed urchin bobbed in from the bakery, his arms full of loaves. "Gimme your jackknife and I'll sharpen it just for luck, so your ma'll see I mean business! Sing you a song, too! Hand it over. My! that's a handsome knife!

"'There was an old man—'"

24

The stroke succeeded. The jackknife brought to murderous sharpness, the mistress of the bakery declared that the others could wait. Soon Pippin was enjoying to the full what he declared a breakfast that a king would cry for: eggs and bacon, coffee and rolls, all excellent of their kind.

"I wonder why they *call* it coffee over there!" he confided to his stick. "'Cause if this is, that ain't, you see! But 'twas good as I deserved! That's the way they look at it, I take it; and I expect they're right. No, ma'am, not another morsel. I'm full as much obliged to you. That sure was a good meal! Now I'm ready to sharpen all the knives and scissors in the county. I'll stand my wheel close to the door where it won't be in folks' way, and then just watch me!"

The baker's wife brought an apronful of knives and scissors, and Pippin set to work, blessing the Old Man, who had put him in the tool shop for six months and made him keep the tools in order while old Grindstone was laid up with rheumatism. Old Grindstone! Pippin wondered what his real name was. "They called him Grindstone, account of a song he used to sing when he was grindin'. He said 'grinstone' where I say 'grindstone,' and I always maintained I had reason, because it grinds; but he thought otherwise, and he'd grind away—wonderful hand he was at it; in for twenty years, and ground all the time except when laid up as he was now and again; arson, though he says he never knew there was any one in the house, and anyway they was got out alive, though some damaged—well—so he'd grind away, the old man would, and all the time he'd sing in a kind of dry, wheezy voice:

"Grin, grinstone, grin!Grin, grinstone, grin!When you're outYou roam about,But it's otherwise when you're in—grin!It's otherwise when you're in! Grin!It's otherwise when you're in!"

Pippin's voice rang out round and full; his wheel turned merrily, the blades flashed in the sun. A little crowd gathered round him, watching the whirling wheel. Looking up, he saw some children among them. Was this quite the song for them? He checked himself and broke out with

"There was an old manAnd he was mad—"

The children clustered nearer.

"Sing another!" said a little flaxen-haired girl in a pink pinafore.

Pippin looked at her approvingly, and reflected that she was the very moral of the "little gal," that little sister he had—or as good as had, almost! He ran over his repertory: most of the prison songs were not what her ma would choose—certainly not! But—there was one the cook's boy used to sing—how did that go?

25

"Dum de rido! dum de rido!I had a little dog, and his name was Fido—"

"What's that?" Something seemed to speak in his heart. "Why not sing one of the Lord's songs? Well, I *am* a duffer! And tryin' to think of some that would do!"

He threw back his head, and let out his voice in a shout that made the listeners start:

"Oh, Mother dear, Jerusalem,When shall I come to thee?When shall my sorrows have an end,Thy joys when shall I see?"

The baker's wife came to the door and stood, wiping her eyes with her apron. The baker, flushed and floury, left his ovens and came to peer over her shoulder, open-mouthed; people appeared in the neighboring windows and doorways, and the crowd on the sidewalk thickened silently. Pippin neither saw nor heard them; his voice poured out in waves of song, longing, rejoicing, triumphant.

"Thy gardens and thy goodly walksContinually are green,Where grow such sweet and pleasant flowersAs nowhere else are seen."

"You bet they do!"

"Right through the streets with silver soundThe living waters flow,And on the banks on either sideThe trees of life do grow."

"There, ma'am, there's your knives and scissors as good as I can do 'em, and I hope it's pretty good, to pay for that good breakfast. I surely do."

"Good land, young man!" cried the baker's wife. "Who learned you to sing like that? Why, you'd sing the heart out of a stone statue!"

Pippin laughed joyously, eyes and teeth flashing together.

"I expect the Lord did, ma'am!" he said. "Anyhow it's His song, and you have to sing it as good as you can, ain't that so? Don't know of a job goin' beggin', do you, ma'am?"

"What kind of job?"

"'Most any kind! I'm lookin' for a trade to work in with my grindin' for a spell. I'm handy, var'ous ways: make brooms, set glass, carpenter or solder, I've done 'em all."

"Ever been in a bakery?"

"Not yet, but I'd admire to, if there was a chance."

Pippin's face kindled, and he looked eagerly from the baker's wife to the baker himself who was considering him gravely. He was a stout, kindly-looking man; his right hand was bandaged, and he wore his arm in a sling.

"I'm in need of an extry hand myself," he said slowly, with a glance at the bandage. "I don't know—" He looked at his wife, who nodded emphatically.

"Step inside a minute, young man! Move on, boys, if you'll be so good! You're cluttering up the whole sidewalk."

The crowd slowly dispersed, one or two neighbors lingering to question the good woman of the shop about the young stranger who sang so wonderfully. Who was he? Where'd he come from? Good-lookin', wasn't he? Their own knives would be none the worse for goin' over—

Inside the neat, fragrant shop, with its tempting display of coffee cakes, brown and varnished, of shapely loaves and rolls, cookies and doughnuts, the baker questioned Pippin. At first the questioning promised to be brief, for when, in response to "Where do you come from?" he heard, "State Prison!" the good man shook his head resolutely.

"I guess that isn't good enough!" he said, not unkindly. "I'm sorry, young feller, for I like your looks, and you sing like a bird; but—my shop has a good name, and—"

"Hold on!" Pippin laid a hand on his arm. "I know how you feel, sir! I'd feel the same in your place; but it would be because I didn't know. I won't hurt your shop, nor you! I'm *straight*! Lemme tell you!"

He told his story briefly, the baker listening with anxious, doubtful looks.

"So you see," he ended, "I couldn't go on the crook again, not if I wanted to, and I don't!"

Still the comfortable-looking baker shook his head. "I've heard pious talk before," he said; "it don't always hold good. I'm afraid—" he rose, as if to close the interview; Pippin rose too. His eyes roved round the pleasant shop, and came back, meeting the baker's squarely. "This is a dandy place!" he said slowly; "and you have the look of a dandy person, if you'll excuse the freedom. I'd like to work for you, and—I'd hate—to think—that you wouldn't help a guy that wanted help and wanted to work for it. I think you make a mistake; but it's your store, and what you say goes."

With a little bow and another regretful look around him, Pippin turned toward the door. A moment, and he would be gone. His hand was on the latch.

"Hold on!" said the baker. "I didn't say positive. I'm not a hard man by nature, only—"

"I bet you ain't!" said Pippin. "That's why I say I think you make a mistake—" He turned back with his smile that seemed to warm and brighten the whole shop. "Try me, Mister! Try me a week, and see for yourself. No satisfaction, no pay, as it says on the medicine bottles. And I couldn't pinch anything off'n you now if I wanted to. I've put you wise, and you'll be on the watch, see?"

The baker laughed in spite of himself. "We'll make it a week, then!" he said. "But not a word to my wife of where you come from. She's timoreous, and she wouldn't sleep a wink all night."

"Now!" said Pippin, "I wouldn't break that good lady's rest, not for all the elegant things in this bakeshop."

CHAPTER IV
PIPPIN GOES TO CYRUS

PIPPIN always looked back on the weeks he spent in Kingdom as one of his good times. Folks were so everlastingly good to him; they couldn't hardly have been better, he thought, not unless they had been your own. Mrs. Baxter, the baker's wife, was like—well, call it an aunt. Yes, she sure was like a good aunt, and equally so was her uncle; as for Buster, the boy—well, that was Pippin's moral of a boy. Buster would grow up a fine man, you see if he didn't. He'd *better*! As to looking for the grace of God like he promised Elder Hadley, why, he didn't have to. It stuck right out of 'em, like—like electric lights!

Pippin lodged with the Baxters and paid his board in work, lighting the fires in the morning, heating the ovens, sweeping out the shop, and doing a "hand's turn" in many directions. Mrs. Baxter declared Providence sent him just at that time, when Father had caught his hand in the oven door and lamed him so; she did not know what upon earth they would have done without Pippin. Indeed he showed himself so handy that after the first week Mr. Baxter offered him a permanent job, declared he would make him the smartest baker in the county. Pippin promised to think it over. He loved the smell of new bread; he loved to handle the dough, and rake out the glowing coals; yes, it was a pleasant trade, it sure was; but yet—but yet—

Other offers came to him. Among the crowd who had gathered to hear him sing that first day were Father O'Brien of St. Bridget's and Elder Stebbins, the Methodist Minister. Both were music-lovers. Both made it in their way to drop in at the bakery in the course of the next few days, and invite the young scissor-grinder to sing in their choir while he sojourned in their midst. Was he a Catholic? Father O'Brien asked. No? More was the pity, but let him come and sing in the church, and 'twould be good for him and the rest besides. Pippin assented joyfully. He would be real pleased to come, and sing the best he knew how. Then came Elder Stebbins, ostensibly to buy a coffee cake for supper. Was his young friend a Christian? "You bet!" replied Pippin, wrapping up the cake with deft fingers. "I'd have to be, wouldn't I? Unless that the Lord had seen fit to have me a Chinee, or like that, and I'm just as glad He didn't!"

Mr. Stebbins hoped his young friend was also a Methodist; but Pippin shook his head; he guessed not. They were all good, he guessed; he presumed he belonged to every church there was, in a general way, you know. Mr. Stebbins looked grave, and said that was not a very safe doctrine. He hoped his young friend would join their service of song on Sunday evening; it might be helpful to him, and would assuredly minister to the enjoyment of others. Pippin assented joyfully, after ascertaining that service would be over in time for him to set his sponge to rise.

So on Sunday, and other happy Sundays, he went to St. Bridget's in the morning, and sang stately old Latin hymns and chants; inhaled incense (which he thought real tasty, but yet nothing to what the Lord could do with a field of white clover), kneeled reverently with the rest, listened respectfully to Father O'Brien's excellent little sermon, and liked it all. And the evening found him behind the green moreen half-curtains in the Methodist meetinghouse, pouring out his soul in gospel hymns and assuring his hearers that they would meet beside the river, the beautiful, the beautiful river, in such tones and with such feeling that every woman in meeting wept, and there was a mighty blowing up of nasal trumpets among the men. Elder Stebbins' discourse was rather long-winded and rambling, but when Pippin lost the thread, he would take refuge in a psalm, or recall one of Elder Hadley's brief, pistol-shot addresses, or think how the buttercups shone in the field that day he found the Lord. And here, too, he loved it all, every bit, and came home in a glow of happiness and fervor that was enough to make the dough rise at the sight of him.

The baker was puzzled at first by his new assistant; as the good man himself expressed it, he didn't get on to Pippin's curves. There were things that jarred—for a time—on his sensibilities; as thus. They were together in the shop one evening, and a customer came in for his evening loaf; the shoemaker it was, Jere Cargo, a man of dry, critical humor. He commented on the loaf; it was a shade deeper brown than usual.

"One minute more, young man, and that loaf would have been burnt, that's what!"

Pippin scanned the loaf carefully. "Is that so?" he said. "Now! Why, I was pleased with this batch, I thought the Lord give me an elegant bake on it: that's what I *thought*! But if folks likes 'em pale, why, pale it is!"

The shoemaker stared; Mr. Baxter coughed apologetically as he accompanied him to the door, and—on a summoning jerk of the head—followed him outside.

"What have you got there?" asked the shoemaker. "A preacher? Where'd you get him?"

"No, he isn't a preacher, though I dare say he might have been, if he'd had education. He's just pious, that's all. It's his way of talking."

His tone was conciliatory, but the shoemaker sniffed.

"'Just pious!'" he repeated. "Look out for 'em, I say, when they're just pious. They'll bear watching. Where'd you say he come from?"

"He's traveling!" Mr. Baxter knew his customer, and had no idea of telling him whence Pippin came. "He's a scissor-grinder by trade, and a master hand at it. I hurt my hand last week, and he come along just in the nick of time and has been helping me since. Real good help he is, too."

"Humph!" said Jere Cargo, shrugging his dry shoulders. "You look out for him, that's all I say. Sharp-looking chap, I call that; he'll bear watching."

Returning to the shop, Mr. Baxter coughed again, this time with his eye on Pippin, who was arranging a tray of creamcakes with a lover's ardor.

"Ain't them handsome?" he cried. "I ask you, Boss, ain't them handsome? And dandy to eat—green grass! Mis' Baxter give me one. *They* drop fatness all right, no two ways about that!"

Here Pippin broke into song, proclaiming joyously that he was a pilgrim, he was a stranger, he could tarry, he could tarry but a night.

"Do not detain me,For I am going—"

"Ahem!" said Mr. Baxter, "I was thinking, Pippin—"

Pippin came to attention instantly. "Yes, sir! You was thinkin'—"

"I was wondering—" the baker spoke slowly, in a tone half admonitory, half conciliatory, and wholly embarrassed—"whether maybe you—just in a manner, you understand, just in a manner—was in the habit of making a mite too free with—with your Maker, so to speak."

Pippin's eye grew very round. "Meanin'—with the Lord?" he said.

"Yes! with—with—as you say, with the Lord!" Mr. Baxter was a godly man, but his Deity lived in the meetinghouse and was rarely to be mentioned except within its four walls. "For example," he went on, "I was wondering whether it was exactly a good plan to bring the—the Almighty—into the bakeshop."

"Gorry!" said Pippin. "I'd hate to leave Him out of it!" His eyes, still round and astonished, traveled slowly about the pleasant place. Three sides of it were filled with glass counters displaying a wealth of pies, pumpkin, apple, mince and custard, with cakes of every variety, from the wedding cake which was Mr. Baxter's special pride, to his wife's creamcakes, eagerly sought by the neighborhood for ten miles round. Behind the counter, on neat shelves, were stacked the loaves of bread, white and brown, the crisp rolls and melting muffins. The shop looked as good as it smelled; "ther nys namoore to seye!"

31

"I'd hate to leave Him out of it!" repeated Pippin. "Dandy place like this! Don't know as I get you this time, Boss!" He turned bewildered brown eyes on Mr. Baxter, who coughed again and reddened slightly.

"What I meant—" the baker ran his eye along a pile of loaves, and straightened one that had slipped out of place—"isn't it making rather free with—ahem! what say?"

"Oh!" Pippin's face lightened. "I get you! Now I get you, sir! Lemme tell you! Lemme tell you just the way it is." Fairly stammering in his eagerness, Pippin leaned across the counter, his eyes shining. "You see, sir, I was raised a crook!"

"Hush!" Mr. Baxter looked over his shoulder. "No need to speak out loud, Pippin. Just as well to keep that between ourselves, you know."

"I was raised," Pippin repeated in a lower tone, "a crook, and I heard—and used—crooks' language. Nor it isn't only crooks!" he cried, smiting the counter. "Where I was raised, 'most everybody had the name of God on their tongues every hour in the day, but not in the way of praisin' Him; no, sir! There's plenty folks—good folks, too—they can't name hardly anything, whatever be it, without 'God damn' before it. You know that, Mr. Baxter. You know what street talk is, sir." The baker nodded gravely. "Well, then! That's what I was raised to, and it run off my tongue like water, till—till I come to know Elder Hadley. I'm tol'able noticin', sir; I expect crooks is, when they're all there; you have to be, to get on. I noticed right off the way he spoke, clean and short and pleasant, no damnin' nor cussin'; and I liked it, same as I liked clean folks and despised dirty ones. That was all there was to it at first. But yet I couldn't stop all of a sudden; it took time, same as anything does, to learn it. Then— come to find the Lord, like I told you, sir, why—I dunno how to put it. I'd ben askin' Him all my life to damn everything, this, that, and the other, folks, and—everything, I say; I didn't mean it, 'twas just a fool way of speakin', but what I thought was, supposin' I was to ask Him to help right along, 'stead of damn, and *make* it mean something! What say? You get my idea, Mr. Baxter, sir?"

Mr. Baxter nodded again. "I get it, Pippin. I won't say anything more."

"But yet—but yet—" Pippin was stammering again, and halfway across the counter in his passion of eagerness. "I get you, too, Boss! I do, sure thing. You mean it brings some folks up short, like that gen'leman that stepped in just now? He's no use for me, I see that right off; I wondered why, and now 'tis clear as print. I'd oughter sized him up better. Take that kind of man, and he may be good as they make 'em, prob'ly is; but yet—well—you say the Lord's name *excep'* in the way of cussin'—I don't mean that he's that kind himself—but—*it's like he stubbed his toe on the Lord's ladder, see?*"

"You've got it! you've got it!" the baker was nodding eagerly in his turn. He laughed and rubbed his hands. "Stubbed his toe on—on the Lord's ladder! I—I expect I stub mine a mite, too, Pippin, but I won't say another word."

"'Cause we're awful glad the ladder's there, ain't we, sir?" Pippin's voice was wistful enough now.

"Ahem! Yes! yes!" The baker took out a clean red handkerchief and rubbed an imaginary spot on the shining glass. "That's all right, Pippin. Do what comes natural to you; only—what *are* you doing now?"

There was a little stove in the shop, behind the middle counter, used for "hotting up" coffee or the like when people were in a hurry. Pippin, after a glance at the clock, had taken some pennies out of the till, and was laying them carefully on the top of the stove, which glowed red hot.

"What are you doing?" repeated the baker. Pippin grinned.

"Tryin' an experiment!" he said. "There was a quarter missin' yesterday, Boss, you rec'lect, and ten cents the day before, and so along back."

"Yes!" Mr. Baxter looked serious. "I'm afraid, Pippin—"

"Don't be afraid, sir! Just watch me!" Pippin tested the pennies carefully and taking them up one by one on the blade of his jackknife, deposited them on the counter. "I've noticed along about this time every night—there they come! Don't say a word, only watch!"

He retired behind the counter as the door opened and two children came in, a boy and a girl. They were poorly dressed, and there was something furtive and slinking about their looks and manner, but they came forward readily, and the girl asked for a five-cent loaf of white bread, putting at the same moment five pennies on the counter, close beside those which already lay there. As Pippin was tying up the bread, the girl began to ask questions. How much was them cookies? Were they molasses or sugar? What was the price of the custard pie, and when was it baked?

"Baked this mornin'!" Pippin replied cheerfully. "Cost you a quarter, and worth a dollar. What—"

A piercing howl interrupted him. The tinkle of metal was heard, and the boy sprang back from the counter and danced about the shop, crying and spluttering, his fingers in his mouth. Pippin vaulted the counter in an instant.

"What's the matter, Bo?" he asked kindly. "Hurt your finger? Lemme see!" The boy clenched his fist, but Pippin forced the fingers open, not ungently. "Why, you've burnt 'em!" he announced. "My! my! that *must* hurt! How in the name—why, you must have made a mistake and took up some of Mr. Baxter's pennies. Yes, sir, that's what you done. Didn't you know that bakeshop pennies was hot? They be, sure thing! There goes Sissy!" as the girl, seizing her loaf, slipped noiselessly out of the door. "Now you foller her, Bo, and go home and tell your ma what I say. *Bakeshop pennies is hot!* Think you'll remember that? Here's something to help your mem'ry!"

Leading the boy to the door, he gave him a carefully modulated kick, and with a friendly, "So long, Bo!" returned to the shop.

"I've had my eye on them kids for two three days!" he explained. "Smart kids! If I met 'em in the city, I should say they was in trainin'. I'll set Father O'Brien on 'em; they go to his gospel shop. I see 'em there."

"I never should have thought it!" said the baker, and he shook his head sadly. "Those little kids! Why, the boy doesn't look to be more than eight years old, and the girl only a year or so older."

"That's the time to start 'em!" Pippin spoke with emphasis. "If you're aimin' to make a first-rate crook, you've got to start in early with him. But Father O'Brien'll see to 'em; he's smart as a jimmy, Father O'Brien is."

"We won't tell the wife!" said Mr. Baxter. "She is nervous, and 'twould ha'nt her, and keep her awake nights. One comfort, they're not Kingdom born, those kids. They belong to them French folks over by the dump, down Devildom way."

Weekday mornings Pippin spent mostly in the bakery, working, singing, whistling, all with a hearty will. After dinner he would take his wheel and go his way through the pretty shady streets of the country town, or out along the green roads that led from it in various directions. When he came to a promising looking corner with houses set within comfortable reach of one another, he would stop, and leaning on his wheel, would put up his shingle, as he called it: in other words, sing his grinding song. He had made it up, bit by bit, as the wheel turned, humming, under his hands. Here it is: but you should hear Pippin sing it!

Knives and scissors to grind, oh!Have 'em done to your mind, oh!Large and small,Damaged and all,Don't leave any behind, oh!

Knives and scissors to grind, oh!Every specie and kind, oh!Bring 'em to me,*And* you will seeSatisfaction you'll find, oh!

"Yes, sir, made it my own self!" he replied to Elder Stebbins' questions on the song. "I don't know how I done it. I expect it was a kind of miracle. I sang the first line through two three times, and lo ye! the next one turned right up matchin' of it. Now that isn't nature, you know, but yet it's *right*, and it fits straight in. When a thing comes like that, I call it a miracle. What say?"

"Very interesting, my young friend! Do you—a—might it perhaps be better to substitute 'species' for 'specie'? The latter means, as you doubtless are aware, current coin; and—"

"Great!" said Pippin. "Current coin is what I'm after every time, so I get it honest. Specie'll do for me, Elder!"

Before he had sung the song through once, doors and windows would be opening, housewives peering out, children running to gather round the magic wheel, listening open-mouthed to the singer. It was all play to Pippin; wonderful, beautiful play.

"I tell you," he would say, "I tell you, seems though just to breathe was enough to keep gay on. Over there to Shoreham—I dunno—I expect the air got discouraged, some way of it. They'd open the windows, but the outside air was shy of comin' in— like the rest of us! But out here in the open—and things lookin' like this—green grass! I'm happy, and don't you forget it!"

Sometimes he got a lift on his way. Solitary drivers, plodding along the road, and seeing the trim, alert figure ahead stepping out briskly with its wheel, were apt to overhaul it, and after a glance at Pippin's face would most likely ask, "Goin' along a piece? Like a lift?" and Pippin, with joyous thanks, would climb eagerly in, all ready to begin a new chapter of human intercourse.

Once, so clambering, he found himself beside a tall man, brown-eyed and brown-haired, who drove a brown horse. Pippin's eyes were brown, too, but they danced and sparkled like running water; the stranger's eyes were like a quiet pool under shady trees, yet there was light in them, too.

"Goin' far?" he asked. His voice was grave, and he spoke slowly.

"Four Corners was what I'd aimed at," said Pippin, "but if you ain't goin' that way—?"

"Goin' right past it, on my reg'lar route! I do business there to the store. I see you carry your trade with you, same as I do!" He jerked his head backward toward a neat arrangement of drawers and tiny cupboards which half filled his roomy wagon. "Nice trade, I expect?"

Pippin laughed his joyous laugh. "Real nice, only it isn't mine, not for keeps, I would say. 'Twas a—well, you might call it a legacy, and you wouldn't be far wrong. It come right to my hand when I was lookin' for a job, and I took it up then and there. Yes, sir, 'tis a good trade, and a man might do well at it, I don't doubt, but yet I don't feel it to be my own trade that I was meant for. So I go about seekin' for that one, and workin' at this one, and helpin' in the bakery—Baxter's to Kingdom; I'm boardin' there—helpin' there mornin's an' evenin's."

The brown eyes studied him carefully.

"About twenty-one years old, son? Twenty-two? I thought about there! Well, what have you been doin' up to now?"

Pippin told him, much as he had told Jacob Bailey. The brown man listened attentively, murmuring, "Sho!" or "Ain't that a sight!" occasionally to himself.

"So you see," Pippin concluded, "I want to be right down sure I've got the real thing before I settle down."

"Sure!" the other assented. "That's right!"

"And I keep feelin' at the back of my head that what I want is work with my hands; not this way, but farmin', or like that. The smell of the earth, and to see things growin', and—don't you know?"

The stranger assented absently.

"Elegant!" he said. "Farmin's elegant, when you've got the gift, but—ever thought of goin' to sea?" he asked; an eager look came into his face.

Pippin shook his head. "Not any!" he said. "I see the sea once, an' honest, it give me the creeps. Cold water mumblin' over the stones, like it wanted to eat 'em; and brown—kind o' like hair it was, floatin' about; and every now and then a big wave would come *Sssss!* up on the shore—well, honest, I run! I was a little shaver, but I've never wanted any more sea in mine!"

The brown man laughed. "You'd feel different, come to get out in blue water!" he said. "Smell the salt, and get the wind in your face, and—gorry! I'm a sea-farin' man," he said simply. "I spent good part of my life at sea. I'm runnin' a candy route at present—have a pep'mint! Do! 'Twon't cost you a cent, and it's real good for the stummick—but where I belong is at sea. Well! you can't do better than farmin', surely. Would you like a temp'ry job pickin' apples? I dunno but Sam—"

"There's more to it than that!" Pippin was speaking absently now; there was a wistful look in his eyes. "There's all that, the smell of the ground, and—and buttercups and—things; but there's more to it. There! You seem so friendly, I'll say it right out. I want to help!"

"That's right!" murmured the brown man. "Help! that's the stuff!"

"I want to help them that needs help. I want there shouldn't be so many kids in cellars, nor so many boys go wrong. Green grass! Tell you what!" Pippin's eyes were shining now, and his hands clenched. "I've been sayin' along, this month past, I'd forget all that time when I was a kid; I'd forget everything up to where I found the Lord. I kind o' think there was where I was wrong, mister—?"

"Call it Parks!" said the brown man. "Calvin Parks is what I was christened, and I'd like to know your name, son."

"Pippin!"

"Meanin'—?"

"Just Pippin!"

"Christian name or surname?"

"All the name there is!"

"But Pippin ain't no given name; it's an apple!"

"That's right! But it's all the name I've got. Fur back as I remember, Granny Faa called me it, and Dod Bashford called me 'pup' or 'snipe.' That's all I have to go by, so you see how 'tis!"

How should you remember anything more, Pippin? You were a baby when Granny Faa, then still able to travel, living in and out of the tilt cart which was home to her, found you by the roadside with your dying mother. The woman was almost past speech. "Don't roof me!" she muttered, flinging her arms out as the old gypsy lifted her. "Don't roof me!" and so died. Granny Faa felt no responsibility for the corpse. She rifled the body methodically, but found nothing of value. The shoes were better than her own, so she put them on. As for the baby, she took it partly because it smiled in her face and made something stir in that withered region where her heart was still alive, but more because her son wished it. Gypsy Gil (short for Gilbert), bent over the child delightedly; he snapped his fingers, and the baby crowed and jumped in the withered arms that held it. "Hell! ain't he a pippin?" said Gil. "Say, kid, ain't you a pippin?" "Goo!" said the baby. That was all. It was very simple. During the week Gil had still to live, he was "wrop up," as his mother said, in the child, and declared twenty times a day, with a new oath each time, that it was a pippin sure enough. Then, a knife thrust in a drunken scuffle sent Gil wherever he was to go; but he had named the baby. The old woman, mourning like a she-wolf, tended the child grimly because Gil had liked it; called it, for the same reason, by the name-that-was-no-name which he had given it. It was all simple enough, you see, had Pippin but known.

"That's mighty queer!" the brown man ruminated. "I don't know as ever I heard of any one without two names to him, and yet it sounds all right, too. Pippin! Well—well, son, I will say you look it. And now, here we are at the Poor Farm, and I'm goin' in here in my reg'lar way."

"Poor Farm! is this a Poor Farm?"

Ever since it came in sight, Pippin had been looking with a lover's eye at the broad low house of mellow brick, standing back from the road under its giant elms, its neat garden skirts gathered round it, its prim, trim gravel path leading to its white steps and green fan-lighted door.

"This a Poor Farm!" he repeated.

"Sure! Jacob Bailey's idea of one, and I wish there was more like it."

"Jacob Bailey!" cried Pippin. "Why, green grass! Why—why, ain't this great? He's a gentleman I'm acquainted with; he asked me to come and see him, and I promised I would. Well, if this ain't a leadin', I never see one. Mr. Parks, I'm pleased enough at meetin' up with you, just your own self; but add on your bringin' me here—why, I don't know how to thank you, sir!"

"Nothin' at all! nothin' at all!" said Calvin Parks. "I'm just as pleased myself. Think of your knowin' Jacob! Well! well! He's pure fruit and cane sugar, Jacob is, not a mite of glucose in his make-up. Here he comes this minute!"

Such a welcome as they had! Good Mr. Bailey, coming out to welcome his old friend, was quite overcome with pleasure and amazement at finding his new one, too. He had been telling the woman about him ever since that day, he assured Pippin. Only this morning he had said he wished that young feller would turn up, and she had said she wished to goodness he would for there was nothing in the house that would cut except Aunt Mandy's tongue.

"One of the inmates!" he explained. "Poor old lady! M' wife was a mite worked up, and she *is* cuterin', times when her rheumatism ketches her. Come in! Come in, the two of ye! Make ye welcome, Pippin, to Cyrus Poor Farm!"

He led them through the neat vestibule, through—with a glance of pride—the chilly splendor of the parlor, with its embossed plush rockers and lace curtains, into the kitchen.

"We'll find the woman here!" he said. "Kitchen's home, I always say."

It was a large, brick-paved room, with four broad windows facing south and east. Most of one side was taken up by a black cavern of a fireplace, which sheltered grimly the shining trimness of a modern cookstove. There was plenty of room for the settles on either side, and warm though the day was, two or three old people were sitting there, rubbing their chilly knees and warming their poor old hands. They looked up, and their faces sharpened into lively curiosity at sight of the visitors; but the girl who sat at the window never glanced at them, only crooned to the cat in her lap. The blind man in the corner, weaving willow baskets, listened, and his face lightened at the sound of the brown man's voice.

"Howdy, folks!" he said. "Well, I am a stranger, as you were saying. Say we have a pep'mint all round, what? Or a marshmallow? Uncle Ammi, I've got a treat for you, come all the way from Cyrus!"

While he gossiped cheerily with the old people, a sweet-faced woman came from an inner room and was introduced by Jacob Bailey as "m' wife."

"This is the young man I was tellin' you about, Lucy!" he said. "Cur'us he should happen along to-day, what say?"

"That's right! Only I should call it providential myself, Jacob. Be seated, won't you, Mr.—now Jacob told me your name!—Pippin—to be sure! Be seated, Mr. Pippin. We'll be having supper soon, and you'll set right down with us, I hope."

"Thank you, ma'am! If there was some knives I could be sharpenin', to earn my supper, sort of, I should be tickled to death to stay. Or if there's anything else you'd rather—what I aim at is to please, you see. Them scissors the young lady has in her lap don't appear to be what I'd call real sharp, now."

Mrs. Bailey laid her hand gently on the girl's fair head.

"Flora May can't have sharp scissors!" she said. "She's good as gold, but she's a little wantin', and she might cut off her lovely hair, mightn't you, Flora?"

The girl raised a sweet, vacant face. "I might cut off my lovely hair!" she repeated in a musical singsong. "My lovely, lovely hair! My—" The quiet hand touched her again, and she was silent.

"After supper we'll have some singin'!" she said. "Flora May admires to sing."

"Does she?" Pippin looked earnestly at the young face, pure and perfect in form and tint. "It's like a lamp when you've blown it out!" he thought.

Now Mrs. Bailey brought an apronful of knives and scissors. Pippin retreated to the yard where he had left his wheel, and was soon grinding and singing away, oblivious of all else save flying wheel and shining steel. Glancing up after a while, he saw all the inhabitants of the Poor Farm gathered in the doorway, listening; he paid little heed; folks always listened. That was the way the Lord had given him, to pay folks for bein' so pleasant to him as they always was. He was real thankful.

"Look at the aidge on this knife, will you? Hardly you can't tell which is it, and which is air; see?"

He broke out into a wild, sweet air:

"Oh! carry me 'long!Dar's no more trouble for me.I's gwine away to a better land,Where all de niggers am free.Long, long hab I worked,I'b handled many a hoe;I'll turn my eye before I die,And see de sugar cane grow."

Something moved near him. He glanced down and saw the girl Flora May. She had crept nearer and nearer, till now she was almost at his feet. She sat, or rather crouched, on the ground, graceful as a creature of the woods, her blue print gown taking the lovely lines of her figure, her masses of fair hair, neatly braided, wound round and round her head. Such a pretty head! Just a little too small, poor Flora May! not for grace, but for other things. Looking at her, Pippin saw, and wondered to see, the face which he had likened to a dead lamp, now full of light, the pale cheeks glowing, the red lips parted, the blue eyes shining.

Yet somehow—what was the matter? They did not shine as other eyes shone; those brown ones, for instance, of the brown man towering in the doorway, or the twinkling gray eyes of Jacob Bailey.

"The lamp's burnin'," said Pippin, "but yet it's went wrong, some ways, but even so—green grass! she's a pictur!"

Coming to the end of his song, he smiled and nodded at the upturned face.

"Sing more for Flora May!" cried the girl. "Sing more!"

40

"Sure!" said Pippin. "Wait till I get a start on this aidge, Miss Flora May—Now! Here's what'll please you, I expect:

"Joseph was an old man,An old man was he;He married sweet Mary,The Queen of Galilee.

"As they went a-walkingIn the garden so gay,Maid Mary spied cherriesHanging over yon tree.

"Mary said to cherry tree,'Bow down to my knee,That I may pluck cherriesBy one, two, and three.'"

A long way back to the cellar, and Granny Faa crooning over her black pot—in her best mood, be sure, or she would not be singing the Cherry Tree Carol. A far longer way back to an English lane in early summer, the gypsy tilt halted under a laden cherry tree, the gypsy mother singing to her little maid as she dangled the cherries over her head. A long, long road to go, and yet as yesterday, as a watch in the night.

"O eat your cherries, Mary,O eat your cherries now,O eat your cherries, Mary,That grow upon the bough."—

"Now, Mr. Pippin," called Mrs. Bailey from the doorway, "it's plain to be seen there'll be no supper in this house till you give over singin'. I'm full loath to ask you to stop, but my cakes have to be eat hot, or they're no good."

CHAPTER V
CYRUS POOR FARM

ANOTHER lifelong possession for Pippin was that first supper at Cyrus Poor Farm. "I never forget a good meal!" he was wont to say. "It's one of the gifts, or so I count it; we've no call to forget 'em, just because we've eat 'em up. I think about 'em oftentimes, travelin', and enjoy 'em over again."

The long table was set in the wide doorway of the shed, "for coolth," Mrs. Bailey said. All around were piles of fragrant wood, birch and oak, with here and there a precious little store of apple wood, fruit of Jacob's thrifty pruning and thinning. The table itself, in the full light of the westering sun, glowed with many colors: rosy pink of boiled ham, dull brown of baked potatoes, rich russet of doughnuts, all set off by the vivid red of the Turkey cotton tablecloth.

Pippin drew a long breath as he surveyed his plate, heaped with the solids of this repast, the lighter eatables ranged round it in nappies shaped like a bird's bath. "Lord, *make* me thankful!" he ejaculated. "If I wasn't thankful, Mr. Bailey, sir, I'd ask you to take me by the scruff and heave me out, I would so!"

"Well, son, well!" responded Jacob comfortably. "We aim to set a good table, m' wife an' I; glad it suits you. You see," he added, "we have advantages over many other institutions. Some of our inmates is payin' boarders, sir, payin' boarders, and behooves us set palatable food before 'em. Why, some of us pays as high as two dollars a week, don't we?" He smiled round the table. Pippin flung a quick glance, saw two sharp noses proudly lifted, two pairs of eyes gleaming with satisfaction, while the serene dignity of the blind man's countenance proclaimed him third of the paying boarders.

"I've allers paid where I boarded!" said Miss Lucilla Pudgkins.

"I would scorn to do otherwise!" said Aunt Mandy Whetstone.

"And others that doesn't pay in money pays in help!" Jacob Bailey went on calmly; "so you see we're all comfortable! A little more of the ham, Pippin? Pass your plate!"

"I don't know," said Pippin, complying, "I don't really know as I ever eat a ham to compare to this, Mr. Bailey. It's—it's *rich*, that's what it is!"

A new voice spoke from the bottom of the table, that of a fat old man with a game leg. "I claim," he said huskily, as if there were crumbs in his throat, "that it's the second best ham I've ever ate here."

"The *third* best!" said the blind man calmly. "The fire got low on me one night, and the smoke was checked. We had a ham last year and one five years ago that was some better than this."

"Green grass!" ejaculated Pippin in amazement. "Do you mean to tell me—"

"We're right proud of Mr. Brand here to the Farm!" said Mrs. Bailey gently. "Wantin' his sight has give him wonderful powers of smell and taste—and touch, too. He has smoked our hams and bacon for twenty years, haven't you, Mr. Brand?"

"I have, ma'am!" said the blind man proudly.

"We make good profit out'n 'em," said Jacob. "Far and near, folks wants our hog p'dooce. Mr. Brand is money in the bank for the Farm and for himself, too."

As they left the table, a little cold hand was slipped into Pippin's.

"Sing!" said the girl. "Please sing for Flora May!"

"Why, sure!" Pippin was beginning; but Jacob Bailey broke in kindly but firmly:

"Not the minute he's finished his supper, he can't sing, Flora May!" he said. "Beside, I promised old Mr. Blossom to fetch Pippin in to see him."

"Old Mr. *who*?" cried Pippin.

"He said you'd know the name," chuckled Jacob. "This way, Pippin! He's pretty feeble, the old man is. Keeps his bed mostly, now."

For one moment Pippin hung back. Another! First Nipper, and now—Old Man Blossom, too! Old boozer, old snipe! Was he goin' to meet up with these folks right along, think? Wouldn't he ever get rid of 'em?

"Shut up! If the Lord can stand 'em, I expect you can!" and Pippin followed Mr. Bailey into a clean bare little room, where, propped on pillows, lay a clean old man. He looked eagerly up as Jacob entered. "You got him with you?" he asked querulously. "You got Pippin? I heard his voice—"

"You did, Daddy Blossom!" Pippin advanced and took the hand that was plucking nervously at the coverlet. "You heard Pippin, and now you see him! Well! well! And who ever thought of meetin' up with you here, Daddy? And sick, too! but if I had to *be* sick, I wouldn't ask no pleasanter place—" He turned to smile at Jacob Bailey, but Jacob had disappeared, and the door was closing softly.

43

"Pardoned out!" whispered the old man in his weak fretful voice. "Pardoned out, 'count of age and sickness. I ain't a well man, Pippin; my vitals is all perished; but that ain't what I want to say. I want you to help me! Say you'll help me, Pippin! I was always friends with you over There—" he nodded vaguely—"and now I'm old and sick, you'll help me, won't you?"

"Sure!" Pippin drew a stool beside the bed and sat down. "Put a name to it, Old Man! What can I do for you?"

"Find my little gal, Pippin, my Mary: you rec'lect her? Sure you do! She used to bring me candy, and poke it in betwixt the bars with her little hand—flowers too, she'd bring: sure you rec'lect little Mary, Pippin?"

Pippin did not, but there was no need of saying so.

"What about her, Old Man?"

"I want her! I ain't a well man, nor yet I ain't goin' to be well, and I want my little gal; I want you to find her, Pippin, and bring her to me."

"Sure!" said Pippin comfortably. "Where would I be likely—"

"I don't know!" cried the old man wildly. "That—" he gave a brief and vivid sketch of his wife's character—a wholly inaccurate sketch—"never would tell me where she sent her. She died herself, and a good job, too, and she sent word to me that Mary was well and doin' well, but now she'd got shet of me she was goin' to keep her shet. Now what a way that was to talk to a father! If little Mary knowed where I was, she'd come like a shot, but she don't know, nor I don't know—You find her, Pip pin! You rec'let the little gal: you'll find her, won't you?"

"Sure!" said Pippin. For some moments he sat absently, running his fingers through his brown curls. Taking out the little file, he considered it unseeingly, tried to whistle a tune on it, and failing, returned it to its hiding place. Then, waking from his reverie, he put the old man through a sharp examination. The answers were feeble and uncertain, but he learned something. Eighteen year old, or mighty nigh it. Yes, red hair, or—naw! it might be darker by now, like her ma's was; color of—there! 'member old Mis' Jennings that lived just over the way from There? Well, sir, she had a heifer, kind o' red brown, like a hoss chestnut when you break it open; and her skin the white of one, too, kind o' soft and creamy; and her eyes like her'n too (the heifer's, Old Man Blossom meant), big and soft and blue with a kind of brown in 'em too—there! he'd know her, Pippin would, by the dimple right corner of her little mouth. Cur'us thing that was. When she wasn't more than a baby, 'bout two year old, he gave her a little sunshade—she see her Ma's and hollered for it, and he said she should have one of her

44

own; pink it was, and she carried it like the Lady of the Land, sir. But bimeby she tumbles down, and the p'int of it went right through her cheek. That's right; instead of a scar, it made a dimple, paint him sky blue striped if it didn't. Prettiest little gal—hair would curl round your finger like 'twas a stick—

The whisper broke into crying, and Pippin had to soothe him and sing "The Factor's Lady, or the Turkish Garland," all through to restore tranquillity. But when Pippin rose to go, the old man clutched him with trembling fingers.

"Whisper!" he said. "Whisper, Pippin! The way you go to work—the way I'd go to work if I wasn't perished in my vitals"—he consigned his vitals to a warm region—"is, take Brand along!"

"Brand?" repeated Pippin.

"The blind man! he has eyes in his fingers. He can—he can tell the way the wind blew yesterday by feelin' of it to-day. If I'd had Brand I'd never been nabbed, and I'd be rollin' in gold to-day, and goin' in my automobile to find my little gal. But you get Brand along, Pippin! talk him round first, he's never been in the sportin' line, but—"

"Hold on! hold on!" Pippin loosed the clutching hands gently, and laid the poor old sinner, still gasping and whispering back on the pillow. "Old Man, you're makin' one big mistake. I'm not in the line any more; I guess not!" He threw back his head and laughed joyously. "You didn't know I found the Lord, did you? Well, I have, and there's no more sport in mine. But—I'll tell you! I'm runnin' a wheel at present, knife-grindin', you know. Why—I've got Nipper's wheel! Nipper was a pal of yours, wasn't he?"

"Nipper's wheel? Where's Nipper? Is he here?"

"He's dead, and before he went he gave me his wheel. It's a real handy—what now?"

He paused, for the old man, after staring at him a moment, broke into a fit of cackling, wheezing laughter.

"Nipper's wheel!" he gasped. "He's got Nipper's wheel, and he's found the Lord, and he isn't in the line no more! Gorry to hemlock, this is rich! You took me in complete, Pippin, you did so! Go on! You're all right!"

He grew purple in the face, and his eyes rolled. Pippin stepped to the door.

"Mr. or Mrs. Bailey!" he called quietly. "Mr. Blossom is having a fit!"

Mrs. Bailey, hastening in, surveyed the situation with practised eyes; lifted the patient, thumped his back gently, administered remedies, enjoined silence.

"You've ben talkin' too much, Mr. Blossom; it always brings on a spasm, and you hadn't ought to. Now lay down and take a nap, that's a good soul."

Obeying a glance of her kind gray eyes, Pippin slipped out, leaving the old man still gasping and gurgling. Many more of them kind, Pippin reflected, would carry the old geezer off, sure thing. He was on the blink, no two ways to that. "Loony too! Hear him laffin' fit to bust when I told him Nipper was dead! Now what do you know about that? That's loony, you see, that is! Behooves me find that little gal pooty quick if I'm goin' to find her. And how—in—Moses' meal-chist—am I goin' to find her?"

Pondering deeply, he went back into the kitchen. The table had been cleared and covered with its decent between-meals cloth of red and white check; beside it, facing the door, sat Miss Amanda Whetstone and Miss Lucilla Pudgkins, diligently mending stockings. These ladies, as has been seen, were paying boarders, and "demeaned themselves accordin'," as they would have said. They helped Mrs. Bailey in housework, mending, etc., but always with a touch of condescension and the understanding that it was "to accommodate." In person they were well contrasted. Miss Whetstone was a thin active little woman, with eyes like black glass and thin lips puckered in a sub-acid smile. She was always neat as wax, in dresses of black and white striped print, the lines so near together that they seemed to waver constantly. ("Throw her away!" Flora May often besought her "Uncle Bailey." "Please throw her away! She dazzles!") But every one knew Aunt Mandy had a black silk in her trunk, and a tatting collar that the minister's wife might have been glad to possess.

Miss Lucilla Pudgkins was billowy in figure and was addicted to purple print, with a string tied round the middle to show that she knew where the waist line ought to be. Her face might have been made by a clever boy out of a large red apple; and if Aunt Mandy's eyes were like glass, Miss Lucilla's were like china, two blue china buttons plumped into the red, on either side of the queerest button of a nose that ever was seen, Pippin thought. She wore a rather pathetic "front," which was seldom quite straight; in fact, she was a pathetic figure altogether, poor Miss Lucilla, but she did not know it, so all was well. She never forgot that at sixteen she had been Queen of the May at a Sunday school festival, and her trunk still held, under the scanty stock of petticoats and aprons, the white muslin frock of her great day. Miss Lucilla was a little greedy, and somewhat foolish, though not so foolish as Aunt Mandy thought her; the attitude of the two towards each other was usually an armed truce, except on occasions of general conflict, when they never failed to combine against the common enemy—usually Mr. Wisk, the fat man, who was greedy too.

The two ladies looked up eagerly as Pippin entered. How was Mr. Blossom? Miss Whetstone asked. He sounded something awful. Was it the death spasm, did Mr. Pippin think? They had been expecting it any day, and wishing his folks would come. Wasn't it awful?

"He's all right!" Pippin reassured her. "Choked up a bit, but Mis' Bailey knows how to handle him. He'll rest easy now, poor old skeezicks. How long has he ben this way, ladies?"

"Sit down, do, Mr. Pippin!" Miss Whetstone hastened to make room for him beside her. "That cheer is comfortable; set right down, now do so! He has been having those spasms ever since he come, a month and more ago, but none so bad as this. Be you kin to him?"

"Me? Not much!" Pippin shook his head vigorously.

"I only asked because one likes to know, you know, about the folks one has to associate with. Of course you can keep yourself to yourself, and oftentimes so do, but any one ought to be sociable when they can, I claim."

"Sure thing!" murmured Pippin absently, his eyes glancing over the speaker's head to where Flora May sat rocking in her corner, her hands folded in her lap, her eyes fixed on him with a curious intentness. She seemed to be calling him, he thought, though she made no sound. He nodded, with a friendly glance which said "Presently!" Impossible to go at this moment, for Miss Whetstone evidently had more to say. She was bridling, and making little clucking noises in her throat, expressive (to herself, at least), of delicacy of feeling. Now speech came, preluded by a genteel titter, and accompanied by a glance round the room, which took in the blind man quietly whittling splints in his own special corner, and Flora May, rocking by the window, the latter with a compassionate depreciatory shrug of Miss Whetstone's shoulders.

"We aim to be as select here as circumstances allow," said the lady. "Of course it is a town institution, I am well aware of that; but Cyrus is a select neighborhood, and there's no one feels any call to take boarders *except* Mr. Bailey. You can see for yourself how it is, Mr. Pippin. The house is large and his own family small. He is well connected, Jacob is; his mother was own cousin to mine, and so—we thought, me and Miss Pudgkins, we'd like you to understand just how we come to be here. Not but what we could of went anywhere we pleased, if we *had* pleased!"

Pippin was aware of a certain wistfulness in the two pairs of eyes fixed on him. Now wouldn't that give you a pain? Poor old ladies!

"I bet you could, ma'am!" he responded heartily. "I expect you could pass all your time visitin' round, and find your welcome runnin' ahead of you like a houn' dog. But if you searched the country over, I bet you wouldn't find as pleasant a place as this. You show your taste, is what I would say."

The wistful eyes brightened as they exchanged glances. There was a point to make with this young man; it had to be made with every newcomer. People *must* know that they were here for convenience' sake, and that alone!

"I knew he would understand!" cried Miss Pudgkins. "He has that way. I see it first thing. And bein' as it is, Mr. Pippin, we try to keep up the*tone*, you see. Now Mr. Blossom—you say he's no kin to you? Well, to speak my mind—and Miss Whetstone holds with me—Mr. Blossom is *not*just the kind Cyrus folks is accustomed to. Has he—has he led a good life, are you aware?"

Pippin smiled at her. "Well, no, lady, he ain't; not exactly to call it *good*, you know; not what *you* would call good, though there never was as much harm in the Old Man as in lots of others. But anyway," he added, "he's on the blink now, you see, liable to croak 'most any day, I should judge, so it don't so much matter, does it?"

"Liable to—I beg your pardon?"

"I beg yours. No expression to use to ladies. Pass away is what I would say. I expect his trick is about up, what say? Dandy place to pass away in, too, when your time's come. Excuse me, ladies, I see Mr. Bailey—"

Pippin saw also his opportunity of escape, and with a little bow of apology, and appreciation, slipped out of the door, thinking to join his host who had just walked past it. But Jacob Bailey had already disappeared in the shed, and it was Flora May's turn. She had followed Pippin, and now stood before him, looking up at him with clear, lovely, empty eyes: empty, yet with that curious shining intentness he had noticed before.

"Sing now for Flora May!" said the girl.

"I will!" Pippin assured her. "Just the moment Mrs. Bailey gets through with Mr. Blossom, we'll have us a reg'lar singsong, we will so. Real fond of singin', ain't you, Miss Flora May? Say, that's a dandy necklace you have on! Them beads are carved elegant, they sure are."

Flora May lifted the beads and glanced carelessly at them. They were of some hard nut wood, each one adorned with flowers and fruit in delicate carving: a pretty ornament enough.

"Uncle Brand made them for me," she said. "Take them!" She had slipped the necklace off and was pressing it into Pippin's hand. He took it and examined it admiringly, then put it gently back over the girl's head.

"I thank you a thousand times!" he said. "I couldn't wear 'em myself, not travelin' like I am, you see, and I like to see 'em round your neck, they look so pretty. It's young ladies ought to wear joolry, you know."

He smiled at her, but her eyes met his anxiously.

"You are not goin' away?" said the girl. "You are goin' to stay? I'll give you my eagle feathers if you will stay. I'm tired of the folks here."

"Now what a way that is to talk! You're just jokin' though, I see. It *would* be a joke if you was tired of Mr. and Mrs. Bailey, wouldn't it now?"

"I'll give you the white duck, if you'll stay!" she went on in her sweet monotonous voice, which yet was strangely eager. "Uncle Bailey gave it to me, it's mine. I'll give you everything I've got if you'll stay."

At this moment, to Pippin's infinite relief, Mr. Bailey emerged from the shed. He laid his hand on the girl's shoulder; instantly her whole form relaxed and she drooped into her customary attitude of listless indifference.

"Anything wrong, little gal?" asked Jacob Bailey, kindly. Flora May shook her head and turned away with a pettish movement of her shoulders.

"She was wantin' me to sing for her," said Pippin. "I will, too, Mr. Bailey, sir, soon as ever you and Mis' Bailey are ready. I don't mean to brag of my singin', don't you think that, but it's what has ben give me, and about all I have to give when folks is so dandy to me as what you folks have been here. So if agreeable, sir, say the word and I'll tune up!"

CHAPTER VI
PIPPIN SINGS FOR HIS SUPPER

SO Pippin sang for his supper, a grateful Tommy Tucker; and the imbecile girl sat at his feet and listened, rocking to and fro, her lovely face so full of joy that it was almost—almost—

He sang about the Young Lady who went a-hunting with her dog and her gun, and about poor bonny sweet Bessie, the Flower of Dundee, and "Silver Threads among the Gold," which made Mrs. Bailey cry and Jacob blow his nose loudly. He was about to give them "Nancy Lee," but checked suddenly. Was he forgetting the Lord, after that elegant supper? Now wouldn't that give you a pain?

"*That's right!*" Pippin spoke so suddenly that everybody started. "Excuse *me!*" he said hastily. "I was thinkin'—leastways I wa'n't thinkin'—well, it don't signify whichever way of it, but if agreeable, I will praise the Lord a spell!"

A murmur of approval greeted him. Mrs. Bailey's kind face lighted up.

"That will surely be a treat!" she cried. "And—oh, Mr. Pippin, wait one moment! If you don't mind standing in the doorway of old Mr. Blossom's room, so he can hear you? He's real quiet now, and I'm sure 'twill do him good—"

So Pippin stood in the doorway, and threw back his head and sang with all his heart and soul:

"When I can read my title clearTo mansions in the skies,I'll bid farewell to every fear,And wipe my weeping eyes."

This hymn is left out of many hymn books nowadays; it is old-fashioned, and some of its lines are patently absurd: but I wish the hymnologists could hear Pippin sing it. His voice goes soaring up, a golden trump of victory and triumph:

"There shall I bathe my weary soulIn seas of heavenly rest;And not a wave of trouble rollAcross my peaceful breast."

As he finished, he swung round, his eyes blazing, every inch of him a-thrill. "Old man," he cried, and the passion in his voice made them all start. "Don't you feel it? Don't you feel somethin' crinklin' all through you, like sap in a sugar maple? That's the grace of God, Old man; let her run! Oh, Lord, let her run!"

There was a moment's silence; then Mr. Blossom snickered. It is not a pretty word, but then it was not a pretty sound.

Pippin was at his side in an instant, his eyes ablaze again, but with a very different light.

"You old skunk!" he cried, gripping the bony shoulders hunched below the leering face. "You darned old son of a broken whisky jug, you dare to snicker before the Lord? For half a quarter of a cent I'd wring your rooster's neck for you, you—"

He stopped, as if somebody had touched him. His head drooped, his arms dropped by his side, and he flushed scarlet from throat to forehead. He stood so for several minutes, no one stirring; then he turned humbly to Jacob Bailey.

"I ask your pardon, sir, and the company's. I lost holt of myself. There! I am fairly ashamed." He leaned over the poor old sinner, who was still gasping from the sudden onslaught. "Hurt you, did I, Old Man? I ask your pardon, too, I do so. Lemme h'ist you a mite!"

With anxious care he raised the shrunken figure and settled the pillows under the palsied head.

"There! That comfy, old geezer? Now you go to sleep! I was a mutt to shake you up that way. Goo' night, Old Man!"

Sitting on his neat bed an hour later, Pippin dealt with himself, as judge with criminal. His vivid fancy saw himself as two distinct beings, one arraigning, the other replying. He desired to know whether he, Pippin, thought he was all creation? Because if so, he took leave to tell him he wasn't, nor anything approachin' it. Reassured on this point, he further observed that perhaps on the whole it might be best for him to go back to Shoreham. Most likely he wasn't prepared yet to live among Christian folks; say he was to go back for another year till he'd learned to hold his tongue and keep his temper! How would he like that?

"Well, then, you behave! If you're a Christian, show up, that's what I say. What was it you promised Elder Hadley? To look for the grace of God in every one you see, wasn't it? Well, then! *Did* you look for it in Old Man Blossom?"

"Why, sure! Didn't I sing, and pray, and all? I couldn't find no grace, not a mite, so help me!"

Silence; the outward man sitting with bent head and knotted brows, the inner— both of him—wrestling with a problem. At last the brows cleared, the head lifted.

"Bonehead!" said Pippin. "You didn't look in the right place. Prayin' an' singin' wasn't his kind, no more than they were a dumb critter's. Didn't he want his little gal,

51

want her real bad? Wasn't that mebbe the way grace took him? I expect the Lord has as many ways as there is folks."

Finally Pippin concluded that he would do well to say his prayers and go to bed and let the Lord run things a spell, as He was full able to do. And start off next morning, sure thing, or the Boss would think he had cut. Gee! he hated to leave this place!

"I don't see how you do it!" said Pippin. "Gorry to 'Liza, Mr. Brand, I don't see *how* you do it!"

Brand was making a broom; Pippin, smoking his after-breakfast and before-departure pipe in the barn doorway, watched him with growing wonder and admiration. His fingers seemed almost to twinkle, they moved so fast, knotting, laying together, binding in the fragrant strands of broom corn.

"I've made many a broom!" Pippin went on. "I was counted a crackerjack at bindin'; but you work twice as fast blind as what I would seein'; that's what gets me!"

The blind man raised his head with a smile, his hands never ceasing their swift motion.

"I sometimes think seeing folks don't have half a chance at broom-making and like that," he said. "There's so many things to take their minds off. Now, take this minute of time. There's a cloud passing over the sun, isn't there?"

"Why, yes!" Pippin looked up involuntarily, shifting his position a little to do so. "Yes, sir, there is. Now how—"

"And you had to look up to see it!" the blind man went on, calmly. "That takes time and attention. Now I *feel* the cloud, and that's all there is to it. There are some advantages in being blind; born blind, that is."

Pippin gave him a helpless look. His eyes wandered over the scene before him: the wide, sunny barnyard, the neat buildings, the trim garden spaces, the green, whispering trees; beyond them the white ribbon of the road, and wave upon wave of fair rolling country, sinking gradually to where the river flowed between its darkly wooded banks; overhead a sky of dazzling blue flecked with cloudlets of no less dazzling white. There was a hawk hovering over the chicken yard. Pippin picked up a stone and threw it at the bird, which vanished with a shrill scream. His eyes came back to the figure in the doorway, with bent head and flying fingers.

"Advantages?" he repeated, and his tone was as helpless as his look had been. "Well, you get me, Mr. Brand, every time. You—you was born blind, sir, do I understand?"

Brand nodded. "Sixty years ago this month. When I say advantages, I don't mean I would have chose—" he made a slight, eloquent gesture toward the clear, sightless eyes. "But since so it is, one looks at it from that end, you see, and one finds—advantages. For one thing, changes don't trouble a born-blind man as they do seeing folks. I hear talk about this person looking poorly, and that one having gone gray, and lost his teeth, and like that; that don't trouble me, you see, not a mite. Folks look to me just as they sound. Now take our folks here—Lucy—I would say Mrs. Bailey—and Jacob: well, their voices tell me what they are like, see? They called Lucy handsome when she was a girl; she's just as handsome to me as she was then."

There was a wistful note in his voice, and Pippin responded instantly.

"She's a fine-appearin' lady, now!" he said heartily. "She sure is."

"I presume likely!" said Brand. "She'd have to be, being what she is. When Lucy first grew up, I made a—a picture (so to say! I never saw a picture) of her in my mind, and I see it as clear to-day as I did then."

He was silent for a time, then went on, in an altered tone: "Then there's other things, things that seeing folks don't have. Take hearing. I hear twice what most folks do, and I hear things no seeing person *can* hear; undertones, our music teacher called them, and overtones, too. Now, you hear a woman's dress rustle, and that's all, isn't it?"

"Ye-yes!" Pippin replied. "That is—I can tell a silk rustle from a calico, and a woolen from either."

"Well, that is more than many men can do. Women, of course; but not many men without training." The blind man leaned forward, and felt carefully of Pippin's ear. "A good ear!" he nodded approvingly. "An excellent good ear! There's many hold that the outer ear has nothing to do with hearing, but I don't know! I don't know! The Doctor told me of a king who wanted to know everything that was said in his house—palace, like!—and he built it in the shape of an ear. Long ago, Doctor said it was, and he didn't say he believed it, but I've often wondered. But you've had training, too; you've learned how to listen, which is more than some folks learn all their lives long."

"You bet I had training!"

Not a vision this time, though a dim, brutal figure lurks in the background; not a vision, but a sound!

"Listen! listen, you cursed pup, or I'll cut your heart out. My ears are thick to-night. Is that a cop's whistle, or a pal's? If you get it wrong, I'll make you sweat blood—"

"Yes, I had training!" said Pippin.

"Then—" Brand's face was fairly glowing as he turned it on his young visitor. It was not often that he could speak of his blindness, but there was something about this boy that seemed to draw speech from him like a magnet. "Then—there's the other senses; smell—why, what wonderful pleasure I have in a delicate smell! Whether it's a flower, or my bacon when it's smoked just to the fine point, or—why, take smoke alone, all the various kinds of it! Wood smoke, and good tobacco, and leaves burning in the fall of the year, and brush fires in spring! And there's herbs, southernwood, mint, lemon balm—wonderful pleasure in odors, yes, sir! And when you come to touch, why there's where a blind man has it over a seeing, almost every time. The pleasure of touching a leaf of mullein, say, or soft hair like the little gal's—Flora May's, I would say—or a fruit, or a baby's cheek—wonderful pleasure! I wonder are your fingers as good as your ears? Let me see!" He held out his hand, and Pippin laid his own in it.

How proud you were of your hands, Pippin! How you used to boast that your fingers needed no sandpaper to sharpen their exquisite touch! Is that why you hang your head, and the blood creeps up to the roots of your hair?

"If he's let to live," a husky voice murmurs, "he'll make a —— —— good un; but I ain't certain but I'll wring his neck yet. There's things about him ain't right!"

Perfectly consistent, Mr. Bashford, and wholly correct from your point of view!

"A fine hand!" says David Brand. "Strong and yet delicate. You can do a great deal with that hand, young man. Why, with that, and your fine ears, you—why—" he laughs his cheery laugh—"I won't go so far as say you'd ought to have been born blind, but you surely would make a first-rate blind man!"

Pippin puffed at his pipe meditatively for a few minutes, considering the serene face and the flying fingers. What a face it was! the calm, thoughtful brow, the well-cut features, the clear eyes, the patient look—well, there! If an Angel could be old—that is to say, gettin' on in years—and blind, this would sure be him! Now—come to see a face like this, you know the Lord has ben there: *is* there, right along, same as the devil

54

was with Dod and Nosey and them. Do a person good, now, to hear what he has to tell, how the Lord has dealt with him, what say? He couldn't more than say no, if—

"Mr. Brand!" Pippin spoke timidly, yet eagerly. "You'll excuse me—but when I like folks, I like to know about 'em; what they've no objection to tellin' is what I would say. You must have a lot that's real interestin'—I hope no offense!" he ended lamely.

"None in the world!" Brand laughed cheerily. "Quite the other way, young man. Old folks don't always find young ones that care to hear their old stories. I should be pleased—find a seat, won't you? I haven't much to tell, but you're welcome to what there is!"

Pippin curled his long legs up on the floor, his back against the door jamb. "This is great!" he murmured. "This certainly is great. I'd ought to be gettin' on, but I don't care. Now if you're ready, Mr. Brand!"

Brand reached for a pile of straws, measured, clipped, laid them in orderly piles ready for binding in.

"I was born in Cyrus," he said; "born and raised. I was the only child, and my parents did everything they could for me. I was a happy youngster and had reason to be. Everybody was good to me; Cyrus is a good, kind neighborly place. Yes, sir, I was a happy boy. Always singing and laughing; I recollect hearing folks say, 'Poor child!' or like that when they came to see mother. I used to wonder what poor child they meant. I asked Lucy one day—Lucy Allen, that's Mrs. Bailey now; we lived next door, and played together always, her and Jacob and me. I says, 'Lucy, who are they always saying "Poor child!" about? Is it you?' And Lucy says, 'I wouldn't wonder, Dave! My front teeth has come out, and I am a sight.' Little girl seven years old: she was that thoughtful always, Lucy was. She was doing me good turns every day and all day when we was little: once, I remember, I had a chance to do her one. We was playing together in Uncle Ivory Cheeseman's candy kitchen—he give us the run of it, Lucy and Jacob and me, because he could trust us, he said; he was a kind old man, though crusty where crust was needed. Well, we was playing there, and Lucy went too near the stove and her dress caught fire. I smelled it before it begun to blaze, and caught it in my two hands and squeezed it out. 'Twas a calico skirt; another minute and 'twould have been in a blaze."

Brand paused, and Pippin looked up inquiringly.

"I've always been thankful for that!" said Brand. "There was a girl at the Institution who lost her sight by burning, just that way, her skirt catching at the stove."

55

"Now wouldn't that give you a pain?" murmured Pippin. "I know what burnin' feels like, just a mite of it. Not meanin' to interrupt, Mr. Brand; I'm just as interested!"

"When I was ten years old, mother died, and father sent me to the Blind Institution. I was there many years, and there I learned all I know—except what I learned before or since!" Brand added with a whimsical smile. "That puts me in mind of the first—no, the second—day I was there. I was to see the Doctor, the head of the Institution—he was away the day I came—and I was left alone in his office to wait for him. I was always keen to see what kind of place I was in, so I was moving about the room, finding out in my own way, when the door opened and two men came in. One of them was tall—what say?"

"Now! now!" cried Pippin. "How in the airthly did you know he was tall?"

"His voice was high up! That's an easy one, Pippin. Why, *you* would know that, with those good ears. He was speaking, and the first sound of that voice stays by me yet. A *master* voice! I've never forgot the words either. 'The first lesson—the hard lesson—you have first to learn is—*to be blind*—to live in the world without light—to look upon your life as still a blessing and a trust, and to resolve to spend it well and cheerfully, in the service of your Maker and for the happiness of those about you.'"

Dr. S.G. Howe to one of his blind pupils.

He paused. Pippin sat spellbound, gazing at the face that was indeed now as the face of an angel.

"The service of your Maker, and the happiness—" he murmured. "Say, that's great! It—it sounds like a song, don't it, Mr. Brand? Or—like Psalms, some way of it! I'd like to learn them words off by heart, sir, if no objection."

"He was a great man!" said Brand reverently. "A great and good man. As he spoke, so he lived, for his Maker and his fellow men. The man he spoke to gave a kind of groan, I remember; he had just lost his sight—a gun that wasn't loaded, the old story! Then the Doctor said a little more, comforting him like, and then he saw me. I had felt all round the room, and now I had my fingers on a raised map that hung on the wall. I had heard of such things and was pleased to death to get hold of one. I suppose it showed in my face, for the Doctor said, 'Here's a little fellow who already knows how to be blind! Come here, my son!' I went straight to him—his voice led me, you understand: I could always follow a voice, from the time I learned to walk. He laid his hand on my head and turned my face up, studying me. I knew that; I felt his eyes, is the only way I can put it. 'Born blind, weren't you, my boy?' he said. 'Twasn't often the Doctor had to be told anything about blind folks—or seeing either, for that matter. Well, sir, that was the beginning of life for me, in a way. I got my education there. 'Twas a happy place, and a happy life. I could tell about it from now till sundown, and not fairly make a beginning. The Doctor was my friend; everybody was my friend. I was quick, and I wanted to learn; and, too, there was a good deal I didn't have to learn, being born blind, you see. There's a passage in the Bible about remembering that 'he was born thus'; I used to think—"

A silence fell, while Brand counted strands, Pippin watching him eagerly. A black hen who had been watching, too, her head cocked, her bright yellow eye fixed on the blind man with the false air of intelligence affected by hens, came up with a quick, rocking step, and uttered a long, reflective "crawk!" scratching meanwhile on the barn floor.

"Hicketty Picketty wants some corn!" said Brand. "Here, Picketty!" He took a handful of corn from a bag and scattered it. The black hen pecked vigorously, trying to get every grain swallowed before any one else should come; but the motion of Brand's hand brought other hens fluttering, squawking, jostling, to get their share, and there was quite a scrimmage before he could resume his work.

"I spoil that hen!" he said apologetically. "Jacob says I oughtn't, and it's true; but she has such a way with her! There's no other hen I'm so partial to, though I love them all.

"Well! Want to hear any more, or are you tired of listening? 'Tisn't much of a story; I warned you in the beginning."

"Tired? Well, I guess nix! Why, I'm—why, it's *great*, Mr. Brand! I'm learnin' something 'most every word you say. Do go on, sir—if I'm not troublin' you!"

"I don't know as there is so very much more to tell, after all. A man's life goes on steady; there don't things keep happening right along, as they do in stories. I've had a quiet life, but a real pleasant one. I stayed on at the Institution quite a spell after I grew up, teaching in the shop. Basketry is what I taught; I liked it best, and was good at it. Then, along when I was thirty years old, father needed me, and I came home. He was getting on in years, and he needed some one, and I was the one. His housekeeper got married, and I was handy about the house. Yes, we made out to do well, father and I, as long as he lived. Spare time and evenings, I'd make brooms and baskets, and the neighbors took all I could make. Sometimes I'd make a trip round other places, same as you do with your wheel, Pippin. I liked that real well. Lucy and Jacob had married by that time—I always knew they would! I—yes, I always knew they would, and right and fitting it was. Jacob's folks had passed on, and he and Lucy lived there next door to us, and was like brother and sister to me, as they always had been. Cyrus is a pleasant place; yes, sir, we've all been happy, only when Lucy lost her little David— named for me, yes, and like my own to me. That was a grief, but grief is part of our lot. Lucy mourned so, Jacob was desirous of making a change for her, and about that time they was changing here, too, and the selectmen beseeched Jacob and Lucy to take the place, and they did. They wanted me to come with them then, but I wouldn't leave father. Bimeby, though, father passed on, and then—I didn't make up my mind right away to the change. I didn't want to be a care to Lucy, and I thought I could get on by myself, and I *could*; but—well—no need to go into that. Along about ten years back I come to make my home here with my good friends, and I've never regretted, nor I hope they haven't."

"No need to go into that!" Quite right, Brand. Impossible for you, being what you are, to tell of the various persons, male and female, who saw your comfortable cottage and few but fertile acres, and "felt a call to do for you." Lucy Bailey sometimes spoke of it to her husband with amused indignation. "Fairly driven out of his home, David was! The idea! Lucky we had one to offer him, or he'd have been saddled with the whole passel of them, like Cap'n Parks was a while back, and no Mercy Lovely to trim 'em out for him."

A doleful squeak was heard, and a wheelbarrow trundled slowly by with Mr. Wisk as the motive power. "You'd think 'twould go faster by itself!" Pippin thought; then reproached himself, the man being afflicted. Brand's fine brows contracted as he listened to the squeak.

"Wisk has been promising to oil that exe for a month!" he said. "It gives me the toothache to hear it."

"Moves kinder moderate, don't he?" said Pippin. "I s'pose his leg henders him."

Brand laughed. "I don't—know! Aunt Mandy Whetstone says the lame leg makes the better time of the two. She's small and spry, you know, and Wisk gets in her way sometimes. He means all right, but he never feels any call to hurry, that I know of."

Here Mr. Wisk, having given up the wheelbarrow as a bad job, came hobbling up, and with a wheeze by way of greeting, planted his shoulders against the door-jamb. "Nice mornin'!" he said.

"Great!" replied Pippin. "It surely is great! I'd oughter ben on the road an hour ago, but Mr. Brand makes it hard to get away, now I tell ye. I must go in and say good-by to the folks, and then I'm off. Mr. Brand, I thank you a thousand times for all you've told me, and you may be sure I shan't forget it, no, sir! You'll see me again pretty soon. I shan't be able to keep away from this place more'n just about so long, I see that plain. Good-by, sir!"

They shook hands warmly, the blind man urging him to come sooner and stay longer every time he could.

"Good-by to you, too, Mister." Pippin turned to the lame man.

"I'm goin' into the house!" said the latter. "I'll step along with you. I want a drink o' water!"

He stumped along beside Pippin. Out of earshot of the barn, he looked back over his shoulder. "Or a drink of something!" he added. "Got a drop about you, young feller?"

"No, I ain't!" said Pippin shortly. He was not drawn toward Mr. Wisk.

"I thought you might have. I'm orful dry, and the water here don't agree with me. Say! Brand ain't the only one is afflicted, young man. I want you should understand that. My limb pains me something fierce; very close veins is what I have. You wouldn't find me in no such place as this if I didn't. Brand's a stand-offish kind of cuss, but he don't measure up so much higher than other folks as what he thinks, mebbe. They make of him because he's blind, but I'll bet a dollar he don't suffer nights the way I do. Got a mite of tobacker to spare? Ain't? When I was in trade—I was a tin-knocker while I had my health—I allers made out to have a drop and a chew for a gen'leman when he asked for it; it helped trade. I was allers called a good feller. Well, so long! Call again!"

Pippin took an affectionate leave of the inmates of Cyrus Poor Farm. They would see him again, he assured them heartily; no fears but they would. All he had to do was say good-by to the Kingdom folks—for a spell. *They'd* see him again, too. Elegant folks!—and go find that little gal, or young woman, or whatever she was, and then just watch him make a bee line for Cyrus! Yes, sir! He would bring back that gal, sure thing! And he would bring Mr. Brand some of that new basket stuff he'd heard tell of.

"Yes, ma'am!" as he shook hands with Miss Lucilla Pudgkins. "You shall have some perfoomery, the best I can lay hands on. And you shall have them buttons, Miss Whetstone, if they are to be had. And Miss Flora May shall—"

He looked about the room, but the girl was not there.

"She's out some place," said Mrs. Bailey. "Feeding the hens, I presume likely. I'll tell her good-by for you, Pippin!"

He shook hands with Old Man Blossom, who was only too eager to be friends. "I'm all friends, Pippin!" he cried in eager, quavering tones. "Honest I am! You find my little gal, and you can pray yourself black in the face and I won't say a word. It just took me that way, you know; you prayin' as slick as a Gospel shark, and Nipper's wheel out in the shed all the time—tee hee! You're smart, Pippin! Ain't any pious goin' to get round you, hey? 'Tother way round, hey? Gorry! that is rich!"

He grew purple, and the bed shook under him.

"Hold on there!" said Pippin. "Don't you go and have another on me. I'm goin'." And he bolted.

"I'm comin' out to the gate with you!" said Jacob. "Take a look at the stock as you go?"

Pippin nodded gravely. The two went out together to the great barn, fragrant with hay; patted the sleek farm horses, rubbed the noses of the calves. Jacob pointed out briefly the merits of each animal; Pippin responded with suitable encomiums. Both men were absent and constrained. It was not till they reached the gate that Jacob Bailey spoke out. Leaning against a post, he drew out his jack knife, looked about for a stick, and finding one, began to whittle.

"Well!" he said at length. "So you found your way here. How do you like?"

"First-rate!" said Pippin. "I never saw a place I liked so well."

Jacob whistled "Yankee Doodle" (his one tune) carefully through; then—

"How about comin' back?" he said. And as Pippin was about to speak, "I mean comin' to stay! There now, I've out with it," he added. "Here it is! Me and m' wife have took a liking to you, and so has all the inmates. I never saw 'em take so to any one, unless 'twas Cap'n Parks, and he's an old friend. What I would say is, Pippin, we're gettin' on in years, and we need young help. We've no boys of our own; I've got a nevy, but—never mind about that now! We'd like first-rate to think that you'd come back bimeby to stay."

"Do you hear that?" Pippin asked himself silently. "He would trust me; knowin' all there is to know, he'd take me right in! Now wouldn't that—" He turned to Mr. Bailey with shining eyes. "You're real good, sir!" he said simply. "You're— you're *darned* good! I don't know how to say what I feel, but I feel it all the same. Now—want me to say what I've ben thinkin'?"

"Sure!" assented Jacob with a grave nod. Pippin looked about him vaguely. "Woodpile yonder!"

Jacob nodded over his shoulder. Pippin went to the pile and selected a stick with great care, squinting along it to observe the straightness of the grain. Returning with his prize, he produced his own knife, and silence reigned for a moment while he removed the bark, Jacob critically regarding him the while.

"I've ben thinkin'—the *chance* of it! Here you've got these folks, and they're nice folks—most of 'em, that is—and you're doin' everything in the world for 'em, and it's *great*. Yes, sir, it's great! And the farm, and the garding—why, it's Mother dear, Jerusalem, right here in Cyrus township, or so it appears to me. But what I'm thinkin' of is the boys!"

A look of pain crossed the kindly face. "The boys!" he repeated.

"Mr. Bailey, I'd love to take care of them old folks, and blind, and like that; but all the time I'm thinkin' of the boys. Boys in the slums, and boys in jug, where I left 'em the other day. It appears to be laid upon me that I am to help the boys; though not to forget the others either, when I git a chance at 'em. Now see! I can't go but a little ways at a time, can I? It's like I was learnin' to walk—if you see what I mean. I don't know just what the Lord has for me to do, 'cept the first thing, to find this old rip's gal. That's plain, ain't it? When I can *see* a thing, right face to, I can do it—sometimes! But after that—all about it, I can't tell, but I expect the Lord has it all laid out for me, and He'll let me know, 'cordin' to."

There was a pause. Pippin looked up expectantly, and saw his companion looking out over the fields with eyes full of trouble. His face had suddenly fallen into lines of age.

"What's wrong, sir?" asked Pippin impulsively. "Have I said anything I shouldn't? I'll ask you to excuse me if I have."

A shake of the head reassured him. Jacob Bailey turned the troubled eyes on him, seemed to hesitate; finally, clearing his throat, spoke in a slow, husky voice.

"There's one boy—" He stopped. "Them oats looks good, don't they?" He nodded toward an adjoining field.

"Fine!" Pippin threw a hasty glance toward the oats. "They are dandy, sure. You was speakin' of a boy, Mr. Bailey! What about him?"

Still the gray-haired man hesitated, looking about him with those troubled eyes. At last he seemed to make up his mind, and looked straight at Pippin.

"There's one boy—" he said; "Pippin, there's one boy needs help the worst way. I expect he's right there in Kingdom, where you're stoppin'."

61

"I want to know!" Pippin was aglow with interest. "Where'll I find him? What's his name? Has he been run in?"

"Speak low!" the farmer glanced about him. "There's no one round, and yet you never can tell; the folks don't know. It's m' wife's nevy I'm speakin' of, Myron Allen, her sister's son. He's been stayin' with us since his mother died—father dead, too—and he got to be like our own to us. He went to school, and he helped me with the chores and helped m' wife with hers, and was handy boy all round. Mebbe we worked him too hard; he's only sixteen. We never thought it, but mebbe we did. Yet he seemed happy—whistlin' all over the place, jokin' and like that; and his cheeks was round and red as a Baldwin apple. Yes, sir, he enjoyed good health, and everybody made of him, and he was good as gold. Yes, sir, no one couldn't ask nor wish for a better boy than what Myron was till last summer. Then—well, 'twas bad company begun it."

"You bet it was!" murmured Pippin. "Go on, sir!"

"'Twas hayin' last year done the mischief. Myron hired out to a man over Tinkham way—that was after he'd got through with the hayin' here—and there he met up with some that was no better than they should be by all accounts. Pippin, that boy left us an innocent boy, that never had a bad word in his mouth that ever *I* heard, nor no one round here. He come back—" the gruff voice faltered—"he come back different, sir. He'd slap through his work and then off he'd go and set down behind the shed and read. He'd got a lot of books from some one he'd met up with; them Sleuth stories, you know, and like that, little paper books. You've seen 'em?"

"I've seen 'em!" Pippin nodded.

"He'd set there by the hour, readin' and readin', and oftentimes the cows bellerin' their hearts out to be milked. I'd come back from the field and find him with his nose in the book, and his eyes startin' out of his head. There warn't no cows nor no farm nor nothin' for him those times. I'd get real worked up, now and then, and give him a good callin' down, and he'd do better for a spell; but that was only the beginning." He glanced round again, and his voice dropped to a whisper.

"There's more to it. Things begun to be missed round here! It's been goin' on all winter; nothin' great, just a little here and a little there. Folks begun to talk, and some claimed 'twas tramps, and some begun to wonder—He's only a boy, you understand, Pippin! Oftentimes the thinkin' part grows up slower than what the bodily part does, ain't that so?"

Pippin met the anxious eyes cheerfully.

"That's so! Why, likely he wasn't more than ten years old, come to look inside of him. Where you'll find one boy that knows just where hookin' ends and stealin' begins, you'll find a dozen that don't. And there's more to it than that; but go on, sir! I'm just as interested as I can be!"

"This spring, a feller come along, and Myron knew him; he was one of them he had met over Tinkham way, and he was trampin'. Lookin' for work, he said, but if I ever saw a countenance that said lookin' for mischief, 'twas his. Young man, too! Well, Myron brought him in and we treated him well, because Myron seemed so taken with him. We give him a bed, and next day I set him to work hoein'—said he *wanted* work, you understand—and he appeared pleased as pie. Myron was hoein', too; we can't keep the witch grass out of that field, try our best. I was busy in the barn that day, choppin' hay, but yet I'd come out now and then jest to let 'em know I was round, and every time I'd find 'em with their heads together, tongues doin' the work and hoes takin' a noon spell: quick as they saw me they'd shut up and go to work. Well! I'd ought to have known then that they was plottin' mischief, but you don't look for your own folks—"

He broke off, and was silent a moment. Pippin assured himself that it was all right; it hurt, and thank the Lord it did! How'd he feel if it didn't?

"That night one of the neighbors was broke into, and money taken from his pants pocket. He woke up jest in time to see a man with a mask on gettin' out of the window. He up and run, but they was too quick for him—he see from the window there was two of 'em—and though he hollered and fired his gun, they got off, and he couldn't find hide nor hair of 'em. Next mornin' the tramp was gone, and Myron with him, and I found—I found in Myron's room some pieces of black cloth, and one of 'em with eyeholes cut in it."

There was a long silence. The two sticks were beautifully smooth by this time; Pippin began polishing his thoughtfully on his coat sleeve. Finally he shut his knife with a snap, and straightened his broad shoulders. The older man, looking up, met his eyes brimful of light and joy.

"Mr. Bailey," said Pippin, "the Lord is awful good to me! What did I tell you just now? That I couldn't see but just one step ahead, wasn't that it? Well, now I see two, and the second one is ahead of the other."

"I don't—quite—" began Jacob doubtfully.

"Don't you? Why do you s'pose the Lord put in your mind to tell me about this? Why, green grass! I got to find the boy as well's the gal! That's plain to see. Look! Where would them two go? They'd strike the nearest town, wouldn't they, so's they could lay up a bit, and spend their swag? Well, what's the nearest town? Kingdom, where I'm stayin' at present; Kingdom, where I'll have to be a spell yet, till I find some one to take my place—Green grass! I believe—"

Silent again, but in great excitement, Pippin pocketed his knife and stick, pulled out his file, and ran it through and through his hair wildly.

"Mr. Bailey, sir," he cried at last, "the Lord is showin' me His hand, and it's a dandy one. Don't say a word; don't ask me anything; but if you can trust me—if you *can* trust me—why, I'm to be trusted, because the Lord has hired me for the job!"

CHAPTER VII
FLORA MAY

SOON after this, Pippin took the road, sober at first, walking slowly with bent head, thinking hard; but as the morning got into his blood it began to tingle, his eyes began to shine, and up went his head.

"Green grass!" he said. "That sure was a nice place, and nice folks. Most of 'em, I would say; Old Man Blossom is a mite yaller sure, but some of the others are white enough to make up for him. Mr. and Mis' Bailey, now, I declare! They are as like as— as peas—to Pa and Ma, that I thought up to myself along back. How do, Pa? How be you, Ma? Don't you go back on me! Gee! and think of that young feller goin' back on them two! If I was him—green grass! wouldn't it have been great if I was! I tell you I'd make things hum to that nice place. I'd make them two forget I wasn't their own son, and twins at that. And them old ladies! Why, all they need is a little humorin'. Real friendly they was to me! And Mr. Brand! He is a peach, sure thing! I expect he could do more for me, blind, than I could for him, seein'. But I'd be—call it a nevy— to him, if I had the chance. And that poor sweet pretty creatur, if I wouldn't be a brother to her, send me back over There and put me in solitary! Try and learn her little things, try and make her eyes look a mite different. Not but they've tried, them good folks, but bein' nearer her age, and she taken with my singin' and like that—why, an angel wouldn't be no handsomer than what she would be if she had her mind. Take and learn her—"

Pippin stopped dead. Something was rustling in the bushes. The dream light faded from his face; he stiffened to attention like a pointer, his eyes fixed on the fringe of woods on his left. Something in there! A critter, or—?

The rustling grew nearer, louder; the bushes crackled, parted; a figure came out, timidly, eagerly, ran forward, fell down before him, seized his hand and looked up with dumb, imploring eyes. Flora May!

There are two men in every one of us. I used to think there were ten in Pippin, but for one instant all ten were paralyzed, looking helplessly into the blue eyes that burned into his; then one of them woke, the one who would have been a physician if Pippin had been reared in a home instead of a cellar.

He took the girl's wrists, and, holding them firmly, raised her to her feet.

"Why, Miss Flora May!" he said cheerfully. "Don't ever tell me this is you! Did you come all this way just to say good-by? Now, if that wasn't pretty of you! I'm just as much obliged as I can be, young lady; and I'll walk back a piece with you, I will so. This wood lot is a mite lonely, 'pears to me."

The girl tried to fling herself down again, but he held her tight. "I wouldn't do that!" His voice was kind, but he spoke with authority. "Get your nice clean dress all dirty! What would Mis' Bailey say? Why, she'll be lookin' for you, I expect. She thought you was 'tendin' to the hens, and all the time—what say?"

"Take me with you!" cried the girl. "I want you! I won't go back. Take me with you!"

"Now what a way that is to talk! You wouldn't leave Mr. and Mis' Bailey, good and kind as they be—"

"I want you!" wailed the girl, and again she would have flung herself down, had not those firm hands held her fast. "Take me with you! Sing to me! Love me! I belong to you!"

Pippin's face had been full of perplexity, but now it lightened.

"Sing to you! Why, sure I will! There's a song you'll just admire to hear, Miss Flora May. We'll walk along and I'll sing as we go. No, I won't let go both your hands; I'll hold this one so—so we can keep step together. Now let's step out lively!"

The girl drew back, her eyes narrowing.

"This isn't the way you were going!" she said sullenly. "I won't go back. I'm a big girl, and they treat me like I was a kid. I won't go back! If you won't take me, I'll drown myself!"

"We'll go along! 'Along' isn't 'back,' is it now? Along, you know: matches up with song, don't you see? Green grass! see those pretty yaller flowers! They're along, too, just a piece! Let's we gather some, see if they're sweet as they are pretty!"

Still holding her wrist in that firm grasp, rambling on about the flowers, he stooped to pluck them, and managed to turn back in the direction of Cyrus.

"Now we'll come along!" he proclaimed. "Here's a good clear stretch of road, and I'll sing—you just listen!"

Never before, it seemed to Pippin, had he let his voice out to its full power. He felt it fly like a bird before him; it must reach all the way, it *must*!

66

"When I can read my title clearTo mansions in the skies,

("He'll hear that sure! he'll sense it in a minute, and know it's all right!")

"I'll bid farewell to every fear,And wipe my weeping eyes!

"So we will, Miss Flora May, won't we? You sing, too, that's a dandy girl! Let her go, Gallagher!"

Two hundred yards away, a man was driving through the woods at top speed of his lumbering horse. Brows bent, lips compressed, deadly fear at his heart, he sat unseeing, silent, save when he urged the clumsy beast to still further effort. Fear at his heart, and anger, and bewilderment; but struggling with all these something that said dazedly over and over,

"I don't believe it! He wasn't that kind! I don't believe it!"

Suddenly he checked the horse and threw up his head, listening. Through the trees, down the wood road, a voice came flying like a bird, ringing like a trumpet, crying like a great wind in his ears:

"I'll bid farewell to every fear,And wipe my weeping eyes!"

"Lord, forgive me!" cried Jacob Bailey. "Lord, have mercy on me, and never let him know!"

A glint of blue among the trees, the jingle of a little bell that hung beside the wheel; next moment they came in sight, Pippin first, chin in air, mouth open, singing as a bird sings, with every fibre of his being; the girl hanging back a little, held close by that strong hand, but singing, too, in a sweet, broken voice.

"Let cares like a wild deluge come,And storms of sorrow fall,May I but safely reach my home,My God, my heaven, my all!"

"Why, if here isn't our Mr. Bailey, this minute of time!" cried Pippin. "Why— why, Miss Flora May, he's cryin'! Mr. Bailey, you sick, sir? Miss Flora May, you climb right in the wagon, and comfort him up pretty!"

"That was a close call!"

Pippin stood rubbing his head with his file, gazing after the retreating wagon. His cheek had blanched under the tan, and his breath came quick and short. Pippin had been frightened, a thing that had hardly happened since the days when fear was his yokefellow, day and night.

"That," he repeated, "was a close call, as close as I want in mine. S'pose I'd got further off, so's he couldn't catch me up. What would he ha' thought? Poor innocent gal! Gee! The Lord stood by me good that time! But—gorry! S'pose I'd ben—Gives me the cold shivers to think of it. Now—now—I wonder—"

Pippin stood fingering his file absently, deep in thought. How to help a person like that? He had wanted to help her, sure thing, and now—'peared like all he had done was to hender. He expected 'twas his being a new person, breakin' in, like that, when she was used to havin' things quiet and all of a piece, so to say. He sighed, and replaced the file. Best leave it, after all, to them dandy folks; they was used to handlin' her and they knowed how. Best he keep away, till he had found the little gal, what say? Yes—but—now a doctor might know things that even Mr. and Mrs. Bailey wouldn't. Then he laughed, in spite of his trouble.

Now! How come he to think of that just now, of all times? Along back—way along back—they'd say White Patter over a person that was like that, not to say crazy, but a little wantin'. Old White Patter! They would, sure! Kind of an old charm; couldn't call it a prayer, but mebbe as nigh one as Granny Faa could manage to come. Pippin had tried to say it late times, but he couldn't seem to fetch it: now—now—

He lifted his head; it was coming back, the age-long jargon. Word by word, dropping into his mind from some limbo of things forgotten; word by word, he said it over aloud, standing in the wood road, the trees arching over his head, the moss curling round his feet.

White paternoster, St. Peter's brother,What hast 'ou i' the left hand?White-book leaves!What hast 'ou i' the right hand?Heaven-gate keys!Open heaven-gate and steek hell-gate!White paternoster, amen!

Back in the cellar! Darkness, foul air, fumes of liquor. Some one singing in drunken tones snatches of song vile as the liquor. The child, on his huddle of rags in the corner, shrinks and shudders, he knows not why. The old woman rises; there is a cuff, a curse, a maudlin whimper; she makes her way to the corner and bends over the child. "When he gets singin'," she whispers, "don't 'ee listen, Pippin! Stop your ears and say White Patter! Hark now, till I larn it 'ee!"

Bending lower, she recites the charm over and over, till the child with faltering lips can say it after her. "That'll keep 'ee safe!" says Granny Faa, and hobbles back to the spark of fire that keeps her old bones alive.

"'Twas all the prayer she knew!" said Pippin. "Green grass! But yet I expect the Lord understood. There's Amen to it, you see."

Joy of the road on a June morning! Who could taste it as Pippin did? It stood to reason that no one who had not been behind the bars could really know what it meant. Blue sky overhead—not a little square patch, but all you wanted, all there was—clear, deep, stainless, from rim to rim of the horizon. That would be enough just itself, wouldn't it, after three years of gray-white walls? But there was all the rest beside; trees still in their young, exquisite green, birds not in cages but flitting from branch to branch, singing, singing—

Flowers along the road: buttercups, Pippin's own flower that the Lord gave him that day; daisies, too; beautiful, wicked orange hawkweed, and good honest dandelions, each one a broad gold piece of Summer's coinage. Grass, too—gorry! 'twas in There ("There" was Shoreham) he got the habit of saying "Green grass!" It did him good just to think of it, and it filled the mouth full as good as swearin', for all he could see. He used to think about it; used to wonder, on breathless days when the gray-white walls radiated heat—and other things than heat—how it would feel to lie down and roll in grass, cool, moist, fragrant.

Ah! and now here it was under his feet, an elastic, emerald carpet. All he wanted of that, too! Were ever such uncountable riches as Pippin's this June morning?

He was to have yet more, Croesus that he was. On the left of the road a glint of rosy purple showed against the black tree trunks. He stepped aside and parted the branches. A little ferny hollow, with a tiny stream babbling through: beside the stream masses of purple blossoms, delicate, glowing, exquisite.

"Green grass!" said Pippin. He stood for some time gazing; asking no questions of Rhodora, being no critic, but taking his fill of delight in simple thankfulness. "Gee!" he murmured, as he let the branches droop again over the enchanted place. "And that's right here, by the side of the road, a reg'lar flower show, and no charge for admission. Now what do you think of that for a world to live in? I tell you, Paradise has got to toe the mark to get ahead of that. What say?"

The trees grew thinner, fell away to a fringe; the road grew broader and more even. Presently a house or two came in sight. Yes, this was the Kingdom road; he remembered that white house. He would be back in time for dinner; then he'd put in two three days—or a week, mebbe—finding that boy, and finding—yes, he sure would—the grace of God in him. Take a boy like that, and he could be no more than egged over with sin, like you do coffee cake: it hadn't had time to grime into him. And—come to get him all clean and nice and steppin' the Lord's way again, what was to hender his steppin' right into his, Pippin's, shoes and bein' handy man to Mr. Baxter? Green grass! Pippin had planned lays before now, but he never planned a prettier one than what this would be if it worked out good—and it would! And then it

69

was the city, and to find that little gal. He had never meant to go back to the city, chaplain had told him not to; but if he knew how things was, he would say go, he sure would, Elder Hadley would. Yes, sir! And when he found her—well! After all, the Old Man was her father, and he wouldn't be lasting long anyhow, and if she was a good gal she wouldn't grudge him a portion of time. Mebbe even she'd be fond of him: you never could tell what a woman wouldn't be fond of. Why, Sheeny's wife was fond of him. Used to come over There once a month reg'lar and cry over him 'cause he was in for a long jolt; now you'd thought, knowin' Sheeny, she'd cry if he wasn't. And, gee! there was the meetin'-house, and if Pippin wasn't holler for his dinner, believe *him*!

CHAPTER VIII
PIPPIN SETS BREAD AND LAYS A PLAN

THE Baxters received Pippin with open arms. 'Peared like he had been away a week, they said, instead of just over night. They certainly had missed him. No, they hadn't set the dough yet: they were just thinking of it, but they thought likely—well, hadn't he better have his supper first? No such great hurry, though of course 'twas *about* time—

"Gimme five minutes," said Pippin, "and then just watch me!"

In five minutes, washed and brushed, spotless in white cap and apron, his arms bare to the shoulder, he appeared shouting for his task.

Everything was white in the bakery; shining white of tiles and vessels, soft white of scoured pine, softer white of snowy flour. The great caldron stood ready, under the chute that led from the upper floor. Pippin pressed a knob, and down came the flour, in a steady stream. Pretty, Pippin thought, to watch it piling up in a soft cone, falling away in tiny avalanches, piling up again.

Another touch; the stream is checked. Now for the salt and sugar. Now yeast, milk and water, half and half: more whiteness, brimming in a white pail. In it goes, with wonderful effects of bubbling and creaming, while snowy clouds float up and settle on Pippin's brown face and sinewy arms.

He touches another knob; down comes the iron dasher—this, too, shining in white enamel—and round and round it goes, tossing, dropping, gathering, tossing again, steadily, patiently; that is the way they mix bread at Baxter's bakery.

Pippin watches it, fascinated; he never tires of the wonder of it. But presently Mrs. Baxter calls. "Supper, Pippin, come now! Buster'll mind Elbert for you."

Elbert is the dasher, named for the brother baker who persuaded Father Baxter to give up hand mixing and take to machinery. Pippin gives the machine a friendly pat. "Good old Elbert!" he says. "Keep it up, old figger-head! I'll be back, time you're ready to lay off. She's all right, Buster," as the boy enters, munching his final doughnut. "In great shape, Elbert is! You want to scrape her down a mite—" give it twenty masculine names, and a machine must still be feminine—"when she gets balled up, that's all. She's just as sensible—why, she can all but talk, this machine can."

"Mourns good and plenty," chuckles Buster, "when she's dry."

71

"Lots of folks mourn when they're dry! I shall be mournin' myself if I wait any longer for that cup o' coffee your ma's got for me. So long, old sport!"

"You said you'd tell me that story about Mike Cooney and the turkey!"

"Sure thing! But I didn't say I'd tell you when your ma was keepin' supper for me. Quit now!"

Seeing he was so late, Mrs. Baxter thought he might as well set right down here at the kitchen table; here was his ham and eggs and coffee, and the pie and doughnuts handy by. She'd been flustrated up all day. Had Pippin heard that there was thieves about? No, Pippin hadn't; he wanted to know if there was! Well, 'twas so. Mis' Wilkins had two pies stole last night right off the butt'ry shelf, and a jug of cider, and matches all over the floor; and night before that they broke into Al Tibbetts's store, broke open the till and made away with two dollars and seventy-five cents. There! She was so nervous she thought she should fly. Did Pippin think the lock was real safe on the bakery door?

Pippin, after reassuring her on this point, grew thoughtful over his supper, so thoughtful that he was reproached for not eating a thing. He roused himself.

"Not eatin'! Just you watch me, Mis' Baxter! Know what ailed the man that wouldn't eat a supper like this? Well, he was dead, that was what troubled him!"

The table cleared, Pippin washed his hands and arms at the sink, and joined Mr. and Mrs. Baxter on the back porch. Soon two pipes were puffing, and three rocking chairs (Buster had unwillingly gone bedward) creaked and whined comfortably. It was a soft, dark night, just cool enough for comfort, Pippin thought, and yet warm enough—well, warm enough for comfort, too. The back porch looked out on a little gully, the bed of a stream that flowed through Kingdom to join the river near at hand. White birches grew on the steep banks—you could see them glimmering through the dark—and the place was full of fireflies; the stream murmured drowsily over its pebbles.

"Green grass!" murmured Pippin. "Now wouldn't it give you a pain to think of leavin' this?"

They were three tired people—Mrs. Baxter had done a big ironing, and the baker had missed Pippin sorely—and for some time were content to sit silent, rocking softly, breathing tranquilly, "just letting go," as Mrs. Baxter put it. But after a half-hour of this pleasant peace, Pippin sighed, knocked the ashes from his pipe, and sat up straight in his chair.

"Now, folks," he said, "I've got to talk."

Mrs. Baxter woke out of a comfortable doze; Mr. Baxter straightened himself and knocked out his own ashes. "That's right!" he said. "We'll be pleased to hear you, Pippin. I heard you tellin' Buster, and it sounded real interestin'. Fire away!"

"Well!" said Pippin ruefully. "I'm in hopes you won't be any *too* well pleased, Father Baxter. The heft of what I have to say is in four words: I got to leave!"

The rocking chairs creaked with startled emphasis.

"You ain't, Pippin!"

"You don't mean it, Pippin!"

"You're jokin'! He's jokin', mother, can't you see?"

"I wish't I was!" sighed Pippin. "I tell you, Mr. and Mrs., I don't want to leave, no way, shape, or manner; but yet I got to. Lemme tell you, and you'll see for yourselves. First place, I got to tell Mis' Baxter about before I come here. Yes, Boss, I just plain *got* to! I meant all along to tell her before I left, but I've kind of put it off—the further I get from that feller I used to be, the worse I hate him! Well!"

Slowly and carefully Pippin rehearsed the familiar story, hiding nothing, glossing nothing over, giving what glory there was to the Lord and Elder Hadley. When he finished this part, the baker was holding one of his hands, his wife the other, both uttering exclamations of pity, sympathy, encouragement.

That wouldn't make no difference, the good people assured him, not the least mite. "Why, he told me the very first day, mother! I didn't want to make you nervous, so I kep' it to myself. It don't cut no ice with us, Pippin, not a—"

Pippin checked them gently; that was only the first chapter. He went on to tell of his visit to Cyrus Poor Farm (omitting only the episode of Flora May), and of his promises to Old Man Blossom and to Jacob Bailey.

"Now you see, you nice folks—you nicest kind of folks—here I be! I *love* bakin'—if I was to work within four walls there's nothin' else I'd choose so soon—but it isn't so intended; I make sure of that. Here I be, promised to the Old Man to find his little gal if she's to be found (and that means if she's alive), and promised to Mr. Bailey to get hold of that boy and give him a boost. You see how 'tis, don't you? Well, of course! I knew you would! Well, now I was studyin' this out all the way home, and the Lord took hold and showed me His idea, and I think 'twill work out real good, if we have luck. I say 'we,' because you folks have got to help."

"For pity's sake, Pippin!"

"Yes, Mis' Baxter, for pity's sake! That's the stuff. And that boy's sake. Suppose it was Buster! This is a good boy, mind you, only weak. Suppose it was Buster! Look at here! This is the way I've worked it out. Mr. Bailey is a dandy man, and Mis' Bailey ekally so woman, but they made a big mistake. What did that boy need? He needed other boys, and there wasn't none round, so happened. There was old folks, and blind folks, and wantin' folks, some good as gold and others—well, the reverse! He didn't want none of 'em; he wanted a pal! Well! He got one, and he got a crook. That was his streak of bad luck, see? And he's in it still. Way I look at it, we got to haul him out, ain't it?"

"I'll do my part, Pippin!" said Mrs. Baxter promptly.

"Count me in!" said the baker. "I don't know what I can do, 'less it's knead the youngster up in a batch of dough and bake him to keep him out of mischief, but count me in!"

"Well!" said Pippin. He leaned forward, a hand on the knee of either. His voice dropped to a whisper. "Now—"

He paused abruptly. Something was moving in the gully beneath them. With a swift gesture of caution, he stole noiselessly to the railing of the porch and looked down. All was soft darkness, save where the birches glimmered dusky white, where the fireflies danced and shone. The stream droned on; the night clung closer. Look! Was that a blacker shadow there, just where the old willow overhung the stream? Was it a shadow that moved, followed by a second stealthy shade? A twig snapped; a branch rustled. Hark! Was that a whisper, a footstep? The fireflies rose in a wild whirl, scattered, came together, resumed their rhythmic dance, filling the little glen with golden sparks. Silence fell like a mantle.

CHAPTER IX
PIPPIN ENCOUNTERS THE RED RUFFIAN

THE days that followed Pippin's disclosure of his plan were troublous ones for Mrs. Baxter. She looked under the bed a dozen times a day; she avoided the broom closet for fear of what might lurk there; if a door resisted her opening, she made sure it was held on the other side. For the first time, terror entered her life. It had been a comfortable life: she had been a good and cheerful baby, child, maiden; she was a good and cheerful woman. She had known that this was a wicked world, and—in a general way—that there were bad people even in Kingdom. They never entered the bakery, but tales of them were whispered over the counter during the tying up of buns and coffee cakes. And we were all miserable sinners, of course, especially on Sunday. But now she was living *in* a tale! Their own Pippin, Pippin of the bright eyes, the winning smile, the pleasant, helpful ways—Pippin had been one of the wicked. And now there were more of them about, walking Kingdom streets, perhaps—she shuddered—looking in the window the moment while her back was turned; and she was to be called upon to help save one of them.

"But I've had no experience!" she would say piteously. "I don't know how to talk to them kind of persons, Pippin. I've had no experience!"

"Well, you're goin' to have!" Pippin told her cheerily. "Woman dear, crooks is just folks, same as other folks; they ain't painted black, outside or in. You know how to talk to me well enough, don't you?"

"Oh, Pippin!"

"Well, then! Just bear in mind that what this boy is, I was, only about a thousand times wuss. Why, he's nothin' *but* a boy! Say to yourself, 'S'pose it was Buster!' Say it over and over till it comes easy as breathin'!"

"Yes, Pippin!" said Susan Baxter.

As for Pippin himself, the days were not long enough for him. He was making the most of his last week of baking. Hitherto he had kept strictly to bread, rolls and doughnuts; but now he essayed loftier flights, wrestled with coffee cake, overcame; made his first batch of pies and glowed with pride to hear them pronounced A No. . Between work hours he ranged the town with his wheel, and at every corner people gathered round him, ostensibly to have their knives sharpened, though by this time there was hardly a dull knife in Kingdom—really to watch Pippin at work and hear him sing. He scanned every group with eager eyes, but saw no strange faces, only the kindly Kingdom Comers, as he called them, who were all his friends. After dark, leaving his wheel at home, he might drop in on Father O'Brien or Elder Stebbins for an hour's chat, and hear what was going on in the two parishes, to both of which he considered himself to belong.

"Say, that was a dandy anthem, wasn't it?" he would say to the good Father. "Suited me down to the ground! Good sermon you preached, too, Father. Common sense! I liked that sermon. Only, wasn't you just a mite hard on the heathen? I've known dandy heathen, sir, simply dandy. I wish't you knew old Sing Lee. He used to tell about a guy they call Confusion, and I never could see why they called him that, for he was plain as print, 'peared to me, and his ideas was dandy, they sure was. Well, so long, Father! Yes, sir, I'd like a blessin' real well; thank you kindly!"

Taking his leave, he would leave the house very quietly, shutting the door after him without a sound. Before going home he would wander, apparently aimlessly, about the town, diving into alleys, coming suddenly round corners, exploring the quarter of the town known familiarly as Devildom.

During this week the pilferings hung fire. Anxious housewives counted their garments on the line, storekeepers looked well to tills, locks and bolts, and slept with their pocketbooks under their pillows; but nothing happened, and it began to be whispered about that "the mean folks" had left town and gone elsewhere.

Toward the end of the week Pippin made an excursion to a neighboring village on urgent representation from one of its inhabitants, "sharpened 'em up good," as he expressed it, all round, gave them a Gospel concert, spent a happy day visiting round among the scattered farms, and started for home with a light heart and a pocketful of dimes. He had covered a good deal of ground, and became aware that he was distinctly "leg weary"; but green grass! he thought, what a dandy time he had had, and how good supper would taste!

It was growing dusk as he drew near Kingdom. There was the patch of woods that was full of violets a month ago. He wondered if there would be any still in bloom. Mrs. Baxter was ter'ble fond of violets (and yet they wa'n't her pattern, you'd think; pineys was more her kind), but if there *was* any violets—

Entering the cool shade of the wood path, he was pacing slowly along, glancing left and right for the "proud virgins of the year," when he heard a rustling among the bushes by the roadside. Thought flashed back to that day—only a week ago, was it? It seemed a month—when those other bushes had rustled. For an instant he dreaded to see the pale, lovely, imploring face of the imbecile girl; then common sense returned. "She couldn't have got so far," was his first thought; "nor yet she wouldn't be wearin' pants!" his second. There was no time for a third. Out from the shadow stepped two masked figures, one of them with a leveled pistol.

"Throw up your hands!"

"That's what!" said Pippin.

The holder of the pistol—a slight, youthful-looking fellow, gave a triumphant laugh, and glanced over his shoulder at his companion. He laughed too soon. In the act of lifting his hands, Pippin made two catlike steps forward, tripped, fell heavily against him, and the two came to the ground together. There was a brief struggle, the two rolling over and over, silent and breathless. When it ended Pippin was sitting on his assailant's head, and it was he who held the pistol. Thus seated, he put two fingers to his mouth and gave a shrill and piercing whistle in three notes: up, down, up. At sound of this, the second, who had been hovering in the background, took to his heels and fled as if for his life.

"Green grass!" said Pippin. "That worked pretty, didn't it?"

The person under him struggled and groaned.

"Like me to move a little ways?" said Pippin, and moved down to his chest. "There! Breathe easier that way, can't ye? Well, what about it?"

"Lemme up!" cried the sufferer. "—— —— you, lemme up!"

Pippin drew out his red handkerchief, and calmly stuffed it into the fellow's mouth. "Just till you can speak pretty!" he said. "You're free to hold me up, if you know enough, which you don't, but I've no call to hear your language when I don't like it. That's square, ain't it?"

Presently he removed the handkerchief and tied the fellow's wrists with it in a workmanlike fashion. "There now, we can chin a spell; what say?"

Quitting his uneasy seat, he helped the other to his feet, and as he did so, twitched the mask from his face. Then he whistled. It was a boy's face that scowled at him, angry and frightened. A boy of sixteen or seventeen, not bad-looking either—

"Green grass!" said Pippin under his breath. "I'll bet—" but he did not say what he would bet. Instead, he bade the other, kindly, to see what a fool he had went and made of himself. It was easy to see he was new to the trade. The other guy was the old hand, eh, what? He judged so from the way he lifted his feet. Lifted—his—feet— Where had Pippin seen feet lift like them, pounding that way? Memory seemed to hover for an instant, but was gone before he could catch it.

"And think of your tryin' it on one of your own trade!" said Pippin comfortably. "Me, that was old to the fancy when you was nussin' your bottle. That was hard luck, wasn't it? And yet—who knows? Mebbe 'twas good luck, too!"

"What—what you mean?" stammered the boy. "Do you mean that you—"

"Well, I guess! Brought up to it from a baby. Ever hear of the Honey Boys of Blankton? Well, I'd like to know who was boss of the Honey Boys, if 'twasn't me. Yes, sir! I could tell you stories—Say we sit down a spell!"

They sat. Pippin told a few stories with apparent gusto. "Now," he said, "let's hear what you have to tell, bo!"

The boy, nothing loth, poured out a wild, foolish tale enough. How he was bred to farming, and despised it; how he meant to make his fortune and come back a rich man, and show them—yes, siree! he'd show them whether he was a lunkhead or not! How he met up with that feller over yonder hayin', and heard how things was done, and they went to Kingdom. There wasn't much doin' there, so to-night Reilly said he'd show him about road work, and let him try his hand.

"But, honest, I don't believe he'd ha' done any better than I did!" cried the boy, his weak, handsome face aglow with admiration. "He wouldn't ha' stood up against you. Say, you done that slick, Mr.——I don't know what your name is!"

"Try Moonlighter," said Pippin—"Moonlighter or Jack-o'-Lantern; I've answered to both names. As to your friend, you're well rid of him. If you ask me, he's a sneak and a skunk. He won't come back; I doubt if he stops this side of the city. What makes me think so? Why, you heard me whistle?"

"Yes; what did it mean?"

"Cop's whistle: look out, there's crooks about. He didn't know I wasn't callin' my mate, did he? No, nor yet you don't know! But I like your looks, bo! You ain't a sneak, are you? You wouldn't give a pal away, if he was to show you a firstrate plant—what say?"

The boy stammered protestations and assurances.

"That's right! Oh, you can tell from a guy's looks, when you're used to sizin' folks up. Now if you really mean business—" Pippin paused, drew out his file, whistled on it softly, winked and replaced it—"if you really mean business, bo—" he said.

When Pippin entered Kingdom town again, it was by a back way little frequented. He trod softly and warily, and at his heels trod his late assailant, now his slave and devotee.

Pippin would show Red Ruffi'n (thus he had named the lad) a place where he could rest safe and easy till next night. Things wouldn't be ready till next night; he had a heap to do. Red Ruffi'n would see; this was a dandy place, where he'd be as safe as he would to home. Just let him show him! Go easy now!

Kingdom, neat, prosperous little town though it was, had its slum; a huddle of ramshackle cottages tumbling up and down a ragged hill. The cottages were in sad need of paint and shingles, their windows held more old hats than glass, the linen that flapped about them on sagging clotheslines did not look particularly clean.

Close by was the village dump, exhaling unsavory odors. By day this spot was haunted by frowsy children and slatternly women, grubbing about the edges of the dump for an orange that might be partly good, a box that would split up for kindling; but now all was quiet in Devildom. The place was the scandal of Kingdom housewives. Pippin had usually avoided it, but now he led the way thither eagerly. Skirting the edge of the dump, he came to a spot where a ledge cropped out, partly overhanging a tiny hollow. He had seen some children playing here once, and had noted the spot as a good hiding hole, thanking the Lord that he never would need to hide, never no more, glory be!

"There!" he said, and turned to his companion. "Here you'll be safe as you would in your own bed. Folks is scared of this place, think it's ha'nted; won't nobody come nigh, you see if there does."

"Is—is it?" asked the Red Ruffian, in a tone that might have sounded timorous had his character been less desperate.

"Is it what? Ha'nted? I dunno. I never see anything here but once, and then I wasn't quite positive. Somethin' white an' misty went past, sort o' groanin' to itself; I couldn't pass no judgment what it was. Anyway, they say if you speak up to 'em, same as you would, they can't do a person no hurt. But say, ain't this a dandy hole? Now you rest easy here, and I'll come to-morrow night and fetch you. Here's some crackers: what say?"

"It—it smells bad, don't it?" The boy was sniffing with evident disrelish.

"Yes!" Pippin glowed enthusiastic. "Don't it? Real bad. That's another thing will keep folks away. Oh, you'll be as snug as—what say? Damp? No, it ain't! It's dry as a

79

lime-burner's wig. Gorry! I wish't I'd had a place like this, when I was—well, goodnight, Red Ruffi'n! Pleasant dreams to ye! You've got the countersign?"

"Ye-es! 'Blood is red!' Are you—are you going, Moonlighter?"

"That's what! Just wait till to-morrow night and you'll see stars! Green grass! we'll—have us—a time!"

His voice died away: the Red Ruffian tried to call him back, but failing, cowered down in his hiding hole and shivered.

The next day it rained; a gentle, steady downpour that evidently meant business. Mrs. Baxter, with looks of dismay, called Pippin's attention to the fact. Pippin chuckled and said it was great.

"But my land! That boy'll be all wet!"

"You bet he will! Wet through to his bones, I tell you!" Pippin chuckled again. "Might I trouble you for a morsel of the pork, Mrs. Baxter?"

Mrs. Baxter passed the pork absently, stirred her coffee absently. Presently: "What's he got for breakfast?" she asked.

"Crackers!" said Pippin gleefully. "Nice dry sody crackers; or mebbe they ain't quite so dry by now; *and* a cigar!"

"Pippin!" Mrs. Baxter looked reproach.

"Yes, ma'am! Nice long black cigar, the strongest I could find in the store. Green grass! Mr. Baxter, where'd you s'pose Ed Nevins got them cigars? Why, they'd knock a bullock stiff!"

"My land! It'll make him *sick*!" cried Mrs. Baxter.

"Well, I guess! If there's a sicker boy in Kingdom than what he'll be, I'm sorry for him!" Pippin threw back his head and laughed gleefully, Mr. Baxter joining in with a deep rumble over his pork and beans.

Mrs. Baxter's dark eyes flashed.

"I'd like to know what *you* find to laugh at, Timothy Baxter! I must say I think you're real unfeelin', both of you." She brushed the crumbs from her apron with hands that trembled. "That boy—and you *said* he was motherless, Pippin, I heard you—out in the rain all day, half starved, and then to make him sick—there! I think menfolks is just *mean*!" She rose from the table. As she turned away, Pippin caught at the corner of her apron.

"Don't be mad with me, Mis' Baxter!" he pleaded.

"Well, I *am*!" Mrs. Baxter turned squarely upon him. "I am mad with both of you, and what's more, I'm disgusted. There!"

"Hold on, Ma!" Father Baxter pushed his chair back and came to lay a calm hand on her shoulder. "Now, Ma, you behave! We agreed to let Pippin run this show, didn't we? Well, then, what I say is, *let* him run it!"

"But I never—" Mrs. Baxter began indignantly.

"Hold on, Ma! Pippin knows this kind of boy, and you don't, nor I don't, over 'n' above. He ain't calculatin' to give him a birthday party, with a frosted cake and seventeen candles and one to grow on; are you, Pippin?"

"You bet I ain't!" Pippin was glowing with earnestness. "I'm goin' to give him— why, look at here, Mis' Baxter! When Buster ate them green apples last week, what was't you give him? A portion of physic, wasn't it? I thought so! Well, you physicked his stummick, 'cause he'd got things in it that didn't belong there; woman dear, I'm goin' to physic this boy's soul, and don't you forget it!"

At the ring in his voice, the kindling light in his eyes, the good woman melted. The tears came into her eyes and her lips quivered.

"That's right!" Pippin was stroking her head now and talking as if to a little child. "You'll see, 'twill all come out nice as pie. And you got your part to do, you know, Mis' Baxter. You're goin' to have the best hot supper, and the warmest bed, and the dryest clothes that ever was, ready by the time we get through to-night. Yes, ma'am! And Mr. Baxter, he's goin' to do his part—"

"I am!" said the baker solemnly. "I don't know yet just what it'll be, but I'm goin' to do it all the same."

"Green grass!" cried Pippin. "You *are* dandy folks, no use talkin' 'bout it!"

CHAPTER X
PIPPIN LOOKS FOR THE GRACE OF GOD

ALL day long the rain fell, softly, steadily, without haste and without rest; all day long the Red Ruffian cowered in his hiding hole, cold, wet, hungry and miserable. The water trickled in streams down the rock behind him and gathered in pools about his feet. The dump near by steamed, and sent off noisome fumes. Rats ran in and out of it; the Ruffian was afraid of rats.

What did the boy think of as he sat huddled under the partial shelter of the ledge, munching his sodden crackers? Did he picture to himself the glories of successful crime, the riches won by skill and daring, the revels with other chosen spirits? No! He thought of Cyrus Poor Farm. He saw the bright, cozy kitchen, the wide fireplace, the cheerful glowing of the stove. He saw the table spread with its homely, hearty fare: baked beans, done to a turn, with that dusky-gold crisp on the pork that none save Aunt Bailey could give; the potatoes roasted in their jackets; the brown bread—at thought of the brown bread the Ruffian groaned aloud and passed the back of his hand across his eyes.

The long day wore on. The slow hours chimed from the church beyond the hill. His one comfort was the thought of the cigar inside his shirt, dry and safe in its oiled paper. The matches were safe, too, in a tin box. He would wait till along towards dark, and then smoke. It would chirk him up good, and when Moonlighter came to fetch him, he'd find him as gay—as gay—a strong shiver seized him, and his teeth chattered. Wasn't it about time? It was growing dusk. At last, with wet, trembling fingers, he drew out his prize. Sheltering it with his body from the pitiless rain, he struck a match and applied it to the cigar. The tiny flame spurted, clung, shrank to a spark, spurted again—the cigar was alight.

It was near midnight. The rain had ceased, and a dense white mist was rising from the drenched earth. A breeze came sighing through the branches of the trees, rustling the grasses round the hiding hole; it was answered by a low moan from the sodden figure that lay stretched in the hollow under the rock. It was his last moan, Myron thought. Death was coming; this white mist was his shroud. They would find him here—or maybe they would not. Maybe his bones would whiten in this dismal spot, and years after, the traveler—Hark! what was that? A sound, that was not wind or trees or grasses: a long, low, wailing cry.

The wretched boy struggled up on one elbow and peered through the thick white curtain, then, with a smothered shriek, he scrambled to his hands and knees. Something was there! Something whiter than the mist; something that moved—

"Help!" cried the Red Ruffian. "Murder! Help!"

"Hush!" said Pippin. "Hold your darned noise! *Steel is sharp!*"

"Oh! oh, dear! oh—*blood is red*! Is it you, Moonlighter? Why are you—why are you all in white?"

"Make folks think I was the ha'nt, bonehead! What'd you s'pose? Cute trick, I thought!"

Pippin stepped down into the hollow and threw off the sheet that covered him.

"Well, how are you, young feller?" he asked cheerfully.

"I'm dyin'!" said the boy feebly. "Tell the folks I—"

"Oh, shucks! Here, set up—so! It's stopped rainin'. My! you are wet, ain't you? Feelin' sick? I expect that cigar *was* a mite—*here!* lean up against the ledge here, and take a drink!"

Reader, have you ever tasted spice-draught? Its basic principle is peppermint. To this is added cinnamon, cloves, cassia, and a liberal dash of cayenne pepper. "Temp'rance toddy," I have heard it called, but there is nothing temperate about it. "S'archin'" is the adjective Pippin used.

"Take a good swig!" he urged, putting the bottle to the boy's lips. "It's hot stuff, I tell ye!"

The boy drank; next moment he was on his feet, coughing, dancing round, and holding his throat. A howl of anguish broke from him, but Pippin checked it with a hand over his mouth.

"Easy, boy, easy! 'Twill het you up good; nothin' like it, Mis'—that is, they claim. Don't you feel it livenin' of you up? That's hearty! Now you'll find your legs. Lean against me if you're wobbly still. Time we was on our job! Foller, Red Ruffi'n!"

As they went along, Pippin explained the nature of the job. A soft snap, just the thing for a green hand. Nice, quiet folks, sound sleepers, old-fashioned lock—pick it with one hand while you eat your dinner with the other. Honest, if he didn't feel that Red Ruffi'n *needed* a soft snap, he wouldn't hardly have had the heart to ease them, they *was* such nice folks. Been real good to him, too, and would be to any one come nigh 'em, but Red Ruffi'n was his pal, and pals were bound to see each other through.

"S'pose—s'pose we was pinched!" said Red Ruffi'n, stumbling along over the plashy ground. "What would—"

"Shoreham!" Pippin gave a lively sketch of the place; the Red Ruffian shuddered and coughed.

"Moonlighter," he said, after a pause; "I hadn't ought to get you into this. I—I ain't feelin' well, either; s'pose we—what say?"

Pippin took his arm with a grip as firm as it was quiet.

"Testin' me, are ye?" he laughed. "Tryin' to see if I'd crawl—what? There's no crawl in me, not an inch! Just wait till we get in where it's warm and dry, and you'll see things different: not but I know you was only foolin'. Crawl *now*, when everything's all ready? Gee! I would be a softy, wouldn't I? Here's the gully! Now you go first and I'll foller and keep watch behind; stop when you hear me peep like a chicken!"

With faltering steps the unhappy Ruffian crept along the gully, keeping well in the shadow, starting at every stray cat, every scrap of wind-whisked paper. Pippin, stepping lightly and softly a few yards behind, whistled noiselessly, and pursued an imaginary conversation with Mrs. Baxter.

"Just you trust me, Mis' Baxter, and you'll see. Why, you don't think I'd take all this trouble, and *give* all this trouble, if I weren't certain sure that I was right? 'He leadeth me,' you know, ma'am, and the Lord is sure leadin' me this time. There's no harm will come of it, but only good, if I'm not a bonehead from Bonetown. Now see—"

He peeped low, like a day-old chicken; the slinking figure in advance stopped.

It was, as Pippin had said, an easy lock to pick. A stout hairpin of Mrs. Baxter's did the trick; a nice tool, Pippin pronounced it gravely. The door swung open, revealing blackness. The Red Ruffian, shrinking back, found himself gently but firmly propelled forward; he stumbled over the threshold and the door closed noiselessly behind him. "This way!" Pippin guided him through a passage, over another threshold. "Here we be!" Closing another door, Pippin produced a match, lighted a bit of candle. "The bakery!" he whispered. "The money is in here! Hush! Take your shoes off; one of 'em squeaks."

The flickering light shone on the white tiles, the glittering enamel, the black doors of the ovens; the further corners of the room were in deep shadow.

"Did it squeak loud? Do you think—do you think any one heard? Hark! What was that?"

"Nothin'! Mouse, mebbe! Now look! The cash is in that box, see? Under the table there; make it out? Now, Red Ruffi'n, this is your job, and you are goin' to have the credit of it. I'll hold the light; you reach down and get the box—"

Mr. Baxter had felt all along that when the time came, he would know what to do. A calm man, he had followed Pippin's instructions implicitly, had now stood patiently for an hour in his dark corner, leaning on his "peel," the long broad-bladed, paddle-like implement which bore the loaves to and from the oven. Mrs. Baxter, in the shop, might palpitate and wring her hands and moan, only restrained by thoughts of Buster slumbering above; Mr. Baxter awaited his moment, and it came.

By the flickering candlelight, he saw a cringing, trembling figure creep forward, and bend over, displaying to his view a broad expanse of trouser. To the father of Buster, that expanse suggested but one thing in the world. Raising the peel, he brought it down with a resounding thwack which sent the boy flat on his face under the table and brought Mrs. Baxter shrieking from the shop.

"Elegant!" said Pippin. "Mr. Baxter, sir, that was simply elegant!"

An hour later the Red Ruffian, full, dry, and warm, a plaster over his injured nose, lay in Pippin's bed; and Pippin ("as per contract with the Elder," he told himself, "lettin' alone its bein' right and fittin' so to do") sat on the edge of the bed and looked for the grace of God.

He began by explaining his plot in full: how he had been at the Poor Farm, heard Mr. Bailey's story, and promised to find the boy if he could; how the Lord had come into it and played right into his hand; how the excellent baker and his wife had agreed to help; how everything had went smooth as greased lightnin'—he never see anything work out neater and prettier.

"Here! Take another drink of the lemonade! 'Tis some different from spice-draught. Gee, wasn't that something fierce! I expect it kep' you from pneumony, though!"

Pippin held the lemonade to the boy's lips, and patted the pillows tenderly, as a woman might. Meeting his eyes, dark with shame, misery, and reproach, he beamed on him benevolently.

"There!" he said. "I know how you feel. Look at it one way, 'twas a mean trick I played you, a mean, low-down trick. I ask your pardon for that! But look at here! I had to stop you, hadn't I? I'd passed my word, and, too, the Lord bid me. No gettin' away from that. Well, now, if I'd sat down there in the wood road that day, talked to you real fatherly and pious, told you thus and so, and asked wouldn't you be a good boy and go back to the farm and hoe potatoes—" The boy made a restless motion. Pippin laid a quiet hand on his arm. "Rest easy! I'll come to that presently! If I'd have done that, would you have listened to me? Not you! You'd ha' laughed at me for a gospel shark, and you'd have up and gone after that mean skunk (you notice he never turned round to look what become of you?) fast as you could pick up your heels. Then what? Say you'd caught up with him and gone on to the next town, and started in breakin' and enterin'! Well, what say? Why, then you'd ben pinched and run in. Yes siree Bob! You never was built for a crook, my lad; you're too slow, and you're too— call it clumpsy. You've no quicksilver in your toes, nor yet in your fingers. You'd ben run in, and then you'd gone to Shoreham. First offense, they might let you off with six months—more likely a year, but *say* six months! For six months, then, you'd worked as you never worked before in your little life, alongside of men—well—the Lord made 'em, amen!—only they ain't the kind you're used to. What I would say, there's no *ro*mance about Shoreham, not a mite, and don't you forget it! (Say, ain't this a dandy bed? I betcher! And all ready for the man that comes after me. We'll come to that bumby, too.) And if you try to hook it, or misbehave anyways, you get put in solitary. Know what that means? It means four walls with nothin' on 'em except the bricks, walls four feet apart one way and seven the other, and a grated door between you and anything else. It means twenty-four hours every day and each of 'em half of the whole, seems though! No! You can't understand, 'cause you haven't ben there. It means no word spoke or heard excep' when your victuals is passed in, and mighty few then, and what there is is no special pleasure to hear. Now, bo, that is what I've ben through, and that is what I've saved you from. Now what about it? Did I do right, or did I do wrong?"

"Right!" faltered the boy. "Oh, Moonlighter—"

"Hold on! Forget that! My name's Pippin, and that's what you call me from now on. I had to *show* you what I used to be, or you'd never have listened to me; *now*, I'm an honest man, and there's nobody I can't look in the face. Pippin's my name, and straight is my natur'. Praise the Lord! Amen! Well, sir, that is what I done. Now the question is, what next? And here comes in Mr. and Mrs. Baxter. Well, those folks are as good as they make 'em; they're as good as your Uncle and Aunt Bailey, and more is not to be said. They know all about me, and all about you. I'm leavin' 'em in a day or two, for good; and gorry, what do you think them two Bakin' Angels is ready to do? They stand ready to take you and make a baker of you. Now—rest easy! I got to get it all off my chest! Bakin' is as nice a trade, as *pretty* an all-round trade, as a man can ask for in this world. If I hadn't other things I'd undertaken to do—well, never mind that! Here you can stay, if you're a mind to, and if you feel like you've had your bellyful of breakin' and enterin', and like that; work in daylight and sunlight and free air, and eat choice food, and hear kind, decent, pleasant language and never anything else. That's what you've ben used to all your life, you'll say; yes, but there's more to it. Here you are in a town, and folks all round you, boys of your own age, nice clean fellers like you—you needn't winch! The dirt ain't grimed into you yet; 'twill wash off, you see!—boys to chin with, and play baseball with, and football; girls too, nice, pretty, refined young ladies, comin' in to buy creamcakes, and—green grass! I certingly shall miss those young ladies!—and—go to singin' school evenin's, and church meetin', and like that, and—well, that, sir, is what we offer, against the life of a crook. You balance them two in your mind, and think it over a bit!"

He made a motion with his hand, and turning his face away, was about to take counsel with himself, when the boy spoke hastily.

"Mr. Pippin," he said, "I—no need to think it over! I thank you a thousand times. I'm a fool, but I didn't know it before. Now I see it clear, and I thank you—I—I can't say what I feel, but I do sure feel it. I'd stay here glad and thankful, and I'd do my best, sir, honestly I would, and try to make good; but—but—"

"Well?" Pippin's eyes were very bright, he bent forward eagerly. "Well, youngster? What stands in the way?"

"Aunt and Uncle!" broke forth the boy. "I've been mean—mean as dirt, and they so good to me. If they'll let me, and if Mr. Baxter can wait, say a week, I'll come back more thankful than I've words to say; but first I must go home—and—"

A thwack upon his shoulders, almost as loud as that of the peel an hour before, sent him half out of bed. Looking up in terror, he saw Pippin standing over him with shining eyes and outstretched hand.

"Shake!" he said simply. "I've found what I was lookin' for. Let us praise the Lord!"

CHAPTER XI
THE CHAPLAIN READS HIS MAIL

THE chaplain was sorting his morning mail. He did it deftly and quickly, opening (with a thin-bladed paper knife; no ripping or tearing with hasty fingers), glancing over, destroying, filing, or laying in the "Answer immediately" pile. All this with his swift, careful fingers and half of his careful mind; the other half was busy over problems. Problems of Tom, of Dick, of Harry; problems mental, moral, physical. If he could only keep them apart, how much simpler it would be! But the three *would* run together, act and react one upon the other. One of his trusties was "wobbling," the guard told him; growing surly, careless, shirking his work here and there, getting up steam, Wilson the guard opined; liable to turn ugly any minute. What had happened? Well, he thought his egg had been smaller than the rest, last egg day; he'd been chewing the rag ever since. The chaplain sighed. What children they were!

He ran his eyes over a letter. It was from a prisoner's wife, begging to know how Nate was. She had been sick; would chaplain please tell Nate that was why she couldn't come last Tuesday? (Tuesday was visitors' day.) The children was smart. Joe and Susy was at school, but Benny had no shoes till she got her pay from the factory; she was working extra time to try and have something left over from the rent. They would get along all right till he, Nate, was out, and he could get a place right off in the mill, she guessed.

The chaplain sighed again, and laid the note on the growing pile of "Answer immediately." Poor Susan! She worked so hard, and was so hopeful! She always thought the last spree would remain the last; better so! He shook his head, seeing Nate's weak, comely face, sodden with drink. Poor Susan! Poor women! God help them all!

He opened another letter, and learned that "yrs. respect'ly, Wm. Billiam," hadn't got no work yet; no wun appeared to want him though he show them the note, sir and sum sed when they was a plaice he shood have it and a Nother man sed there wos not work enuf for strate men and he gessed crooks wood haf to wate till the pigs begin to fly "but I ramember wot you sed chapple In and i will keep strate sir you betcher life excusin bad writin'." This letter, written all downhill with no sign of punctuation, smudged and smeared by a not too clean shirtsleeve, might have brought a smile to some faces, but the chaplain's face was grave enough. The endless problem, the riddle without an answer. Not work enough for the honest men; yet if the discharged criminal cannot get work, how to prevent him from relapsing into crime? Who can blame him? He goes out with his little newborn resolve, a feeble, tottering thing, and tries for honest work. He has learned a trade behind the bars, perhaps; he can make brooms and mats, weave rough baskets, cobble shoes. He finds a dozen applicants before him. Questions are asked: Where has he worked? What references can he give? If he tells the truth, seven employers out of ten shake their heads. If he lies, he is found out after a time and the result is the same; he is "bounced." Who can blame the boss? Who can blame the man if—Round and round, over and over! No royal road anywhere. Nothing to do but keep on trying.

The chaplain raised his head, and the fighting look came into his eyes. Keep on! Never say die! The scroll—his eyes fell on the letter with its forlorn smudges; that one looked as if a tear had fallen and been wiped off with a grimy hand—the scroll was growing clearer; slowly, yes, but steadily. You had only to look back twenty years, ten years, five! Line upon line, precept upon precept; here a little and there a little—

"Aha!" The word was spoken aloud, in a tone of pleased surprise. "Pippin, I verily believe!" said the chaplain. He studied the superscription a moment. How he had labored over those upstrokes! It was a good hand now, though the scamp would never be a professor of calligraphy. Then he opened the envelope and read as follows:

DEAR FRIEND ELDER HADLEY RESPECTED SIR,

This is to state that I am first rate and hoping the same in regard to yourself and all friends there. Well Elder I am having a bully time right straight along. I am still to Kingdom in the bakery and grindin same as I last wrote but dont think I shall stop much longer, though I like first-rate and if I felt the Lord intended bakin for mine there's no dandier place, no sir nor one where I'd feel more at home. If they was my own folks they couldn't be kinder to me than what Mr. and Mrs. Baxter is. But I have fixed them all right with a nice boy will step right along and make an A baker if he has his health which appears rugged up to the present and he likes real well and so do they.

Well Elder you said to tell you when I found a Leadin; well sir I have, and it seems to squint like the Lord was showin me His hand. I found a dandy place sir, the dandyest you ever see and folks ekally so, and plenty of room; and savin this boy like, or the Lord savin him through me is what I would say, made me feel Elder I wanted to do *sompin for the boys.* Yes sir when I see that dandy place and only a few old folks that pooty soon their time would be up I thought fill that nice big house up with boys and learn em farmin and gardenin and like that, why twould be *great* elder. Take kids like I was with no folks of their own or bum ones which is worse; what I mean take em away from the city and give em hens to take care of and feed the pigs and learn ploughin and sowin and like that and live out doors with a good house to come in nights and good food and some person that knows boys and *feels for* em and knows what some of em has ben through, I think it would be great sir dont you. I tell you Elder there's guys in there, and lifers some of 'em, if they'd ben handled different when they was kids they'd *stayed* different yes sir they would and you said the same often. Now what I mean is when I've got this present job done and found that kid Im going to follow this lead, because I feel Elder the Lord is leadin me yes sir He sure is. I opened the lids of the Testament you give me and looked and first thing I see was "This should ye have done and not to leave the other undone." Now wouldn't that give you a pain and so it did me and I said lo here was I like Samuel and I am Elder so help me. Mr. Bailey would like it firstrate but he thinks twould take time I tell him I want to start right in soon as I have this job done. I am leavin tomorrow so no more from yours in the Lord and thanking you kindly Elder I am sure for all you done.

Yours resp'y.
PIPPIN.

The chaplain read this effusion through twice, a thoughtful frown knitting his brow, a smile curling the corners of his mouth.

He tilted his chair back against the wall, and looked out of the window. Pippin had been much in his mind since their parting two months before. This was the second letter he had received from him. The first had been written within a week of Pippin's leaving Shoreham, and told of his finding Nipper Crewe dying by the roadside, and of the wheel that he considered rightly his. That was a singular meeting, the chaplain thought. The old sinner, full of evil deeds and memories, suspected of many crimes large and small, yet so crafty withal and so passionately bent on keeping out of prison that for the most part he had succeeded. The chaplain shook his head, recalling one inmate and another, who, shaking an impotent fist, choking with rage, had told how after the "deal" for which he was "pinched," Nipper, the instigator of it, had slipped quietly off under the very noses of the police. While his mate and dupe was there, raging and choking, Nipper would be roaming the country at large with his wheel, grinding more or less, observing a great deal, planning the next neat little job. Yes, Nipper was a bad one! And strange to think of Pippin's being chosen to comfort the old sinner in his last hour and inherit the wheel that had been an innocent *particeps criminis* in so many "deals"! Well, Pippin could comfort him if anyone could, thought the chaplain.

Still looking out of the window, he let his thoughts run back to the day—could it be two years ago? It seemed hardly more than as many months—when he first saw Pippin. His first Sunday as prison chaplain! He had accepted the call because it seemed right; a new hand seemed needed—his thoughts ran off the track, as other visions came crowding in; he brought them back with an effort.

He felt anew, with almost the same shock of strangeness, the first impression of seeing his new flock in chapel that day. The rows on rows of faces, sharp or lowering, weak or silly or vacant, degenerate or sodden, a few that were actually vicious—they were seldom *really* vicious, his poor boys. Suddenly a head lifted, and he saw the face as of a strayed seraph; then presently heard the voice, as of the same seraph at home, singing. The chaplain broke into a little laugh.

Let the bright seraphim in burning row—

That line came insistently to his mind whenever he heard Pippin sing; yet he knew perfectly well that Milton's seraphim were not singing, but blowing their loud uplifted angel trumpets. Perhaps—perhaps voices and trumpets were more alike there?—Anyhow, Pippin's voice had a trumpet note in certain hymns that he specially loved.

The process of Pippin's conversion—to call it that; the chaplain sought for a better word, rejecting in turn a dozen or more—had been the happiest episode of the two years. Plenty of good and cheerful and hopeful things, but that—what *had* it been like? Chipping off the baked ashes—in Herculaneum, say—and coming upon the lucid marble of some perfect statue? No! A statue was after all a statue, and could give back no warmth. Mining, then, in dark and cold and foul air—poor boys! there was so much good in the worst of them, though!—and finding a vein of virgin gold— No! Gold was nothing but gold, after all. What—Ah! Here it was! Fumbling with the keys of an organ in the dark, feeling about, waking here a mutter, there a discord, there again a shriek—till suddenly one struck the true chord and the music broke out like sunlight—Or wasn't it after all just that, just sunlight, breaking from a cloud—

"Come in!" the chair was brought hastily to its normal position. A guard touched his cap in the doorway. "Beg pardon, sir, but French Bill has broke loose. Keeper said you was to be told—"

The chaplain was on his feet in an instant. "What has happened? Tell me as we go along!"

"Fell foul of Tom Packard with his bucket, and mauled him consid'able. I've been lookin' for it these two days. Tom was waitin' at his table, and Bill thought he give him a small egg o' purpose."

"Dear me, sirs! Who is with him now?"

The guard chuckled. "There's no one *with* him! Anybody wouldn't be very comf'table there just now. Jones is handy by, lookin' after him. You can hear him now!"

They could. A muffled roar, rising now and then into a bellow. As they drew nearer, the roar became articulate, and resolved itself into a sustained and passionate request for the blood, liver, and other vital adjuncts of Thomas Packard. "Lemmegetaholdofhim—lemmegetaholdofhim!" Coming down B corridor the clamor was deafening, echoed back from side to side of the narrow passage; accompanied moreover by banging of fists, kicking of feet against iron bars. The chaplain sighed and longed for Pippin. Nobody could manage Bill like Pippin. He usually knocked him down and sat on his chest singing "Onward, Christian Soldiers!" till the fit was over. There wasn't a mite of harm in Bill, Pippin always maintained, only he was nervous, and come to get worked up, he b'iled right over.

The other inmates of B corridor were listening to the uproar, some laughing, others sympathizing with Bill or Tom, as the case might be. Opposite the grated door of the cell a turnkey leaned against the wall, a stolid, unmoved figure. "Here comes chaplain!" the murmur ran from cell to cell; and every face was pressed eagerly against the grating. "Here's chaplain! Chaplain'll sort him!"

Bill himself seemed wholly unconscious of Mr. Hadley's approach. He was a French Canadian, a slender, active fellow. In repose, his face was gentle and rather pensive; now it was the face of a mad wildcat. Shaking the bars with all his strength, he continued to pour out in a monotonous roar his request for the vital organs, amply detailed and characterized, of "Tompack*ard*!"

The chaplain surveyed him quietly for a few minutes in silence; then drew a small square phial from his pocket, and unscrewing the metal top, held it between the bars to the man's nose. With a howl of twenty-wildcat power the fellow let go the bars and staggered backward. Instantly Hadley unlocked the door and stepped inside, closing it quickly after him.

"Now then, Bill," he said quietly, "what's all this row?"

Shaking and glaring, the man cowered in the farthest corner, rubbing his nose, clutching his throat.

"W'at you kill me for?" he muttered hoarsely. "W'at you kill me for, *mon père*? I do you no harm!"

"I haven't killed you. Sit down, Bill. You've been making a horrid row, do you know it? And you've kicked the toe right out of your boot. Now look at that! Those boots were new last month. You'll have to put a new toe cap over that, or the Warden will have you up for untidiness." He bent to examine the toe. "That's too bad! those new boots!"

"I mend heem!" Bill bent eagerly beside him. "I mend heem good, *mon père!* Warden nevaire see; I mak heem better as new."

"Well, see you do! And while you're about it, I wish you would look over my shoes, the pair you resoled for me, and see if you can't take the squeak out of them. It doesn't do for the chaplain to go round with squeaking boots, you know; he might disturb quiet fellows like you. By the way, what was your row about, Bill? I heard you had been pitching into Tom Packard."

They had sat down on the bed, the better to examine the injured toe cap. Bill looked up with a shrug, half ashamed, half sulky, wholly Gallic. "He been treatin' me mean, long time, two t'ree days. He geeve me de smalles' egg he can find for my breakfast; leetle, leetle, like pigeon's egg."

"Well, I got a bad egg the other day; halfway to a chicken it was; but I didn't break the cook's head, as I understand you broke poor Tom's."

"Yes! yes! I break hees head; I kill heem if I could. Yes, sir!"

"And now you're ashamed, eh? You know you are, Bill, you may as well own up." After some argument, Bill owned that he was ashamed and promised amendment. "Then that's all right!" The chaplain rose with an air of relief. "I'll speak a word to Father O'Neill, and he'll give you a nice little penance, and you'll make it up with Tom. I'm going to see him now, and I shall tell him you are sorry—yes, I shall, because you are, you know, sorry and ashamed. But remember!" He drew out the square green phial and held it up. "The next time you'll get it stronger!"

The man recoiled in terror, clasping his hands over his nose. "*Non! non, mon père!* Not kill me again! W'at ees eet? W'at you call eet?"

"Aromatic spirits of ammonia." The chaplain eyed the bottle gravely, shook his head, and put it back into his pocket. "No joke, is it, Bill! Well, good-by, old sport. Remember!"

CHAPTER XII
NIPPER

A wealthy young Squire of Plymouth, we hear,He courted a nobleman's daughter so dear,And for to be married it was their intent,All friends and relations had given their consent.

SO sang Pippin, on a July morning when all the world was singing too. Bobolinks hovering, trilling, lighting, half mad with glee; catbirds giving grand opera in the willows; thrushes quiring psalms in the birches. Pippin stopped short as a dignified robin with the waistcoat of an alderman perched on a blackberry vine at his elbow and poured out a flood of liquid melody. "Like out of a jug!" said Pippin. "How d'you s'pose he does it? Gorry to 'Liza, how *do* you s'pose he does it!

"A day was appointed to be the wedding day,A young farmer was chosen to give her away;But soon as the lady this farmer did spy,She cried in her heart, "Oh, my heart!" she did cry.

"Rest easy a spell, Nipper, and I'll rest too, and listen how he does that."

Nipper was the wheel. Setting it on the ground, Pippin sat down under a wide-branching oak and listened while the robin, like a certain wise thrush we know of, sang his song twice over, carefully and thoroughly. Pippin, his head cocked much as the singer's was, noted each cadence, and when the music ceased, repeated it in a clear, mellow whistle. Robin, much intrigued, sang a third time, and a fourth, cocked his head still further and listened critically. Pippin replied more correctly than before; so it might have gone on indefinitely, but for an inquisitive crow who came bustling down to see what it was all about. Robin flew away scornfully, repudiating intercourse with crows; Pippin flirted his handkerchief and told the intruder to be off with himself for an old black juggins.

Leaning against the oak bole, at peace with all mankind, Pippin listened and looked, looked and listened. Presently he became aware of an undertone of sound which made so perfect an accompaniment to the bird concert that he had not at first distinguished it. In the fringe of weeds beside the road a brook was murmuring over pebbles, gently, persistently, wooingly. The July sun was hot; he had been walking since sunrise.

"I'll have me a wash!" quoth Pippin.

"I'll have me a drink, and I'll have me a wash,And then I'll be clean as a whistle, by—"

He stopped abruptly: he had promised Mrs. Baxter not to say "gosh"; it wasn't an expression she cared to hear him use, not real nice someways.

"And Nipper shall have a bath too!" he said gleefully. "Nip, all the bath you've had these two days is squatterin' in the dust like a hen. I'll show you; just you wait!" Carrying the wheel, he plunged into the green covert; the trees closed behind him. "Green grass!" said Pippin.

There was grass, certainly, long rank grass, such as leans over in graceful curves and dips into brooks. There were sweet rushes too, and jewel weed, and cardinal flowers, which Pippin viewed with respectful admiration, asking, now honestly did you ever? Flowing between these lovely things, taking them quite as a matter of course, was the brook, clear and brown—something like Pippin's eyes, I declare!— babbling over mossy stones, with here a fairy cataract all cream and silver, there a round pool where Pippin might have found a trout, if he had known enough. But he did not know enough, knew in fact nothing whatever about trout; they are not found in cellars, nor in any part of a slum. Kneeling on a flat stone, he drank long draughts of delight, now from his cupped palms, now in sheer boyish glee, putting his mouth to the bubbling silver, letting it splash and tinkle over his face. No thought of germs disturbed his joy; he knew no more of germs than of trout.

Next he pulled off his shirt, pulled out his file and bestowed it safely in a pocket, and producing a bit of soap, fell to splashing about at a tremendous rate, sending trout, lucky bugs, germs and all helter-skelter off in a fright.

A sculptor, watching Pippin at his ablutions, would have wondered how the child of the slums should have developed such muscles as rippled under his brown satin skin. Pippin could have told him. Dod Bashford kept his boys lithe and active as young eels; if they didn't move quick, the rawhide curled about their backs and legs in good shape, Pippin could tell the sculptor. Sometimes the vision would come back even now: boys fighting in a cellar or in the reeking court outside, rolling over and over on the ground, pommelling, kicking, scratching, biting—there were no sporting rules in Bashford's gang. The big brute would stand watching the little ones with an occasional "Go it, pup!" till he was tired or bored, when "Hook it!" followed by the hiss and sting of the rawhide, sent them apart, bleeding, cursing, often weeping with sheer rage and unsated lust of battle. Gee! Remember that fight he had with Nosey, last winter he was with Bashford? Slim, long-legged, snaky kind of guy, Nosey was. Some like a fox; some like a rat, too, a sandy rat: sharp p'inted nose on him. Gee! Pippin gave him a good one on that p'inted nose. Gee! He didn't guess it had p'inted so straight since!

95

Far enough from Bashford's, here in the green thicket, Pippin splashed to his heart's content: at last, dripping and joyous, he rose and shook himself like a water-dog, spattering the leaves and rushes with crystal drops. "Green grass!" he sighed, "that was great!" Next he washed his red handkerchief and his "other" pair of socks, and hung them on a bush to dry; filed a callous on the sole of his foot that had made him walk "pumple-footed" the last day or two; ran his fingers through and through his hair till it curled like that of the Borghese Hermes.

"Now it's Nipper's turn; come on, Nip!"

He had grown fond of the wheel. It was a faithful creature, following obediently whither he would, whizzing cheerfully, singing, Pippin made no doubt, the only song was give it to sing. This last day or two, though, it had developed a squeak and rattle that was new to him; behooved him look her over and see what was loose.

Having wiped the dust off and oiled the whole apparatus, he proceeded to examine it carefully, inch by inch. He had done this many times before; had in fact kept the little machine in apple-pie order, partly for its own sake and his, partly as in duty bound to the departed Nipper. Old Nipper! He had been a rip, Pippin reflected, same as Old Man Blossom; but yet he sure had done him a good turn leaving him the wheel. Now—here was a thing had oftentimes puzzled him of late—what did Old Man Blossom know about Nipper? They might have been pals, he presumed likely; birds of a feather, you know! Well, yes, that; but Old Man seemed to have some hunch about the wheel; laffed fitterbust, and said them things, you rec'lect. Pippin had studied 'em over and studied 'em over, but he didn't get no—

A clock strikes when it is ready, not before. Pippin's clock struck now. Something he had never yet touched, or never in the right way, moved under his hand. A click, and the metal plate bearing the maker's name slid aside, revealing a long narrow cavity. Who could have guessed such a possibility in the compact little contrivance? With a smothered "Gee!" Pippin peered eagerly into the hole or box, thrust in his hand, and brought out a small object. He turned it over and over in his hand, still muttering suppressed "Gee's!" opened it, and sat staring, motionless.

A leather case containing a set of small tools. Nothing strange about that, Pippin, is there? Very ingenious to pack in this little space the tools needed for his trade! Clever Nipper! Why do you stare so, Pippin, and why does your face flush under its wholesome tan?

His eyes riveted to the tools, Pippin sank down on the grass. He handled them, one by one, and a bright spark came into his eye.

"Green grass!" he muttered. "Now wouldn't that—"

If you or I had looked over his shoulder, we should have seen at once that some of these were unfamiliar tools. A screw driver—yes! a pair of nippers—yes! a file—yes! but what were these three little shining objects which Pippin was fitting together with eager, trembling fingers? Now they are joined and make a slender bar of solid steel, one end flattened to a sharp edge. That is a jimmy, and Pippin is looking with shining eyes at a miniature but perfect set of burglar's tools.

"Now wouldn't that—" said Pippin. Sitting back on his heels, he took the tools out one by one and examined them carefully, handling them like a lover, whistling meantime, slowly and thoughtfully, the air devoted to the aged steeple-climber. He ran his eye along their edges; he rang them on a stone to test their perfection. "*Complete!*" he muttered. "These certingly are a complete outfit. Now I ask you honest, would—not—that—give you a pain in your—" Pippin confused the human interior with the gallinaceous. How should he know that we have no gizzard?

"Old Nipper!" he continued. "Only to think of the slickness of him! Went round with his wheel, innocent appearin' as you please, and when he saw a likely crib, he'd up and crack it with these little daisies, just as easy—"

He stopped abruptly, as a light broke in upon him. *This* was what Old Man Blossom meant. This was why he laffed and 'most had a pupplectic fit; and no wonder! Here was he, Pippin, singing and praying, and all the time taking a cracksman's kit along with him wherever he went! No wonder the old rip laughed! Now question was, what to do with 'em?

What say? No one was near; he was alone in the green murmuring place; yet some one did certainly seem to be speaking. Pippin cocked his ear to listen.

A shame to destroy good tools, pretty set like this, prettiest he ever saw or like to see? Might come in handy for any kind of work—even the jimmy? Any one might want to use a bar—farmin' like, or—

The strong brown fingers seemed to close of themselves, without will of his, round the tools, fondling them. Something like quicksilver ran crinkling through him—

"Now HONEST!" said Pippin. "Just watch me, will you?"

A flash in the sunlight where it broke through the leafy screen; a silver splash—the lucky bugs scattered in terror, and a solemn bullfrog tumbled headfirst off the stone from which he had been watching. Another flash and splash, and now a whole shower of them. Sang Pippin:

"There was an old man,And he was mad,And he ran up the steeple.He took offHis great big hat,And waved it over the people!"

Later, he sat under the wayside oak and communed with himself. How did he account for that? he asked. Honest, now, wouldn't it gave you a pain? Here he was, the Lord's boy, a professin' Christian, belongin' to every church they was, he expected, startin' out all so gay to do the Lord's work, and Him knowledgeable to it, and helpin' along; and then all in a minute some part of him—something he couldn't get a holt of—give a jump, and *wanted* them things, wanted 'em like—Gorry to 'Liza! You couldn't have no idea *how* he wanted 'em! and yet 'twasn't him, neither: all the time he was lookin' on, you might say, struck all of a heap. Now how would you make that out? Honest, how would you?

After some thought, Pippin expected that it was the devil. He was always round, you know, like a roarin' line, seekin' whom he could devour 'em up. Behooved him keep a sharp lookout!

But, said another part of his brain, ekally the Lord was round, and more so, let him bear in mind. The Lord was mindful of His own; Elder Hadley had wrote that in the Testament and Psalms he give him, and 'twas *so*; and the Lord was stronger than the devil, never let Pippin have no doubts about that.

"You bet He is!" Up went Pippin's head; he smote his knee with a resounding smack. "You bet He is! Satan, you beat it while your shoes are new! I've got no more use for you, and don't you forget it!"

CHAPTER XIII
ENTER MARY-IN-THE-KITCHEN

IN a certain pleasant suburb—yes, the city has pleasant suburbs, though when you are in the slums you do not believe it—stands a white house with green blinds. It stands in the middle of a square yard (by which I mean an inclosure, not a measure of space); its front looks on a pleasant street, with a sidewalk, and sentinel maples set at regular intervals; the back gives, as the French say, on a road that is not yet paved, with neither sidewalk nor maples, only a straggling procession of elms, with grass or dust, as may happen, under foot. Yet it is more sympathetic, some people think, than the proper street, and Mary-in-the-kitchen, whose windows both above and below stairs look out upon it, privately thinks she has the best part of the house. So thinks the visitor in the back corner room, too; but we have not come to him yet.

Mary-in-the-kitchen is not in it just now. She is in the yard, hanging out the clothes, for all the world like the maid in the nursery song. She is standing on a raised platform; her face is toward the house, her back toward the road. So standing, with her arms raised, pinning linen along a line, Mary is such a picture that you really must stop and look at her. She is neither tall nor short, but just the right height, and her blue cotton gown takes the lines and curves of as pretty a figure as ever sculptor sighed for. Her forehead is broad and smooth, and her hair ripples round it as if for pure pleasure. Her brows are black and straight, her lashes black and curled, and her eyes violet blue with brown shadows; you may see the color in clear water when the wind ruffles it. A short straight nose, a chin like Mary Donnelly's, "very neat and pert, and smooth as a china cup," a mouth with kisses tucked in at the corners: all these things Mary has, and her hair beside. Hair too dark for gold, too bright for brown; rather like October oak leaves when the sun shines through them at a certain angle—but you must know the right kind of oak. Well, then, like a red heifer, a yearling, when her coat is new and glossy in the spring. There is so much of it that Mary hardly knows what to do with it; being a very tidy girl, she has it well braided and pinned in shining coils at the back of her head, but little tendrils will escape and curl round her face just because they cannot keep away; and on the nape of her neck are two little curls that know themselves for the prettiest in the world.

If you asked Mary what she was, she would reply promptly, "A scientific general." By this she would not mean that she was prepared to conduct warfare on approved modern principles; not at all. She means that she has taken courses in General Housework at a certain Institute; and that she is able to do (and does) the work of two "domestics" of yesterday's class, with ease and precision. It stands to reason—Mary's favorite phrase—that she would. Knowing not only how but why a thing should be done, you know what came next, and there you were, all ready. So

Mary was the joy and comfort of her employers ("the nicest folks in the world!") and the distraction of all the youthful tradesmen of the suburbs. And here I am still keeping her standing on that platform with her arms uplifted, pinning the tablecloth on the line. Scientific generals do not wash clothes nowadays, nor any other generals for that matter, but this was the employeress's best tablecloth, and Mary knew the stuff the laundry put in, and see beautiful linen destroyed was a thing she could not; it stood to reason.

The intelligent reader knows why I am keeping her there; I do not even attempt to deceive him. Yes, Pippin is coming round the corner this moment. Here he is, wheel and all; high time, too, says the intelligent reader. He is walking slowly, not looking round him, as is his wont, with quick, darting glances, but with intent look fixed on the ground a little way ahead, as if he were searching for something; as indeed he is. Pippin is very busy this morning. He has just established ten or twenty boys (he is not sure which) in Cyrus Poor Farm, and he is now looking for the right kind of guy to teach them the use of their hands. He has never heard of manual training—Bashford taught it in a way, but it was called by other names—but there were several guys in There (remember that this meant Shoreham) that would have made first-rate mechanics, give 'em the chance. Now take 'em young, and—why—why—

At this point Fate tapped Pippin smartly on the shoulder. He looked up, and saw Mary on the platform, with her back to him, pinning out the tablecloth.

Cyrus Poor Farm vanished, boys and all! "Green grass!" said Pippin. He stopped short, and silently bade himself see if there wasn't some pictur to look at. He joyfully absorbed Mary, from head to trim feet and back again, his eyes resting finally on the nape of her neck where the two little curls were displaying themselves, and on the heavy coils of shining hair. Now *there* was a color! 'Twas the color of a hoss chestnut—no! lighter than that. A bay hoss, then—bright bay, kind o' squintin' toward sorrel; no! lighter than that. Green grass! 'Twas like a heifer, a yearlin' heifer. Now— Pippin smote his thigh lightly—that was the very color Old Man Blossom named in regards to his little gal. Now would you call that a reminder, p'inter like, fear he should forget? Or was it showin' him that gals as had a chance might grow up beauts like this young lady? No, he hadn't see her face, that was a fact, but—here Mary turned round.

Probably neither thought anything in that minute they stood at gaze, save that here was the goodliest person ever seen of their respective eyes; as to how the Fates busied themselves at the time, I am not in a position to say, but the next moment, when Pippin pulled off his cap and smiled, and Mary smiled back, possibly—I cannot say—exceptionally keen ears might have heard the whir of Clotho's distaff.

To both the smile seemed somehow familiar; it was as if—this was not thought, only a sunlit gleam of something too far and bright to recognize—as if each had known how the other would smile; thus, and not otherwise the gracious lines would curve and melt and deepen. How is this? Is there no flash of vision, Pippin? Think! Pippin is too bewildered to think.

"Mornin'!" said Pippin. "Nice day!"

"Real nice!" Mary assented.

"Havin' nice weather right along; seasonable, you might say. Any knives or scissors to grind, lady?"

"Why, I don't know!" Mary came daintily down the steps of the platform (demonstrating the while a seeming impossibility, that her foot was as pretty as the rest of her), and advanced, looking from Pippin to the wheel and back again. "Are you a p'fessional?" she asked.

"That's what! I expect I can give satisfaction, knives, scissors, or tools; anything except razors; them I don't undertake. Like to have a look at the wheel, lady? She's a beaut, too—what I would say, Nipper is her name, not a female name, but all she's got—same as me."

"Nipper!" the girl paused a fraction of a second. It was as if some faint air stirred, not enough to ruffle ever so delicately the clear pool of memory; it passed and was gone. "'Tis a pretty wheel!" said Mary.

"Take it from me, lady, she's O.K., the Nipper is. Runs slick as greased lightning; I'd show you if you had a knife handy."

"I'll fetch the carving knife!" said Mary. "It's dull as anything."

She vanished, to the perceptible darkening of the daylight, but soon reappeared, bringing not only the sun but a handful of knives, big and little.

Looking at them, and still more closely at the strong shapely hand that proffered the first of them, an idea came to Pippin, which he withheld for the moment. He took the carving knife, pronounced it a dandy but been used some.

"Now watch me, lady!" he said.

A pretty trade! Temp'ry, as Pippin never failed to assure himself, but pretty. See now how lovingly he lays the blade to the wheel. His foot presses the pedal, and the wheel turns; slowly at first, then faster and ever faster till all Mary sees is a blur of gray and blue with now and then a darting spark. Pippin, holding the blade tenderly yet firmly against the flying stone, bends over it intent; then as the edge begins to fine and taper, he whistles, then hums under his breath, finally breaks out into full-throated song:

"Knives and scissors to grind, oh!Have 'em done to your mind, oh!Large and small,Damaged and all,Don't leave any behind, oh!

"Knives and scissors to grind, oh!Every specie and kind, oh!Bring 'em to me,*And* you will seeSatisfaction, you'll find, oh!"

Mary looks and listens; looks first at the wheel, then at the man. On him her eyes linger, studying his trim khaki-clad figure (his new road suit, a parting gift from Mrs. Baxter, a good wish set in every stitch), his close-curling hair, the sharp, bold chiseling of cheek and chin. My! thinks Mary, if he's as good as he is lookin'!

A distant whistle sounds; a clock in the kitchen strikes twelve, with an insistence almost personal. Mary jumps up from the step where she has been sitting with her feet tucked under her and her hands clasping her knees. There! She's no idea 'twas so late. She must go in and get dinner. She thanks him ever so; that is an elegant edge. How much, please?

Pippin, resisting the impulse to say, "Nothing at all to *you*!" names his lowest price. Mary runs into the house for the change, and again the sun goes and comes with her. "How about the other knives?" she asks, a little breathless with her run. Will he finish them now, and bring them in, or—

Pippin will come again, if 'tis all the same to her. He does not think it necessary to say that this was the idea that had come to him, winning his instant approval. If he times his coming so as to do one knife a day—why—there's quite a plenty of knives and mebbe she'd scare up some scissors too—Pippin sees a long vista of Mary-brightened days stretching before him. He bids her good day—since it must be so—almost cheerfully. Then, if agreeable, he'll see her again soon. "So long, lady!"

Mary stands looking after him—it is strange (or not, 'cordin' to, as Mrs. Baxter would say) how often people stand looking after Pippin when he goes away—till conscience nips her sharply; and she flies into the kitchen and all in a moment becomes severely scientific and unbelievably general, executing amazing manœuvres with saucepans and double-boilers. So scientific is she that when an amorous greengrocer looks in with suggestions of spinach and strawberries, he is hustled off in short order with a curt, "Nothing to-day, thank you!" He hesitating in the doorway with the information that it is a fine day, Mary, with some asperity, presumes likely, but has not time to look. Now, Mary! As if you had not been a good half-hour out on that clothes platform!

She is even a little—a very little short with her employeress, who saw the departing grocer from her window and thinks they might have liked a box of strawberries. Her brother is fond of—

"He's fonder of shortcake!" Mary says briefly, "and it's all ready in the 'frigerator." Relenting, she explains with her own particular smile that there was enough strawberries left from supper last night, and she remembered that the Elder liked her shortcake last time he was here. "Besides," she adds irrelevantly, "'twas that fellow with the crooked nose, and I do despise him. He's always making excuses to hang round when I'm extra busy."

This was not really meant as a hint, but still the employeress vanished promptly; to see to something, she said. Mary's smile was even more in evidence at dinner, when the employer complimented her on the carving knife.

"Mary, what have you been doing to this knife? It was dull as a hoe yesterday, and now it's a Toledo blade. I didn't get you the steel you asked for, either!"

Mary, standing at attention with an extra plate, an entrancing vision in blue and white, just enough flushed from her manœuvres over the stove, dimples and smiles and says it *is* a lovely edge, she does think. A knife-grinder came along, this morning, and he did appear to be a master hand. He did it just as easy!

"Knows his business!" The employer, who is "in" wholesale cutlery, runs the eye of a connoisseur along the blade. "I'd like to turn him on to my pruning shears. Keep a lookout for him, will you, Mary? He may come by again!"

Mary demurely promises to do so. The visitor, who is the employeress's brother, a quiet man in clerical dress, yet with a certain military air and carriage, and blue eyes as keen as they are kind, notices that the girl's color deepens a little, and that a new and distracting dimple appears at the corner of her mouth, as if a smile were trying to escape.

"If I were in the habit of betting," he says when Mary has left the room, "I would lay a considerable sum that the knife-grinder will come again, and moreover, that he is young and possibly not ill looking!"

"I certainly would if I were he!" says the employer heartily. "I'd go round a block just to look at Mary!"

The employeress here develops dimples of her own, and says there is a pair of them, and they'd better let her Mary alone, or there will be trouble.

"There are enough people going round blocks to look at Mary as it is!" she says. "She's not that kind, either. She huffed Babbitt's man right out of the kitchen to-day, before I had time to get downstairs."

The visitor says nothing. He did not see the knife-grinder, being too busy with his writing—he was preparing a paper for a conference—to look out of the window; but he has a strong impression that he, the knife-grinder, had not been huffed out of the yard an hour or so ago. And here was Mary with the shortcake!

CHAPTER XIV
PIPPIN LOOKS FOR OLD MAN BLOSSOM'S LITTLE GAL

BACK to the city, Pippin! Leafy suburbs, irradiated by clothes-hanging goddesses, are all very well, but they are not your affair; or if they are, you do not know it. All you know is that you have to find a girl, a girl whose rightful name is May Blossom, but likely changed o' purpose to keep the old man from finding the kid, and small blame to her Ma for that.

Pippin goes over in his mind such scant information as he possesses. May Blossom was put in some kind of a Home joint, being then, the Old Man would judge, six year old, or a year off or on it. Pretty little gal—pretty little gal—Pippin's mind comes to a dead stop.

He brushes his hand across his eyes. The vision is upon him, but only to confuse and bewilder. An alley, or narrow court, where clothes are drying. A mite of a girl trying to take the clothes down. She cannot reach them, stamps her feet, cries; a boy comes and takes them down for her.

"Thank you, boy!" she says.

"Say 'Pippin!'"

"Pip-*pin*!"

"Green grass!" Pippin murmurs. "Now—now—could that have been her? He always said he'd knowed me from a baby; said he lived neighbor to Granny Faa—I never believed him special; but he sure was a pal of Bashford's. Now wouldn't it give you a pain if that little gal was his little gal; wouldn't it?"

What he had to do now was find what Homes there was, and ask what become of a little gal name of May Blossom—or anyways looking thus and so. Pippin smote his thigh, and threw back his head.

"One thing at a time,You'll earn a dime:Six things in a pickleYou'll lose a nickel!

like Mr. Baxter says. Now watch me find that joint!"

We cannot watch Pippin through this search, which took several days. True, there were only two Children's Homes in the city; but the approaches to them were devious, and Pippin's methods were his own. First he must find a bakery in the neighborhood of the Home, the one most nearly approaching the perfection of Baxter's. Here he must linger for an hour or more, talking bakery gossip, discussing yeast, milk powder, rotary ovens, and dough dividers; sharpening the knives, too, mostly for brotherly love, for was not he a (temp'ry) baker as well as knife-grinder? Here he would ask casually about the joint whose red brick or gray stone walls towered near by. Home for kids, was it? Well, that was a dandy *i*dea, sure! Did the baker supply—did? Had their own baker, but took his buns and coffee-cake reg'lar? He wanted to know! Well, talkin' of coffee-cake—here yarns might be swapped for a matter of half an hour. Then the baker would be asked what kind of a man the boss was? Or was she a woman? Was? Well—well, even if so! Thursday was visitors' day, was it? Well, he wouldn't wonder a mite but what he'd look in there some Thursday. Pretty to see a lot of kids together, what?

His first visit to the stone Home with the mullioned windows was a short one. The black-robed superintendent was courteous, but cool; she was not interested in either grinding or bakeries. There had been several red-haired girls at the Home in her time, but none named Mary Blossom, none corresponding with Pippin's description. Was he a relative? No? She was much occupied—"Good morning!"

"She don't want no boes in hers!" said Pippin thoughtfully, as he bore Nipper out of the paved courtyard. "I don't blame her, not a mite!"

At the red-brick Home with the green fanlight over the door his reception was more cordial. The kindly, rosy face of the Matron beamed responsive to his smile. The morning was bright, and she had just heard of a thousand-dollar legacy coming to the Home, so her own particular shears needed sharpening, and she superintended the process (she had a grass plot to stand on, too, instead of a pavement) and they had a good dish of talk, as she told the Assistant later.

Hearing Pippin's brief account of his quest, she meditated, her mind running swiftly back over the years of her superintendence.

"A child of six or eight!" she repeated thoughtfully. "With hair like a yearling heifer's! Why, we have had many children with red hair; the sandy kind, and the bricky, and the carrotty—*and* the auburn; but none of them sound just like the child you describe. Then, the parents! You never saw the mother, you say? What was the father like?"

"Like a crook!" said Pippin promptly.

"Dear me! That is a pity. Can you describe him? Not that I ever saw him, but the child might have resembled him—"

"Not her!" Pippin averred confidently. "The old man never looked like anything but—well, call it mud and plaster, and you won't be far off. Now the little gal was a pictur. Hair like I said, and eyes—well, first they'd be blue and then they'd be brown, like in runnin' water; know what I mean? And the prettiest way of speakin' you ever—"

"*Why, you've seen her!* You didn't say you had seen her."

Pippin looked helplessly into the clear gray eyes that had suddenly grown sharp and piercing. "I—don't—know!" he said.

"Don't know what?"

"Whether I see her, or whether I just—" He stopped to sigh and run his fingers through his hair, almost knocking his file out. "I expect I'll have to explain!" he said.

"I think you will!" The tone was not harsh, but it was firm and decided. The Matron had seen many people, and was not to be beguiled by the brightest eyes or the most winning smile. Moreover, the "pictur" Pippin had conjured up had brought a corresponding image on her mental kinetoscope; she, too, saw the child with eyes like running water and the prettiest way of speaking; saw and recognized.

Pippin sighed again.

"When I say I don't know," he said slowly, "it's because I don't! Just plain that! When I said the way that gal looked, it—well, it's like it wasn't me that said it, but somebody else inside me. Why, I spoke it right off like it was a piece: 'twas as if *somebody* knew all along what that little gal looked like. Now—"

The Matron took him up sharply. "As if somebody knew? What do you mean by 'somebody'?"

Light came to Pippin. Why, of course!

"I expect it's a boy!" he said.

"What boy?"

"I expect it's the boy I used to be. I forget him most of the time, but nows and thens he speaks up and gives me to understand he's there all right. You see, lady, when I was a boy, there was a little gal—somewheres near where I lived, I expect; and she had—yes, she sure had hair that color, and eyes that same kind. And when you spoke just now, it all come back, and seemed like 'twas the boy tellin', not me in a present way of speakin'. I don't know as you see what I'm drivin' at, but I don't know as I can put it any plainer."

"What kind of boy were you?"

"Guttersnipe!"

"Where did you live?"

Pippin described the cellar as well as he could. It was no longer in existence, he had ascertained that. Where it had yawned and stunk, a model tenement now stood prim and cheerful.

The Matron looked grave. Her clear gaze pierced through and through the man, as if—his own homely simile—she would count the buttons on the back of his shirt.

"What references have you?" she asked presently.

"References?" Pippin looked vague.

"Yes! I don't know anything about you—except that you are certainly a good scissor-grinder!" she smiled, half relenting. "You want to know about one of our girls—about some one who might have been one of our girls—" she corrected herself hastily—"and you say you were a guttersnipe and her father was a crook. Young man, our girls have nothing to do with crooks or guttersnipes, you must understand that. Unless you can refer me to some one—" her pause was eloquent.

"I wish't Elder Hadley was here!" said Pippin. "He'd speak for me, lady!"

"Elder Hadley? Where does he live?"

Pippin sighed, fingered his file, sighed again. Easy to tell his story to Jacob Bailey and Calvin Parks, the good plain men who had known good and evil and chosen good all their lives long; less easy, but still not too hard, to tell it to the kind Baxters who knew and loved him: but here, in the city, to a woman who knew crooks and guttersnipes and probably feared or despised them—not easy! Still—

"You see, lady," said Pippin, "'tis this way."

The Matron heard his story, listening attentively, now and then putting a shrewd question. When it was over, she excused herself, not unkindly but with a grave formality unlike her first cheerful aspect. She must attend to something in the house. If he could wait ten or fifteen minutes—

"Sure!" said Pippin. "And I might be sharpening the meat knife or like that? I'll throw it in for luck."

While he was sharpening the meat knife (which, he said to himself, had been used something awful; you'd think they'd gone over it with a crosscut saw!), he heard a cheerful hubbub in the street outside; distant at first, then louder, as turning a corner; louder still, as close at hand; till with a deafening outburst of treble and alto the gate of the courtyard was flung open, and—

"Green grass!" cried Pippin. "Here's the kids!"

Here they were indeed, just out of school, rosy, tousled, jubilant: boys and girls, the former small, the latter all sizes from kindergarten toddlers to the big sixteen-year-old maiden to whose skirts they clung. At sight of a strange man they checked, and the hubbub fell into sudden silence; only for a moment, though, for Pippin smiled, and in another minute they were all around him, hustling and elbowing to get the closest sight of the wheel.

"Easy!" said Pippin. "Easy does it! Don't come too nigh her; she bites!" There was an instant recoil, with symptoms of possible flight. "What I would say," he went on, "she'll bite if you touch her; no other ways. Look with your eyes and not your hands! *And not your hands!*"

A swift shove of his elbow saved the fingers of a small boy who thought he knew better, and sent him back upon his more prudent neighbors. Shouts resounded.

"Jimmy got his!"

"Yeh! Jim-*may*! You got yours!"

The culprit faced round with crimson cheeks and doubled fists. He had only been at the Home a few weeks, and fighting was still his one form of argument; a snub-nosed, freckled bull pup of a boy. Pippin observed him, and liked his looks.

"Say!" said Pippin. "Look at here! Want to hear her sing?"

"Hear who sing, Mister?"

"The wheel! Stow your noise a sec., while I ask her." He bent over the wheel and seemed to speak and listen. The children waited open-mouthed, goggle-eyed. "Says she's got a cold," he announced cheerfully, "and feels bashful beside! Say, I'll have to sing for her. What say?"

"Yep, Mister! Do, Mister! Sing, Mister!" came in chorus.

"O.K. You'll have to keep still, though. I'm bashful myself, you see. Now then— Where's the smallest kid? Here, kiddy! Come to Pippin! Don't be skeered, he won't bite nuther. Gimme your hands—that's a daisy! Now then—

"There was an old man,And he was mad—"

When the Matron appeared again, accompanied by an older woman of severe aspect, Pippin was sitting on the cellar door, half-buried in children. One little imp was sitting astride his neck, hammering time on his chest with sturdy heels; a six-year-old girl clung to either shoulder, two or three more were on his knees, the rest sat or knelt or squatted as close as they could get; and Pippin, his head thrown back, his eyes fixed on the maple leaves overhead, was shouting at the top of his lungs:

"Darling, I am growing o-hold!Silver threads among the goldShine upon my brow to-day-hay,Life is fading fast away!"

As the song ended, before the Matron could make her presence known, the bull pup known as Jimmy fell silently upon his nearest neighbor, a boy somewhat bigger than himself, and pommeled him ferociously. The victim shrieking aloud, Pippin seized the pup by the scruff of his neck, dragged him off, and held him at arm's length, wriggling and clawing the air, his eyes darting fire.

"What ails you?" demanded Pippin. "What d'he do?"

"Didn't do nothin'!" wailed the bigger boy.

"He picked on me!" raged the smaller.

"Didn't neither!"

"Did teither! And pinched m' leg beside! Lemme go!"

"Yeth, Mithter!" piped a five-year-old. "He did pinch him! I thee him do it!"

"Hold still, pup! hold still! I'm bigger'n you be. Now then, you, leave him be, you hear me? I expect you did pinch him all right, all right; you look like a pincher. Now look at here! Can you wrestle, you two?"

"Betcher life!" "Nope!" came in a fiery yap and anguished yelp from the two.

"Green grass! What are you made of? Putty, or dough-scrapin's?" This to the yelper, while still holding the yapper well in hand. "Now if we could make a ring, and leave you fight it out sensible, and—"

The Matron stepped quickly forward. Pippin, aware of her, scrambled to his feet, shaking off (very gently, be sure) all but the urchin on his neck, who only clung the tighter; and still holding the bull pup—by the collar now—he beamed on the Matron.

"I was sayin', lady," he said, "that if you'd leave me make a ring, and these two pups fight it out, we'd see which would lick, and they'd be friends from now on. What say?"

The Matron said, "No!" decidedly, and at a word from her the children scuttled into the house by their side door, albeit with many a backward glance.

Pippin looked longingly after the freckled pup. "There's a kid I like!" he said. "I could do something with that kid if I had him. 'Tother one's a low-down skeezicks by the look of him. Here's the knife, lady; I hope it's satisfactory."

It was; but the two ladies desired a word with Pippin indoors, if he could leave his wheel. Pippin expected he could; he'd never knowed the Nipper to bolt, nor even shy. "After you, ladies!" Now who taught Pippin to hold the door open and bow with the grace of a young birch in the wind?

The Matron wondered, but said nothing. The three passed into a cool inexpressive parlor which had no opinion about anything, and sat down on three Mission chairs to match.

"This is Mrs. Faulkner," said the Matron; "the Assistant Matron. I am Mrs. Appleby. Your name is—?"

"Pippin, ma'am!"

"Pippin—what?"

"Pippin Nix—what I would say, it's all the name I've got. Not bein' acquainted with my parents—you see—"

"I see! It seems a curious name—The point is this. Mrs. Faulkner and I think we know—"

"Think we may possibly know!" struck in Mrs. Faulkner, speaking for the first time, and then shutting her mouth with a snap as if she feared a word too much might escape.

"—May possibly know," Mrs. Appleby corrected herself, "the girl you are looking for."

"*Green grass!* Is that so?" Pippin smote his thigh, was confounded, and asked pardon, all in a breath.

Mrs. Faulkner bent severe brows on him, and Pippin reflected what a blessing it was Mrs. Baxter didn't ever look like that.

"We keep in touch with our girls," Mrs. Appleby continued, "till they marry or reach the age of twenty-five. The young woman we have now in mind is eighteen years old, and a very fine girl."

"Gee! Ain't that great? Where'll I find her, lady?"

"Remain seated, if you please! We will come to that presently. We know her under a name slightly different from the one you have heard. Mrs. Faulkner remembers that her mother told her she had altered the name in order that the father should not trace the child."

"Now wouldn't that—" murmured Pippin. "Say, she was a daisy, wasn't she?"

"She was perfectly right!" Mrs. Faulkner's aspect was rigid to the point of awfulness. "She was a decent woman, and wished her child decently brought up. Her husband was a reprobate!"

"Meanin' long for 'rip'?" Pippin leaned forward eagerly, with pleading eyes and voice. "He sure was, lady! Yep, Old Man Blossom was a rip from Riptown, and so remains; but yet there never was any *harm* in him. What I would say—he's a crook, and a bo, and not the guy for family life anyways you look at it; but he never was a *mean* guy. He never hit from behind; there was no sandbaggin' in his; just he'd give you one on the jaw if he couldn't cop the swag without, you see. Now that's square, you see, *for* a crook! But—" Mrs. Faulkner's eyes glared wholly unresponsive. He glanced at Mrs. Appleby, and seeing, or thinking he saw, a faint glimmer that might mean an inward twinkle, addressed himself to her.

"You see how 'tis, lady! And now he's on the blink—that is, near his end, you see, and he wants his little gal; wants her bad. And—bein' a bo myself, it ain't for me to p'int out things to ladies like youse, but if she's the kind of gal like you say, mightn't she think, say, 'Well, after all, he's my dad, and I'm his kid, and 'twon't do me a mite of harm to give him a look in.' What say?"

"You say he is dying?" said the elder woman. "Has he suffered any change of heart? Does he repent of his evil ways?"

"Not yet he ain't!" Pippin flushed and his hands clenched; he seemed to hear the snicker once more. "But the way I look at it is this, lady!" He bent forward again, all shyness gone now, his brown face aglow. "'Look out for the grace of God!' says Elder Hadley to me. 'Wherever you look for it, you'll find it!' he says. 'If you don't,' he says, 'it's your own fault, for it's sure there somewhere!' he says. Well, I tried, honest I did, to find grace in Old Man Blossom, and all I could find was he wanted his little gal. So—well! What I would say, God moves in a myster'ous way, His wonders to *perform*; (sung to 'Albayno,' common metre, fine hymn, though a mite sober!) and how do I know but wantin' his little gal was the way was took by—by Them as has the handlin' of things—" a reverent jerk of the head toward the sky—"and—well—that's the way it struck me!" Pippin concluded lamely.

The tears stood in Mrs. Appleby's kind eyes, and even Mrs. Faulkner's severity was perceptibly abated.

"We only want to be sure—" faltered the former.

"We *must* be sure!" said the latter.

"Yes—of course we must. Pippin, I believe all you say—" she glanced a trifle defiantly at her assistant—"because I cannot help it. I am sure you have told us the truth; but we cannot take action—we cannot tell you where Mary Fl—where the young woman is, until we have *proof* of your respectability and the steadiness of your purpose. You will understand that, I am sure. Well—now! Bring us a note from Mr. Hadley, and we will tell you where she is, and will recommend her employ—that is, the people with whom she is staying—to allow her to visit her father. This is all we can do!"

She rose as she spoke, and held out her hand; Pippin grasped it heartily.

"You're a perfect lady, ma'am!" he said. "I see that the minute I laid eyes on you. I'll get that note if it takes a leg! 'Twon't take above a week to get to Shoreham—say a day there, and another week back—walkin', you understand—say two weeks, and I'll be back if I'm alive. I'm a thousand times obliged to you, lady—and you too, ma'am!" His smile loosened the strictures about Mrs. Faulkner's heart—a good heart, but over-institutionalized by years of routine—and sent a warm glow through her.

"I'll wish you good day—say!" he stopped suddenly. "About that pup—I would say kid: him with the freckles and the bull-dog grip. I like that kid. He's got sand, a whole bag of it. If you was lookin' for a home for him when he leaves this joint—but I

113

guess we better leave that till I bring that note, what say? Good day, ladies! Come up, Nipper!" And with a comprehensive wave and smile that took in every eager face glued to the playroom window, Pippin went his way.

CHAPTER XV
PIPPIN MEETS AN OLD ACQUAINTANCE

PIPPIN went his way, planning his expedition as he went. He would start that evening, in the cool. Pay up at his joint, and he might leave Nipper there, mebbe. Decent folks, and he could travel quicker—No! he would take Nipper along, and give 'em a good sharpenin' up all round over there. The Warden's boys—they'd be glad to see him, he expected. A boy's knife always needed 'tendin' to; and the Warden! He was real good, he might have some tools, and he could go into the shop—green grass! he really believed he'd be glad to see the old place again! Now wouldn't that give you a pain?

Was that because he warn't obleeged to go, think, or because he found the Lord there, and there was a manner of blessin' on the place for him?—"Easy there!"

The last remark was not addressed to himself. He was crossing the street with perhaps a dozen other persons, between two halted phalanxes of motor cars, drays, wagons; midway a monumental policeman held a fraction of the world in the hollow of his hand. Just in front of Pippin was a stout gentleman, puffing nervously, his gold-framed gaze fixed intently on the sidewalk haven before him. Suddenly a boy—he was no more—stumbled over Pippin's feet, lurched forward, and fell heavily against the stout gentleman with a cry of alarm. The gentleman turned quickly. As he did so, Pippin's left arm shot out; he caught the boy and held him, struggling and kicking.

"Nix on the swipe, my darlin'," he said quietly.

"Lemme go!" spluttered the boy. "—— you, lemme go!"

"Is he hurt?" asked the stout gentleman. "Is the poor lad hurt?"

"Not yet he ain't," said Pippin grimly, "but he's liable to be."

"Step lively!" thundered the policeman, his eye on the pawing motor cars.

Pippin nodded toward the further sidewalk, and made his way thither, dragging his prisoner by the collar. The stout gentleman followed, bewildered.

"I don't understand—" he began.

"You wouldn't," said Pippin gently. "His hand was in your pocket, that's all, sir. Easy, bo! Nix on the fade-away, neither; I've got your shirt, too, see? Why not take it easy?"

The boy, who had been trying to wriggle out of his jacket, gave it up and stood sullen and silent, with clenched hands. The stout gentleman looked distressed. "You mean—" he said "—you fear the lad is a pickpocket?"

"That's what! Open your fins, Jimmy! drop the swagglekins! What? Need a little help, do you?"

Pippin was standing discreetly in the gutter that he might not obstruct traffic. Now with his free hand he drew out his file and gave a smart rap on the boy's knuckles. The boy uttered a yelp of pain, the hand opened involuntarily. Pippin deftly caught its contents as they dropped, and handed them to the gentleman with a little bow.

"Pocketbook an' wipe—I would say handkerchief! O.K., Governor?"

"God bless me! Yes, they are mine! Thank you!" cried the stout gentleman. "Is it possible? This young lad! I am distressed. Young man, I am deeply indebted to you. Shall you—a—deliver him over to the authorities?"

"Run him in?" Pippin eyed the boy thoughtfully. "I ain't quite sure yet. Me an' Jimmy'll have a little talk first, I expect. Mebbe—"

A bell clanged. There was a rush and a swirl in the crowd. As the fire-engine came thundering by, the boy suddenly dropped and hung limp and nerveless in Pippin's grasp; then, as the grasp shifted a little to gain a better hold, he gave a violent jerk, a shove, a spring, and was off, under the very wheels of the advancing hose-carriage.

Pippin looked after him regretfully.

"Slick kid!" he said. "He's ben well trained, that kid has. I couldn't have done that better myself. But there wasn't no chance to look for no grace in that one," he added. "Now I leave it to any one! But—what was I tellin' you? That's the second one to-day. You leave me get hold of them boys, this one and that pup to the Home joint, and I could do somepin with 'em. I could so!"

The trip to Shoreham, so carefully planned, was not to come off; the ladies of distaff and shears had ordained otherwise. It occurred to Pippin that in common politeness he could not leave town for a fortnight without "sharpenin' up" that young lady, bein' he had said he would call again. That afternoon, accordingly, he and Nipper took their way to the green lane in the pleasant suburb, and turned in at the white gate. There was no clothes-hanging nymph in the yard this time—it was Monday afternoon, and the clothes were lying in neat snowy rolls in a basket within, ready for the morrow's ironing—so Pippin knocked at the door, and Mary-in-the-kitchen opened it. A rather stern looking Mary, until she saw who it was; then she dimpled and smiled in a delightful way, and wanted to know if that was he.

"I was sort of looking for you to-day!" she added.

"You was!" Pippin glowed responsive. "Now that sounds good to me. Something in my line to-day?"

"There was a woman come to clean Saturday, and what must she do but take my best potato knife to pry off the top of a jar! 'Twas a screw-top, too, so she had her trouble for her pains, and broke the knife besides—Just the tip; I thought perhaps you could grind it off?"

"Well, I guess! just watch me! If there's one job I like better than another, it's grind a new tip."

Mary brought the knife, which he pronounced a dandy from Dandyville. He didn't suppose she would care to see him do it? Some thought 'twas pretty to watch. Mary, with a glance at the clock, thought she had time. Soon, bright head and dark were bending over Nipper, the wheel was flying, the rough edge of blue steel was fining, thinning, brightening, shaping—yes, it certainly was pretty to watch. Pippin had a strong notion that something else would have been pretty to watch, too, could he have looked two ways at once; it was rather wonderful to feel a soft breath on your cheek, to be conscious that within six or eight inches of your own brown head was that bright efflorescence of light and color and softness, but Pippin did not say this.

When the knife was done, he looked up, and met his reward in a soft glow of admiration and wonder that almost took his breath.

"You surely are a master hand!" cried Mary. "Why, it's better than when it came from the shop."

"I'm real pleased if it's satisfactory!" said Pippin modestly. "'Twould be better still if I had a bit of shammy skin; I did have a piece, but I can't seem to—"

"Why, step right in! I've got shammy skin and to spare. Step in and set down, do! I'd be pleased to have you!"

But not so pleased as Pippin was to step! He wiped his shoes as elaborately as if he had not indulged in "the best shine in town, five cents!" before coming; he brushed imaginary dust off his neat brown clothes; finally he made his little bow of a young birch in the wind, and followed Mary into the kitchen.

Very different, Pippin, from the kitchen at Cyrus Poor Farm: for space, compactness; for mellow warmth of brick and timbers, brilliant white of paint and tile and enamel, set off by the blurred or shining silver of aluminum or nickel; for Mrs. Bailey, kindly and wrinkled, in her purple print, this vision of blue and white and gold.

"Green grass!" said Pippin. "This is some, ain't it?"

He was to sit right down at this little table, Mary said. There! Here was the "shammy," and if he would excuse her, she would make up her rolls. That way they'd both be busy, wouldn't they? And no time wasted! Mary's laugh seemed to tinkle all round the room, striking little bell-like notes here and there, just as her smile—or so it seemed to Pippin—woke new lights on the shining kettles and saucepans. Then, standing at the large table next to his small one, she lifted the cover from a yellow bowl full of creamy, bubbling dough, and went to work.

Have you ever watched a pretty girl making rolls? There are few more attractive sights. First she tumbles the soft mass out on the board; then she kneads it, with much play of dimpled elbow and slender wrist. The bubbles heave and swell, but she catches them, breaks them down, works them in, till the whole is like smooth creamy velvet, delightful to see, more delightful to handle. Now she cuts off a piece, cups it in her hands, pats, moulds, shapes, tucks in a bit of butter; behold the perfect roll! Into the pan it goes, with its fellows, and so into the oven, to emerge in due time with the perfection of a "pale bake," tenderest fawn color deepening at the top, say to the hue of a winter beech leaf.

Pippin certainly was a long time over that knife tip. He rubbed it hard for a minute or two, till it shone like Mary's own particular coffeepot; then he paused, lost in contemplation of Mary's wrists and elbows, her clear-cut profile, and waving hair. Whenever she turned toward him, he rubbed the knife tip vigorously, only to relapse again when she turned away. So absorbed was he, he did not notice how rapidly the mass of dough was diminishing; and when Mary, having plumped the last roll into place, turned suddenly full upon him with a "There! *That's* done!" he started with a guilty flush, and almost cut himself with the knife, now more like a razor than a kitchen implement. Mary, meeting the full gaze of his dark bright eyes, flushed, too, and then laughed a little. "I think my work's pretty, too!" she said. "I guess you like to watch it same as I do yours."

"I sure do! And if you'll excuse me sayin' so, I never see rolls handled so elegant in my life. I'm part baker myself," he added apologetically, "and I've seen a many rolls handled." Mary kindled with interest. She wanted to know if he was a baker. Then why—

"Why ain't I bakin'?" Pippin laughed. "I'll have to tell you about that some day—lemme put 'em in for you! Dandy oven you've got; dandy outfit all round! That's if I might take the liberty of callin' again, Miss—"

"Mary Flower is my name!" said the girl. "I should be pleased to know yours!"

"Pippin is what they call me!" Pippin, for the first time in his life, felt the need of two names. Now why?

"Mr. Pippin, I should be pleased to have you call again." She spoke a little formally; these were proper conventions, since there was no third party by to introduce them.

"Well, now, Miss Flower, I shall be glad to come, and more than glad, sure thing, the very day I come back. What I came special to-day was to say—"

But Pippin never said it. At that moment the screen door swung open, and a man entered. A man about Pippin's age, in linen duster and straw hat, carrying a basket of vegetables. A grocer's assistant, evidently; his wagon stood at the gate. The first thing that struck Pippin was the eager glance the man threw about the room, and the sharp flash of—was it suspicion or jealousy?—as his eyes fell upon him, Pippin. This was the first impression; the second was that Mary did not like him; the third that the man's nose was crooked. Having received these three impressions, Pippin bent over his potato knife, and polished it assiduously. Where *had* he seen that nose? Where *had* he seen that nose? It couldn't be—was it?—green grass! now wouldn't that—

He glanced warily up, and seeing the man's attention engrossed by Mary, took a good look at him. A thin, sharp face, eyes too near together, a straight slit of a mouth; but the nose was what interested Pippin. It was certainly *very* crooked! A long sharp nose; that must have been a powerful blow which had turned it from the straight course. Pippin's right fist clenched involuntarily, with a reminiscent thrill; the corners of his mouth twitched, and his eyes twinkled.

"Green grass!" he murmured again.

"No, I guess we shan't want anything to-morrow!" said Mary, in cool, flute-like tones. "No, you needn't call, thank you. We'll telephone when we need anything."

"Got company, I see!" the man directed an ugly scowl at Pippin. Pippin looked up cheerfully.

119

"Hello, Nosey!" he said. "That you? Quite a stranger, ain't you?" Again the man's eyes flashed, and this time there was recognition in them; the next moment his face was a wooden mask.

"Guess you've got me!" he said. "Stranger to me, far as I know. That your wheel out there?" He spoke with a curious mixture of eagerness and sullenness.

"Sure thing! Forgot me, have you, Nosey? Say 'Pippin,' and see if you don't fetch it?"

"We don't carry apples at this season," stolidly. "Berries is what we carry now, and early peaches."

"That so? Well, you're a peach, all right, all right. Well, Miss Flower, I expect I—" He was about to rise and make his adieux, when a look from Mary tingled through him to his toes; it said, "Stay!" He settled back in his seat. "I expect I'm ready for those other things you spoke of," he said slowly. "Scissors, was they, or knives?"

"Scissors!" said Mary. "I'll get them!"

She vanished. As the door closed behind her, the man made a step toward Pippin, and spoke low and savagely.

"You quit, do you hear? Quit and stay quit! If I catch you here again, I'll—" he indicated measures which would seriously incommode Pippin's internal economy.

"That so?" said Pippin in an easy drawl. He tilted his chair back on two legs, and smiled amiably at his interlocutor. "Why, Nosey, I'm sorry you feel that way. I never meant to spile it permanent, but it does seem to have got a kind of a twist, don't it? I wouldn't bear malice, though, if I was you!"

"—— —— you!" hissed the man. "I'll have your—"

The door opened; he dropped back against the table, and his face became once more a wooden mask.

Mary, her hands full of scissors, looked from one to the other; her breath came a little quickly, as if she had hurried. "You two gentlemen know each other?" she asked doubtfully.

"Why," said Pippin slowly, "I thought he was a boy I used to know, but he seems to think different. What is your handsome name, Mister, since Nosey Bashford won't do you?"

"My name's Brown!" said the man hoarsely.

"Well, they both begin with B," said Pippin. "I don't know as it matters any."

"Was there anything else you wanted to say, Mr. Brown?" asked Mary civilly.

At this palpable hint, the man could but take up his basket and start for the door. He gave Pippin one venomous look; Pippin replied with a slight but friendly nod.

"So long, bo!" he said cheerfully.

At the door the man paused, as if struck by a sudden thought. He had some extra fine tomato plants in the cart, he said. They was an order for Goodwins, next door, but the boss thought likely Mr. Aymer (Mary's employer) would like some. Wouldn't Mary step out and look at them? 'Twouldn't take but a minute, if she wasn't afraid to leave—a significant glance toward Pippin finished the sentence and decided Mary's answer. She had meant to say, "No!" with some asperity. As it was, she said, "Yes!" and followed him out to the gate, leaving Pippin alone.

Now, the latter asked himself, wouldn't that give you a pain? Honest, now, wouldn't it? What did he suppose that skeezicks was sayin' to her. If he came the give-away, he, Pippin, expected he could give him as good. Even if Dod was dead, and it wasn't likely he was—

If Pippin had been a cultivated person, he would have said,

"The gods are just, and of our pleasant vicesMake instruments to plague us!"

Being a plain person, he said, no two ways about it, that was what come of startin' mean. Yes; but, he reminded himself, the start was not of his own making. Let him be straight and keep straight, and things would come round 'cordin' to!

"That's right!" said Pippin aloud. "I'm only makin' a beginnin', so to say. *My* start is right now, see? Let Dod and Nosey get what they can out of theirs. Last week's dough-scrapin's needn't trouble me!"

Mary came back with her head high, a flush on her cheek and a sparkle in her eye.

"Gorry to 'Liza!" said Pippin, but not aloud. "She looks some-er when she's mad than when she's pleased!"

"Known Nosey long?" asked Pippin, rising as she entered.

"No, nor want to! He's not my style, nor I his. Did you really know him, Mr. Pippin?"

"Did I? Do I know a skunk by the sm—Yes, I knew him when we was boys. 'Twas I give him his crooked nose. I'll tell you about it some day, if you'll let me. I must be goin' now."

Was it quite by accident, I wonder, that Mrs. Aymer came into the kitchen to get a cup of hot water? She greeted Pippin pleasantly, admired the rehabilitated potato knife, thought his must be a pleasant trade in summer weather. She thought it very possible that Mr. Aymer might like his pocketknife sharpened. Could Pippin wait a moment?

"That's what I'm here for!" Pippin smilingly assured her. Mr. Aymer being summoned, shortly appeared: tall, thin, kindly-faced, looking more like a college professor than a hardware dealer. He, too, after looking Pippin well over, praised his skill and discussed various aspects of cutlery with him. They agreed heartily on the fundamental fact that when you wanted a knife, you wanted it good. Followed commendation of certain makes, disparagement of others. Bugler's goods, Pippin opined, wasn't worth the price of the handles; he'd make as good a knife out of lead pipe. Now take Porter's, and *there* you had a knife. Both men began to glow with responsive ardor, and it required a discreet cough and glance from Mrs. Aymer to convey to both the fact that supper time was drawing near and that Mary had her work to do. Pippin withdrew with many apologies, but not before both householders had cordially asked him to call again. Mary, in her corner, remained demurely mute, but to be sure she had already invited him; and her farewell glance and smile sent him away trailing clouds of glory.

Later, on the comfortable little screened porch, the householders told their guest about the handsome lad who was so clever with tools, and who had evidently "taken such a shine" to their pretty Mary.

"I called John out on purpose!" said the lady. "Of course we feel responsible about Mary; and you liked him, didn't you, John?"

"I certainly did: mighty decent looking fellow. Intelligent, too! Knows good steel when he sees it."

"You ought to have seen him, Lawrence! You are so interested in young men. If he comes again, you must be sure to want your knife sharpened—if this old Conference is going to give you *any* time for us!" she added with a smiling pout. "Of course if there should be anything serious between him and Mary, we should want to be *very* careful!"

"Aren't you a little ahead of the game, Lucy?" her husband laughed. "The boy has been here once, I understand—twice? Oh, well! I don't know that Lawrence can count on the wedding fee, even so. But you would like him, Larry, that's a fact. I took to him at once, and you know Lucy thinks me hard to please, especially about young fellows."

"I wish I had seen him!" said the guest heartily. "I've seen nothing but gray heads all day long, and a boy would be refreshing."

But if he had seen Pippin, the course of my story would have been different.

Meanwhile, as they talked, Mary-in-the-kitchen sat on her back steps in the moonlight, and thought her own thoughts. Happy thoughts! Mary was always happy. If some of them were of dark eyes and a kindling smile, of quaintly chosen words—He had as sweet a voice, Mary must say, as ever she heard; she wished Mrs. Aymer had heard him sing; when he came again—oh, yes, he would come. The queer thing was, he didn't seem a bit of a stranger. Appeared like she had known him always.

What would you say, Mary, if you knew that the dark eyes were watching you now, in the shadow of that big elm across the road? You would be surprised, but possibly not displeased, Mary? Ah! But what if another pair of eyes were watching, too, sharply, eagerly, greedily; little red eyes, set too near together across a crooked nose? What then, Mary-in-the-kitchen?

CHAPTER XVI
PIPPIN ENCOUNTERS THE GIDEONS

PIPPIN spent the evening sitting on the edge of his bed, whistling on his file, as was his custom when perturbed in spirit, and taking counsel with himself. He had had a shock. Two hours ago, after leaving the white house, he felt the need of a pipe; a smoke of tribute, call it, to whatever gods might be interested in youth and beauty, in dimples and waving hair. Nearly opposite the house, across the lane, was a huge elm whose branches drooped low over the roadside. Its roots formed a comfortable seat neatly cushioned with moss. Pippin had already observed this natural retreat; now he sought it, and lighting his pipe, was at peace with the world.

Silently he communed with himself about the "young lady." He did not venture to think of her by any other title, though it must be confessed that he said "Mary" to himself now and then, just to be sure that it sounded like the prettiest name in the world, though of course he always knew it was. And he always knew—now, how did he know it was her name?—that she could have no other. If Pippin had put his thoughts into words—but he could not! His heart beat quick and hard in his ears, and there was something the matter with his breathing; and anyway, who was he to set up thinking of her at all? But if he had found words, they might have shaped themselves thus.

Honest, now! Had he ever, in all his life, seen a young lady that was a patch on her? Believe him, nix! It wasn't only her looks, though they was out of sight, clear; it was the way she moved, and spoke—notice how the corners of her mouth curled up round the words as if she loved 'em—And the sound of her voice, and the goodness that shined right out of her—my! my! *that* lamp is burnin' all right, all right! He paused, for beside the bright face that shone so clear before him, he seemed to see another, a face no less fair, more perfect indeed in line and tint and carving, but, as he had once said, like a lamp unlighted. "Poor Flora May!" he murmured. "Poor gal! Now wouldn't that young lady be a sister to her if she had the chance? You bet she would!"

Thus musing, he chanced to look up, and was aware of a man coming slowly along the road; very slowly, with a singular gait, half limp, half lurch. He was dressed like a day laborer, and carried a dinner pail; a pickaxe was slung over his shoulder. It was the gait that caught Pippin's eye; he stopped building air-castles, and looked narrowly at the advancing figure.

The man shambled slowly along, and paused near the gate of the white house. Drawing out a clay pipe, he proceeded to light it; a clumsy business he made of it, fumbling long for his matches, then making several vain attempts to strike a light, his eyes meantime roaming over house and grounds with sharp, searching glances. Pippin, always so ready to help, might easily have given him a light—but a moment before Pippin had extinguished his own pipe with a swift, silent motion. He sat perfectly still under his tree, not to be distinguished from it in the dusk, under the drooping branches, his eyes riveted to the slouching figure. So absorbed was he that he saw nothing of the quiet approach of another figure, until it stood close beside the first; a lighter, slimmer figure, that of a young man. Pippin could see no more till the newcomer, turning his profile to the rising moon, displayed a crooked nose.

If the two exchanged words, it was in a whisper so low that Pippin could not catch it. The younger man also pulled out a pipe, and seemed to ask for a light; there was more fumbling and scratching, then the elder nodded slightly and went limping and lurching along the road.

Why did the younger man linger? Why did he, too, slip under a drooping tree—not fifty feet away from Pippin's own, I declare—and stand there, silent and hidden as Pippin himself?

Why, Pippin, a man may have feelings, even if his nose is crooked. If a pretty girl comes out to sit on her steps and look at the rising moon and think sweet, girl-moonlight thoughts, why—be reasonable, Pippin! Why should not Nosey Bashford like to watch her as well as you? Nosey's nose is shockingly crooked, and his eyes are crooked, too, little and red and too near together; he is crooked inside and out, but he has his feelings, and it is well for you, Pippin, seeing that you are entirely unarmed, whereas Nosey is never without a sandbag or a brass knuckle or some such pretty trifle, that he does not know of your being only fifty feet away from him.

"That's right!" said Pippin, sitting on his bed, as above mentioned, whistling on his file; "that may be all so, and likely 'tis: but that don't explain Dod happenin' along just that minute, nor yet them two with their heads together. Dod has aged some—well, he would! Must be sixty year old, or nigh it—but he don't look no handsomer nor no—well, say piouser—than he did. What I say is, I believe them two has a game on. I hate to keep the Old Man waitin', but I rather guess I'll have to hang round here a spell, and see what they're up to. What say?"

When in need of sympathy, Pippin was apt to call up his dream family and demand it of them, never failing of a response. He did so now, and Ma, blue-eyed and pink-cheeked, and Pa, brown and stalwart, appeared promptly. Pippin, absurd fellow that he was, saw them sitting beside him, and appealed to Pa to confirm his last remark. Pa said he was right, things did appear to squint that way a mite. He expected Pippin had better keep his eye on them two.

"But I stuck him out!" Pippin slapped his thigh joyously. "I stuck him out, folks! And I would have if he'd have set there all night. Another thing!" His voice was grave again. "Notice what happened just before he left? Why, the Boss—Mr. Aymer, that is—come home. Didn't you hear some one step kind of quick along the sidewalk front of the house, whistlin' a little, but not so as to disturb folks, and then the latchkey rattle a mite as he put in? I tell you, 'twasn't all feelin's in Nosey's. He wanted to know what time the Boss was liable to come home, and he found out. Oh, they're smart, Bashfords; you got to keep your eye peeled when you watch them!"

Pippin stopped suddenly. Some one seemed to be talking; Ma this time, her blue eyes bright and serious. Had he looked for grace in them two?

"Green grass!" Pippin laughed aloud. "Grace, in Bashford's gang! If there's as much grace in e'er a one of 'em as would raise a biscuit, one solitary, little weeny biscuit, I'll—I'll—"

He stopped again, for again the voice seemed to speak.

"I didn't know as the Elder made any exception. Fellow creatures, he said—"

Pippin dropped his head. If he had been differently brought up, he might have beaten his breast and cried, "*Mea culpa!*" As it was, he said, "Green grass!" again, several times. The last exclamation was in a different tone. He raised his head, and his eyes shone.

"I'll try!" he said. "Honest, I will! Now behooves me get a mite o' sleep. But first—"

The room was a small and plain one, in a meek by-street which had to work hard to prove that it was not a slum, but did prove it. There were curtains in most of the windows, faded, patched, darned, but whole and clean (Mrs. Morrissey's were Nottingham lace, the street would have you know, but then Mr. Morrissey was on the Force), and not a house but had a geranium or a straggle of nasturtiums in window-box or tin can or broken pitcher.

Besides all this, not a lodging room in the street but had a Bible; the Gideons had seen to that. Pippin took the fat black book from the little light-stand beside the bed. He had his own little Testament that Elder Hadley had given him, but this was handy by, and besides, he admired to read about them Old Testament guys. Elijah was "some," he thought; as for Elisha, he had no opinion of him. Gettin' them kids all stove up just because they was a mite cheeky! Likely he *was* bald-headed!

The volume opening at the title page revealed a printed slip pasted inside the cover, on which Pippin read as follows:

This Holy Book, whose leaves display
the Life, the Light, the Truth, the Way,
is placed in this room by
The Gideons,
The Christian Commercial Travelers' Association of America,
Aided by
The Christian Forces of this City
with the hope also that by means of this Book
many may be brought to know the love of
Christ which passeth knowledge.

* The Ancient Gideon's Test and Triumph—Judges and .

* The Modern Gideon's Motto—Judges :.

* The Greatest Sermon ever preached—Matthew , , and .

* BLESSED TRUTH—ACCEPT IT—Luke :; John :.

* The Supreme Sacrifice for all—Isaiah .

* The Universal Invitation to all—Isaiah .

* If lonesome or blue and friends untrue, read Psalms and , Luke .

* If trade is poor, read Psalm , John .

* If discouraged or in trouble, read Psalm ; John .

* If you are all out of sorts, read Hebrews .

* If you are losing confidence in men, read I Cor. .

* If skeptical, read John :, :; Phil. :-.

* If you can't have your own way, read James .

* If tired of sin, read Luke :-, -, John .

* If very prosperous, read I Cor. :, .

- The WONDERFUL RESULT—Isaiah —Psalm —Romans .

We earnestly solicit free-will offerings for the aid of our
Bible work.
Christian Traveling Men, Join Us, Help Us.
For particulars, inquire of any man wearing the button, or
THE GIDEONS,
West Quincy Street, Chicago, Ill.

"Green grass!" said Pippin. "Now wouldn't that—" He read it again, slowly and carefully. "Now wouldn't that—well, the reverse of give you a pain! Lemme see! What fits me special in this outfit?" His finger following the table of contents, Pippin knit his brows and set his teeth, murmuring as he went, "'If trade is poor,'—that ain't me! I made three dollars to-day, and two yesterday. Fifteen a week wouldn't be far from it, and five of that in the bank reg'lar every week. I tell you!

"'If discouraged or in trouble;' nope!

"'If you are all out of sorts;' not a mite!

"'If you are losing confidence in man'—There! Isn't that a leadin'? Bet your life!" said Pippin. He turned to the appointed passage and read:

"'Though I speak with the tongues of men and of angels, and have not charity, I am become as sounding brass, or a tinkling cymbal.

"'And though I have the gift of prophecy, and understand all mysteries, and all knowledge; and though I have all faith, so that I could remove mountains, and have not charity, I am nothing.

"'And though I bestow all my goods to feed the poor, and though I give my body to be burned, and have not charity, it profiteth me nothing.'

"I expect that is so," said Pippin gravely. "I certainly expect that that is so, and I will act as near that as is give me, 'cordin' to. Say I learn it off, so I'll have it handy by and not forget it, what say? 'Though I speak with the tongues of men and of angels, and have not charity, I am become as sounding brass, or a tinkling—'"

At this point there was a rap on the wall, and an angry voice asked whether there was a prayer meeting going on, or what? Couldn't a man get a wink of sleep without condemned galoots hollering their prayers through a megaphone?

128

"I'm real sorry, brother!" said Pippin pacifically. "I didn't know I'd riz my voice."

"Riz your voice! You go hire yourself out as foghorn to a Sound boat, and you'll make your fortune!"

"You've got a powerful organ of your own," replied Pippin. "If you'd like to have a prayer meetin', I'd be pleased to have you join in. Are you a Gideon?"

"Are you a goat that wants its hide took off?" roared the other. "If you don't shut your head—"

"I've shut and padlocked it! I'm just whisperin' through a knothole. Go to by-by, bo! Pleasant dreams!"

Pippin's chance came the very next day. As he was carrying Nipper past the white house—he was not going in, but somehow his way seemed to lie mostly through the lane—the grocery wagon stood at the gate, and even as he looked, the door opened and shut, rather hastily, and the crooked-nosed man—his given name was William, by the way—came out with his empty basket. He greeted Pippin with a scowl that blackened his never too attractive face. Pippin gave him a friendly nod.

"Mornin', Nosey!" he said.

Nosey's only reply was a snarl that might have meant anything—except friendliness.

"Say, Nosey, quit the grouch, what? I'm sorry I sp'iled your beak, bo. There! I'd mend it if I knew how, honest I would!"

Nosey's reply was intelligible this time, but unprintable. It was to the general effect that if Pippin didn't light out pretty condemned quick, he would "get his," whatever that might mean.

"That so?" said Pippin. "All right, bo! I just wanted to say that I hadn't no grouch against you. I'm on the straight now, Bill, see? Mebbe you are, too?"

"Yes, you are!" with an ugly sneer. "You and your wheel! You look out, that's all I say to you! Gidap!" The last remark was addressed to the horse, and was accompanied by a savage blow of the whip; the startled animal sprang forward and the wagon rattled out of sight.

"Well, I tried!" said Pippin. "Honest, I did!"

A day or two after, Mrs. Appleby received a letter that puzzled her somewhat. It was signed, "Yours in the Lord, Pippin," and was to the effect that she was please not to be sore because the writer had to hold up that job a mite. He would pull it off quick as he could, but they was some guys trying to make a deal out of some folks he knew that was dandy folks, he could tell her, and he felt a call to hang round a spell so as he would be ready in case an extra hand was needed, for them guys was mean as they grow, and if that young lady or her boss come to any harm, he'd never get over it, sure thing. But quick as he got this off his chest, he'd make tracks for Shoreham and get that letter, if it took a leg.

Mrs. Appleby smiled over this effusion, which was carefully written on heavily ruled paper. The handwriting was stiff and official—had not Pippin learned to write in the office of the Warden, under the eye of that kindly potentate?—the spelling occasionally quaint, but she seemed well pleased as she laid it away methodically.

"I am sure that boy is genuine!" she said with a little nod. "I would trust him— what is it, Jane?"

A pupil-teacher was standing before her, red-cheeked, round-eyed, and out of breath.

"Jimmy 'as run away again, Mam!"

"Jimmy! dear! dear! Played hookey from school, you mean?"

"Yes, Mam! I 'ad 'im be the 'and"—Jane was but one remove from London—"and we was steppin' along quite-like, wen 'e 'eard a horgan, and 'e was horf!"

"Dear! dear!" said Mrs. Appleby again. "That is the third time; I will notify the police at once." Stepping to the telephone, she gave notice of the truant, "Ten years old, small and wiry, red hair and freckles; khaki pants, gray flannel shirt; will probably answer to any name except his own, which is James Mather. Do have him found, Mr. Inspector! He isn't a bad boy, and he is sure to have the nightmare to-night."

Turning back, she spoke to Mrs. Faulkner who was just entering the room.

"Jimmy Mather has run away *again*, Mrs. Faulkner! I really don't know what to do with the boy."

"I should send him to the Farm School!" said Mrs. Faulkner promptly. "He is a very bad influence here. Last evening, when the cook was going to church, he pinned a dishcloth to her cloak, and she never found it out till she got back. She has given notice. I was just coming to tell you. I think she will stay if the boy is sent away."

"Little Jim!" cried Mrs. Appleby. "Oh, Mrs. Faulkner! He is too young for the Farm School, even if—"

"Mary is a very valuable woman!" said Mrs. Faulkner severely. "It is matter of knowledge to me that she has been offered fifteen dollars a week, and we get her for ten because of her little niece being here. James Mather is worth nothing at all that I can see, and is a nuisance besides."

"Oh, Mrs. Faulkner!" said Mrs. Appleby again.

As she stood perplexed, what was this vision that flashed suddenly before her eyes? Two brown, bright eyes in a face that seemed to smile all over, brow to chin; a musical voice saying,

"There's a kid I like! I could do something with that kid if I had him!"

"Dear! dear!" said Mrs. Appleby aloud. "I do wish he would!" and happening to glance out of the window, she saw Pippin entering the courtyard with Jimmy Mather beside him. Yes, things happen that way sometimes. Mrs. Appleby did not try to analyze her feeling of relief when Mrs. Faulkner was called out of the room just as Pippin entered it.

"Run straight into me!" said Pippin, when the culprit had been welcomed, rebuked, provisionally pardoned and sent to bed. "Follerin' a Dago with an organ and a monkey. Gee! Run just the way I used to run after a monkey. I knew the pup in a minute, and I had him by his slack and scruff before he knew what had got him. Green grass! he was surprised, that kid was! Then he bawled, and wanted to go with me, but nix on that, so I said I'd fetch him home, and he come along like pie. But say, lady, you rec'lect what I told you that day?"

"I was just thinking of it when you came in! Your coming seemed providential."

"Can you show me anything that ain't, in a manner of speakin'? Well, I say it again. This is a dandy place for some kids, but it's no place for that one. You want to let me take him—"

"Where? Where would you take him, Pippin?"

"To Cyrus Poor Farm!"

"A poorhouse?" The matron's face fell.

"It's that, but it's more than that, and it's goin' to be more than what it is now. Leave me have that boy and a dozen more like him, and gee! I tell you we'll make things hum there to Cyrus! That's the kind I want; smart little kids, the kind that makes the smartest crook. Catch 'em little, and make 'em grow straight instead of crooked—what do you know about that? Wouldn't that be mince pie atop of roast turkey and cranberry sauce? I tell you!"

Thus Pippin, glowing with ardor, sure that everyone must see his project as he saw it; but now the gay fire died out of his face. "I forgot!" he said. "I can't take him just yet, lady. I—you got a letter from me? Did? Well, there's where it is, you see! I ain't free to go just yet. This job to Mr. Aymer's—"

"Mr. *Who*?" Mrs. Appleby started.

"Mr. Aymer: John E. Lives corner of Smith and Brown Street. Maybe you might know him, Mis' Appleby? They sure are dandy folks!"

"I know Mr. Aymer," drily. "How came you to know him, Pippin?"

"There's a young lady works for him!" Pippin was blushing hotly, but he met the inquiring look bravely. "Miss Flower, her name is. I happened along by—in the way of business, you understand—and she had a carver needed sharpenin', and so we made acquaintance. She's—well, there! Mebbe you might know her, too? Do?" as Mrs. Appleby nodded. "Now isn't that great! Well, honest now, isn't she—did you ever see a dandier young lady than that?"

"She is a nice girl!" Mrs. Appleby's mouth was under strict control, but her eyes twinkled. "Have you been at the house more than once? You say you have met Mr. Aymer—and Mrs. Aymer?"

"I have, ma'am! They were more than kind to me, I must say. Yes, I've been there four or five times. I—I didn't do all the knives the first day I was there, nor yet the second. Their knives was in poor shape—" He paused and looked helplessly into the kind, shrewd gray eyes. "I—I don't know as I was in any too great hurry about them knives!" he faltered. "I—fact is, I give consid'able time to 'em; took a couple one day and another couple another. Pleasant place, and nice folks, you understand—and—I told you about them two mean guys—"

Mrs. Appleby said she did understand. And what did Pippin propose to do next? she asked. Why, that was just what he was studyin' over; he was just puttin' that up to himself when he ran across the kiddo just now. Whether to wait round a bit and watch till he was a mite surer than what he was—and yet he *was* sure, knowin' them two and their ways—or up and tell the Boss thus and so, and let him do as he der—as he thought fit.

"I've got a hunch," said Pippin, "that I'd better tell him right away. What say?"

"I say you are right!" Mrs. Appleby spoke with decision.

"I'll do it! I'll do it before I sleep to-night. Maybe he'll think of some way to hasten matters up a mite. If they're goin' to do him up, I wish't they'd get at it, so's we can round 'em up and me get off on my business. Not but it *is* my business to stop such doin's every time I see a chance. I wish you good mornin' lady, and I'm a thousand times obliged to you."

He departed, and Mrs. Appleby sat down and wrote a note to Miss Mary Flower, care of John E. Aymer, Esq., Cor. Smith and Brown Streets, City.

CHAPTER XVII
THREE TETE-A-TETES

IT'S a rum start!" said Mr. John Aymer.

"It certainly is queer!" said Mrs. John Aymer. "I don't like it one bit, John. I do wish Lawrence was back."

"Sent for him over there, did they? One of his pet lambs in trouble? Well, he'll be back on the night train, for to-morrow is the final cakewalk of his old Conference. But as far as immediate plans are concerned, I'm afraid, my dear, you will have to put up with yours truly. Now, this—what's his name? Lippitt? Pippit?"

"Something like that! I didn't quite make it out."

"Say Pippit! Certainly *seems* to be a decent chap. Tells a straight story, too. Knows this fellow Brown for a crook. We didn't ask him *how* he knew—"

"It wasn't necessary, John. I have *never* liked the man's looks. I spoke to Babbitt about him, and he said he had taken him on trial for three months, and he seemed a smart fellow, and that was all he knew. Of course I couldn't ask Babbitt to discharge him because I didn't like his looks, now could I?"

"—but we can find out about that later!" Mr. Aymer went on calmly. "Has seen Brown chinning with a pal—"

"John! I do wish you were not so slangy!"

"Has seen Brown holding sweet converse with a comrade tried and true, of specially obnoxious character. Look here, Lucy!" Mr. Aymer blew a smoke ring and looked inquiringly at his wife, knitting briskly in her corner by the rose-shaded lamp. "How *does* your friend Nippitt know all this? I want to go a little bit slow here."

"Oh, John! you *are* so tiresome! I am sure, and so is Mary, that Pippit is perfectly truthful. Why, you have only to look at him! When he smiles—John, you needn't laugh! I would believe anything that boy said. And here he offers of his own free will to watch the house at night for a week, or as long as is necessary, if we will just give him a shakedown in the shed. I am sure the least we can do is to accept such an offer as that. The old night watchman would never offer to do such a thing."

"The night watchman is not paid to sleep in people's sheds, my dear!"

"Well, he might as well. He never comes through this street at all, that I know of. *Well*, John, did you tell Lippitt—Pippit—he was to come? I shall feel *so* safe if he is there!"

"Yes!" said Mr. Aymer slowly. "I told him he might come, and now the question is whether I am only a plain fool, or a—"

"And now we need not lose our sleep!" Mrs. Aymer laid down her knitting, and came forward to rumple her John's hair affectionately, and deposit a kiss on his forehead. "You ought not to lose one wink of sleep just now, John, with stock-taking just coming on, and if I lie awake I am such a *fright* next day, and you don't like me to be a fright, do you, dear?"

"Neither to be nor to have!" said John. "Sooner shall Pippit occupy the shed for life."

"The loft could be made into a perfectly good bedroom if ever—" Mrs. Aymer cast a guilty glance at her husband, and went to fetch the cribbage board.

While this conversation was going on in the parlor with its rose chintz hangings, another dialogue was being held in the kitchen. Mary admired the parlor, dusted reverentially its *bibelots*, plumped its cushions to perfection; but for coziness, she must say, give her her kitchen!

It certainly was cozy this evening, with the red half-curtains drawn, and the lamplight shining on white enamel and blue crockery; shining on Mary, too, sitting in her low rocking-chair, knitting as swiftly and steadily as was the lady in the parlor. They were fast friends, mistress and maid, and it was a race between them which should produce the more socks and mufflers in this year when all the world was knitting.

Pippin, sitting as near as he thought manners would allow, watched the flying fingers and glittering needles, and wished that he might be a sock, just for a minute, to feel how soft her hands would be. Now Mary's hands were not soft; she would have been ashamed if they had been: firm, strong little hands, used to work ever since she could remember.

The two had just been preparing Pippin's shakedown in the shed, she deprecating, fearing he would sleep but poorly on a straw mattress, he glowing with praise of as dandy an outfit as anyone would want to see.

"Straw mattress!" he repeated. "Straw'll do for me, Miss Flower. Why, come to think of it, I don't know as I hardly ever slep' on anything *but*straw except while I was to Mis' Baxter's, over to Kingdom. She had wool tops to her beds, and they were surely elegant. I have heard of folks havin' curled hair, horses' hair, in their beds; did ever you hear of that?"

Yes, Mary had heard of that. She forbore to say that her own neat white bed upstairs boasted a hair mattress. As Mrs. Aymer said, it was real economy, but still—and in her heart she was wondering how and where this young man had grown up. Of course they had wool top mattresses at the Home—and mother had had nothing but straw—poor mother! Mary shivered a little. She too saw visions sometimes; one came upon her now, of the straw mattress being taken away, with its scanty coverings, and sold by Him for drink. 'Twas summer, he said; no need of beds and bedclothes in summer. "Sleep floor, nice 'n' cool!" It was after that that mother left him, and took her to the Home. Poor mother!

Mary became aware that a silence had fallen. Looking up, she met Pippin's bright eyes fixed on her with a look half eager, half appealing.

"What is it?" she asked involuntarily. "Did you ask me something, Mr. Pippin? I—I was just thinking—"

"I didn't!" Pippin spoke slowly, and his voice had not its usual joyous ring. "But I'd like to ask you something, Miss Flower; or perhaps tell you would be more what I mean. But maybe I'm keepin' you up?" He made as if to rise.

Mary glanced at the clock.

"No indeed!" she said. "It's only nine, Mr. Pippin. I don't hardly ever go up before half past. I'd be glad to hear anything you have to tell me."

"I don't know as you will!" Pippin spoke rather ruefully. "Be glad, I mean. I—I haven't been quite square with your Boss, Miss Flower. I haven't, that's a fact. No!" as Mary looked up, startled. "I don't mean I've told him anything that wasn't so. I believe it's all as I think and more so; but what I would say is, there's a heap I haven't told him. You see I—I dunno just how to put it—I felt to help him through this deal that I knew them fellers was puttin' up; and—and—what I would say—if I'd told him the whole of what there was to tell, mebbe he wouldn't have let me help. I'm doin' the right thing, young lady, no fears of that; the Lord showed me; but I'm scared, fear mebbe I ain't doin' it the right way. So I thought if I might tell you the way I was fixed—what say?"

"Certainly, Mr. Pippin! I'll be pleased to hear, as I said."

Mary laid down her work, and looked straight at Pippin with her honest blue eyes. That made Pippin blush and feel as if a blue knife had gone through him. To cover his confusion, he felt for his file, drew it out and whistled softly on it; then, seeing Mary's look change to one of open amazement, he fell into still deeper confusion.

"It's a file!" he explained. "I always carry it. It's handy—" He broke off short, and made a desperate plunge. "I wondered if—if *you* wondered—how I come to be so cocksure of that guy's bein' a crook. Did you?"

"Well!" Mary hesitated a moment. "Yes! I didn't doubt but you did know, but—yes, I did wonder some."

"That's what I've got to tell you. I've knowed that guy ever since we was little shavers. We was—you may say—raised together, for a spell; that is, we was learned together, anyway."

"You mean—you went to school together?"

Pippin leaned forward, his eyes very bright.

"Bashford's school!" he said. "Bashford's gang. Sneak-thievin', pocket-pickin', breakin' and enterin'. Instruction warranted *com*plete. That's the school we went to, young lady. I know Nosey Bashford because I was a crook like him—only I will say I could do a better job—" Pippin's chin lifted a little—"till the Lord took holt of me. Now you know where I stand! And gorry to 'Liza!'" he added silently; "do you s'pose I've got to git off this song and dance every time I meet any person that I value their good opinion? I want you to understand the Lord ain't lettin' me off any too easy, now I tell you!"

"But think," he assured himself, "how much easier you breathe when it's off your chest! I expect the Lord knows full well just who ought to be told things, and plans accordin'."

But Pippin had never heard of the *Ancient Mariner*.

Mary Flower had gone very pale, and her sweet face was grave; but her eyes still met Pippin's frankly. "Go on!" she said. "You've said too much, or you've said too little; either way you'll have to finish now. But be careful, for I shall believe everything you say."

"Now wouldn't that—" murmured Pippin; then he was silent for a little, fingering his file absently. Mary thought he must hear the beating of her heart, but he did not, for his own was sounding trip hammers in his ears. She would believe everything—

137

she would *believe*! Lord make him worthy—at least not leave him be more un-so than—Pippin drew a long, sobbing breath. At last he lifted his head.

"I left that gang when I was eighteen years old. I'd broke Nosey's beak for him long before that, fightin' when we was kids. He was a mean kid. I see he has it in for me still, and though I'm sorry, in the way of a Christian, that I broke it, still I'm kind o' glad too."

"So am I!" Mary spoke impulsively.

Pippin looked up in surprise, and a smile broke over his anxious face. "Is that so?" he said. "Well, Nosey never was real attractive, any time that I remember. Anyhow, come to grow to my stren'th, I quit. I didn't like them nor their ways; low-down is what I call Bashford's. But yet I didn't quit the trade: no, ma'am! Not then. The Lord didn't judge me ready by then. I stayed in it, and I done well in it—"

"Excuse me!" Mary's voice faltered a little. "What trade? I don't quite understand—"

Pippin stared at her.

"Like I said. Sneakin', breakin' and enterin'—burglary, to say the real word. There! I wasn't ashamed to do it then, nor I won't be afraid to say it now. I told you I was a crook, and I was—till goin' on four year ago. Then—" a curious softness always came into Pippin's voice when he reached this part of his story—"I found the Lord! Yes, young lady, I found the Lord, for keeps. I—" he glanced at the clock. "'Twould take too long to tell you all about it to-night; some day I will, if you'll take time to listen. I was in prison, and He visited me. All along of a good man who *cared*, and took holt of me and raised me up where I could see and hear, and know it *was* the Lord. If ever you hear of a man named Elder Hadley—"

"*What!*" said Mary Flower.

Had Pippin seen her face at that moment, he might have stopped; but he stooped to pick up the ball she dropped. Mary opened her lips, hesitated, seemed to reflect, finally thanked him for the ball and went on with her work.

"That's his name!" Pippin was looking at the table now, his chin propped in his hands. "Best man the Lord ever made, bar none. I was in darkness, and he brought me out. He brought me out. Amen!"

There was another pause, while the clock ticked and the kettle purred gently on the stove. Presently Pippin pushed his chair back and rose to his feet, his shoulders very square, his chin well up.

"I'll ask you to believe that I've kep' straight since then!" he said gravely.

"I do believe it!" said Mary Flower. Again brown eyes and blue met in a long earnest look; again Pippin drew a long breath.

"That sounds good to me!" he said simply. "I thank the Lord for that, Miss Flower. I don't know what I'd have done if you—had felt otherways. Now—" he glanced at the clock—"I mustn't stay another moment, keepin' you up like this. It's nigh on ten o'clock. There's more to it, a heap more. I'd like you to know why I come here to the city, and what I'm tryin' to do, and all about it. You—you'll try to—I'd like to regard you as a friend, if I might take the liberty. I've never had a lady friend, except Mis' Baxter, and though she is a wonder, and more than kind, yet she's—"

Married and stout, and middle-aged, and altogether aunt-like; speak out, Pippin. But Pippin did not speak out; he stood and looked with bright, asking eyes, at once brave and timid. Mary held out her hand frankly.

"Sure, we will be friends!" she said. "I haven't ever—that is—I'll be glad of your friendship, I am sure, Mr. Pippin. And now I will say good night, and hoping you will sleep well and no disturbance for anyone."

Having witnessed two *tête-à-têtes*, we may as well glance at a third, which was held about the same time, though in a place wholly unlike either rose-shaded parlor or shining kitchen.

A back room in a slum grog shop: dingy, dirty, reeking with stale tobacco, steeped in fumes of vilest liquor. Some of the liquor is on the table now, in two glasses; some of the tobacco is in the pipes, which two men are smoking as they sit, one sprawling, the other hunched, in their respective chairs. An elderly man, low-browed, heavy-jawed, the brutal-criminal type that every prison knows; the other young, slight, narrow-chested, with a crooked nose and small eyes set too near together.

"All ready for to-night?" the elder was saying, in a hoarse, whispering voice, that matched his face. "What's your hurry, Bill? I'm takin' things easy these days. I'm gettin' on in years, and when I take on a night job, I want to be sure it's all slick as grease. What's your hurry?"

The other clenched his fist and brought it down on the table with an oath.

"I want Pippin!" he said. "That's what I'm after. You can have the swag, Dad; it's all straight, I tell you—silver locked up nights in the sideboard, locks that a kid could

139

pick. No money kep' in the house, but good silver; you can have the whole bag, but let—me—get—my hands on Pippin!"

The elder ruffian looked at him curiously. The little eyes were aflame with something more than greed and cunning.

"Go slow, Bill!" said the affectionate father. "Go slow and easy! You don't want to get twenty years for a job like this."

"I'd take hell," said the other, "to smash his face for him!"

"That's it, is it?" the older man whistled, and a grim smile broke over his countenance. "He did maul you bad, Bill, no mistake. Not that you ever were a beauty!" he added musingly. "Your mother's folks is all homely. Well, if that's all you want, to get even with Pippin, why not happen on him in that lane some night and— hey? Then we could take our time about gettin' the swag, and he be out of the way, see?"

"That ain't all!" The young man's face flamed with passion as he bent forward. "I want to get him *there*, Dad! I want to show her—to show them folks—that he's a crook from way back. Didn't I tell you he'd got old Nipper Crewe's wheel? Goin' about smilin' and singin'—damn him!—workin' his way in smooth as oil, and all the time fitted out with the best set of tools in the city. He's ben watchin' the house all the week, an' I've a hunch he's there to-night. I want to show him up! I want they should see his face when I do it—see it before I smash—" He choked with passion; his upper lip curled back, and his breath hissed through the bared teeth.

The older Bashford laughed outright. "Boys is boys!" he said. "You're really mad, ain't you, Bill? Well, I shan't stand in your way. I owe Pippin one myself, ---- —— him! But—hell! he is a slick one, no two ways about that. Joshin' on the pious, is he? And Nipper's kit handy by? That's good, that is! We'll get in ahead of him, Bill, sure thing we will. Now le's go home and get a mou'ful of sleep before we start in."

And all this time, while these three couples were spinning their unconscious threads for the Shuttle, under the quiet starlit sky the night train was drawing nearer and nearer, bringing among its hundred-odd passengers a quiet, bright-eyed man in clerical dress.

140

CHAPTER XVIII
PIPPIN KEEPS WATCH, WITH RESULTS

MARY was a long time going to bed that night. In the first place she could not find her blue ribbon bow, and being as economical as she was methodical, this distressed her. It was a new ribbon, bought at a special sale, and marked down almost unbelievably low, because there was a flaw in the weaving which would never be seen when made up. It was a good bow too; it is not everyone who can make a pretty bow; and Mary was perfectly sure that she had pinned it on her neat collar this evening. She searched the room thoroughly—such a pretty, tidy room, all white and blue like her kitchen—even peeping under bed and bureau, but no blue bow was to be found.

Then there was her chapter to be read; hard reading to-night, though it was Ruth, which she loved; hard to keep her mind on the text, her eyes on the page. Everything was all a-flutter, somehow. Mary sighed, and put her bookmark in soberly. She was not a very good girl, she thought, to be thinking of—other things—when she was reading her Bible. Then—blue kimono substituted for blue one-piece dress—out came Mary's hairpins and down came Mary's hair. It took a good while to do Mary's hair. It was not only the quantity of it—it flowed down and about her like a cloak—it was the quality. It *would* curl up round the brush, and break into ripples in the very teeth of the comb. It was a storage battery of electricity, and if a thunderstorm were to come on now, while it was down, you would see long golden strands separate themselves from the mass and fly straight up from her head. There being no thunderstorms this night, Mary, with firm, long strokes of the brush, with searching arguments of the comb, brought all the unruly gold into subjection, made it lie as nearly smooth as it could over her shoulders, finally braided it tight in two massive braids to be tossed back over her shoulders with a little sigh.

"*That's* done!" said Mary.

But even then, and even when her prayers were said and herself composed in her narrow white bed, as Saint Ursula in her wide one in the Parmegianino picture (looking rather like her, I declare!), Mary was not ready for sleep.

But through her brain of weal and woeSo many thoughts went to and fro,That vain it were her eyes to close.

Most of her thoughts hovered, it must be confessed, about Pippin on his straw mattress in the shed. Why did she think about him so much? Mary asked herself, and found no answer, unless the blood tingling in her cheeks were an answer.

Mary's had been a cool, detached, impersonal little life, in the years of her girlhood. Life at the Home, pleasant, regular, unconnected with emotions in any way, had changed the trembling, palpitating child who started at every sudden sound into a calm, self-possessed, rather matter-of-fact young woman. She did not often think of the old days. Why should she? They were gone, and where was the sense in stirring herself all up when it did no good to any one? It stood to reason!

But Pippin's story to-night brought the old time back whether she would or no. She lay still, staring out into the starlit night. His story—how strange that he should have had such a childhood! Was that why she seemed to have known him all her life? The old times! Perhaps it was the straw mattress that brought it back so clear. She could smell that musty straw now, so unlike the clean, fresh smell of that nice new one out in the shed.

She saw her mother, the little gray shawl drawn tightly over her shoulders, the fair hair strained back from the face with its too early lines of pain and grief; saw her eyes as they followed the poor bed dragged almost from under their feet by the shambling figure. Oh! how she had hated that sodden, stumbling figure! And the child, clinging passionately to those poor skirts—thin, worn to shreds, but always clean; poor mother was always clean!—clinging, crying, shaken with a passion of anger, grief, tenderness, which swept away all power of speech—could that child be herself? Yet he was kind, when he was sober; yes, father was kind—indeed, he had never been hard to her. Often and often he would call her to him, caress her, call her his little gal—while her flesh shrank from him, loathing the smell of liquor—he always smelled of liquor, even when sober—of rank tobacco—pah!

Mary supposed she was hard-hearted: how could she love a man like that? She adored her mother; the tears came smarting into her eyes at the thought of her. But for him, mother might be alive to-day; poverty, hunger, hard work, had aged her, killed her, long before her time, poor mother! Look at her there; see her eyes following the mattress.

Mary turned in her bed, and a sigh that was almost a sob broke from her. She hated wicked people—yes, she hated them; and weak people, too, people who made others suffer just because they were too feeble to deny themselves the drink that was poison—

"I *hate* them!" said Mary aloud. Then she thought of Pippin, and blushed again. Pippin did not hate wicked or weak people. He seemed to love them. How was it? Mary, cool, kind, a little aloof, did not understand it. They had talked together a good deal during these past two weeks, and she had wondered at the glow in his eyes, the thrill in his voice, when he spoke of his religion. Mary was a good Congregationalist;

she went to church, and said her prayers, and read her Bible. She supposed—why, of course she loved the Lord; she would be a wicked girl if she didn't; but—well, she was different, that was all. Of course, with all he had gone through—how bright his eyes were! How strong his faith must be! She supposed she was cold-hearted; yet when Pippin sang a hymn, she felt as if Heaven was close by. It surely was a privilege to know a person like that. And to think that he had once been—how to believe it? How not to believe anything he said, with those bright eyes looking straight into her? Perhaps the Lord would soften her heart— Pippin was right down there in the shed— think of it! She hoped he wouldn't lie cold; it felt so safe, having him there! She put an extra comforter—she did hope he would sleep well—

At this point Mary went to sleep herself.

She slept peacefully for some hours, lying still and straight as Saint Ursula herself; then she began to dream. Pippin was not sleeping well, out there in the shed; likely it had come up cold in the night. He had got up and come into the house, for warmth, of course. She heard him stumbling about among the chairs and tables; if she had only shown him the switch! Hark! He was whistling, calling out—*hark!*

Mary sprang up, broad awake. Something was going on downstairs. Voices, low and angry, hasty steps—the house on fire? She was up in an instant, slipped on the blue kimono and over it a heavy cloak, ran down the back stairs just as John Aymer ran down the front. Opening opposite doors quietly, they came upon a strange sight.

In the middle of the kitchen was Pippin, at grips with another man of slighter build than himself; at one side stood a third man, older and heavier than either, watching the two.

They struggled silently for a moment; then Pippin's greater strength prevailing, he forced the other back toward the wall. Suddenly the latter wrenched his right hand free; wrenched himself round; there was a flash of bright metal—Pippin ducked, and the brass knuckles crashed into the smooth plaster, cracking and starring it. Pippin had been struggling cheerfully and composedly up to now, but when his eye caught the brazen flash, he went dead white under his tan. With a sharp blow he beat down the murderous hand, caught the ruffian by the throat, ran him back across the room and dashed him against the opposite wall with a violence that shook the house. The man dropped like lead, and Pippin, towering over him like Michael over the dragon, turned to face the other. At this moment, before any one could move, the outer door was opened and a giant form appeared in the doorway, lantern in one hand, truncheon in the other.

"What's going on here?" asked Dennis Cassidy, the night watchman.

The elder man stepped quickly between him and the others.

"Officer, I give this man in charge!" his voice was quiet, but venomous. "Assault and battery, mebbe manslaughter, too. He's half killed my son, a respectable tradesman."

The policeman looked from one to the other; then, as Bashford stretched his hand toward Pippin's collar, he motioned him back.

"Hold still!" he commanded. "Everybody stand where they be!" Turning for a moment in the doorway, he drew forth his whistle and sounded a long, piercing note. "Now then, you!" he nodded to Bashford. "What are you and your respectable tradesman son doing here this time o' night? Hallo, young chap!" as he recognized Pippin. "*You* in this game?"

Mr. Aymer stepped forward.

"Good evening, Cassidy. This is the young man I told you about, who was going to watch the house for me. These are the men he found—I suppose—breaking and entering. I think—I am *sure* of his honesty!" The last phrase was uttered somewhat explosively. Mrs. Aymer had crept downstairs after him, and pinched his arm violently.

"That's as may be, sir! Don't you say anything yet, my bo!" to Pippin. "I asked *you*," he spoke to Bashford, "what you and your son were doing here this time o' night."

"Watchin' him!" the reply came coolly. "I give him in charge, officer, and it's your dooty to arrest him. If you don't know him, ask the Third District force! Ask 'em what they know about Pippin the Kid, alias Moonlighter, alias Jack-o'-lantern—he's well known to every cop in that district. Me and my son have seen him wormin' his way in here, deceivin' this good gentleman and his family; me and my son have knowed him from a—" Mr. Bashford paused a moment—"knowed him for a crook from way back."

"I don't believe a word of it!" said John Aymer.

Pippin looked up, white to the lips, but his chin held high.

"It's true!" he said.

There was a moment of dead silence, broken only by a tiny squeak from the stairs where Mrs. Aymer crouched invisible. All eyes were fixed on Pippin, and he held them all, glancing from one to the other.

144

"Up to three years ago," he said slowly, "I was all that. I'm straight now. I'm an honest man. Mr. Aymer, sir, I'd ought to have told you before; I ask your pardon! But I'm an honest man, and I come here to-night to protect your property."

"You *ought* to have told me, Lippitt!" Mr. Aymer spoke in a troubled voice. "I ought to have known if there was anything like this behind you."

A little blue figure came forward, a little warm hand was slipped into Pippin's.

"I knew!" said Mary-in-the-kitchen. "He told me!"

"God bless you!" Pippin grasped the little hand and squeezed it till Mary had to bite her lips to keep back a scream.

But now the younger Bashford, regaining the senses which had been knocked out of him, struggled up on his elbow and pointed a shaking finger at Pippin.

"Yes, he's straight!" he cried in a voice broken with passion. "Yes, he's an honest man all right, all right! Get his wheel, his innercent little scissor-grinder's wheel! Bring it in from the shed where he's kep' it handy. Nipper Crewe's wheel, well known to every burglar in the state, with the finest kit of breakin' tools made by man hid away in it! Fetch the wheel, somebody! The—— skunk has broke my leg or I'd go."

What is this? From dead white Pippin has gone vivid scarlet from brow to neck. He steps forward hastily.

"I'll bring the wheel!" he says.

"No you don't!" the giant policeman fills the doorway, seeming to expand till it is a close fit on either side. "No, nor you either!" as the elder Bashford made a motion. "You three stay where you be! Yes, sir, if you'll be so kind!" This to John Aymer, who has silently indicated his readiness to go.

No one speaks while the householder slips out. Pippin, still holding the little hand, has dropped his brave crest and stands with hanging head and downcast looks. What can it mean? Mary casts little anxious glances at him. Mrs. Aymer weeps audibly on the stairs; the Bashfords, father and son, seem to swell with anticipatory triumph; Dennis Cassidy, thoroughly puzzled, glowers at the three from under his shaggy eyebrows.

As the light rattle of the wheel was heard, Pippin started, and darted a strange look at Mary.

"I ask your pardon, Miss Mary!" he muttered. "I hadn't ought—"

145

Mr. Aymer entered with the wheel, and Nosey Bashford struggled to his knees, still pointing his shaking finger.

"Fetch it here!" he shrieked. "I know the trick of it. Here!" In his eagerness he scrambled up and hopped on one foot (his leg was not broken, by the way, only twisted in falling) to where John Aymer stood. His fingers hovered over the wheel, clutching and clawing with eagerness; his breath whistled through his teeth. John Aymer looked at him and turned away with a shudder of disgust. "Here! Here it is! See, copper? See, Governor? You shove back this plate—look! look, now, and see how straight he is! He, he! What—damn!—what's this?"

He broke short off, and stood glaring. All the others pressed eagerly forward, save Pippin, who stood like a statue, looking at the floor. Dennis Cassidy, with a massive shove, sent Nosey staggering back, then thrust his finger into the narrow cavity and drew out, and held up—a little bow of blue ribbon.

It was at this instant, before any one had time to speak, that a firm, quick foot crunched on the gravel outside. Some one came up the step, and looking over the policeman's shoulder, stood in silent amazement. Pippin looked up, uttered a great cry, and sprang forward.

"Elder!" he cried. "Elder Hadley, sir! I'm straight! As God is above us in Heaven, sir! I'm straight."

The air turned black about him, and for a moment he saw nothing but whirling sparks of fire. When his vision cleared, he found himself leaning on Lawrence Hadley's shoulder. A sob broke from him.

"I'm straight, Elder!" he repeated.

"Of course you are straight, Pippin! Easy, old chap. Take it easy! Look out, officer!"

Mr. Dod Bashford, after one glance at the contents of the secret compartment, had been edging unostentatiously toward the door. As Cassidy stepped aside to let the chaplain enter, he made a sudden dash, amazingly swift for so heavy a man, and diving between the colossal legs, got halfway out of the door; but calculating his chance a little too closely, he upset the equilibrium of Mr. Cassidy, who sat down suddenly and heavily, blocking the doorway more completely than before.

"Hold on, Dod!" he said, seizing Mr. Bashford's legs in a grip of iron. "Hold on! I ain't sure about young Pippin, or whatever his name is, but I've no doubts about you, my man. You're wanted on several counts, and I don't doubt but your respectable son is too. *Hold still!* You don't want I should have to knock you out before the ladies, do you? I'm ashamed of you!"

Bashford struggled savagely, desperately, muttering curses under his breath. His son moved quietly to the window and investigated the firmness of the fly screen.

But now more footsteps were heard. Two men came running along the lane, into the yard, up the steps; stars shone, truncheons waved, handcuffs clinked. In two minutes all was over, and the Bashfords, relapsing instantly into the hunch, skulk, cringe of the habitual criminal, stood in apparent humility before the Force.

One of the newcomers, surveying the group, broke into a jovial laugh.

"Well done, Dennis Cassidy!" he cried. "Bully for you! Let's hear anyone say again that you go to sleep on your beat!"

CHAPTER XIX
A KNOT IN THE THREAD

IT was afternoon of the next day. Mary's kitchen was in its customary trim perfection, so far as Mary could make it so. She had scrubbed and polished all the morning, determined to remove every trace of the hateful doings of the night before. Such actions going on in her kitchen! Real *bad folks* there, and policemen, and all! Of course the room needed cleaning; it stood to reason. One trace, however, could not be scrubbed or polished away. It would need more than brush and mop to mend that plaster, cracked and starred where the savage blow had struck it. Mary, gazing at it over her broom, found herself suddenly sobbing, the tears running down her cheek.

"He would have been killed!" she murmured. "But for being so quick, he would have been killed. *My soul!* Oh, I thank the Lord for saving him. I do thank Him!"

But that was morning. Now, as I said, it was afternoon, and Mary, in her afternoon apron with its saucy pockets and bewildering blue ribbons, was putting away the newly washed luncheon dishes. Pippin had helped her wash them; he would not take no for an answer. Coming a little early for his promised talk with the Elder, he had found Mary still at work, in blue pinafore, and had taken a hand as a matter of course. They were very silent at first over the dishes. Both were shaken by the events of the night. Pippin still felt the theft of the blue ribbon heavy on his soul. Mary, stealing glances at him under her eyelashes, saw again the flash of the brass knuckles; saw—in thought only, thank God! Oh, all her life she would be thanking God—the bright face all crushed and shattered—

She gave a little scream under her breath, lifting her head quickly. Pippin stooped at the same moment to set down a dish, and their heads came together smartly. This brought laughter, and thereafter things went much better. They talked—of trivial things, to be sure, the weather, and crockery, and hardware. Both instinctively avoided the depths, but somehow each found an astonishing quality in the mere sound of the other's voice, something soothing, cheering, uplifting, all at once. So the dishwashing was a singularly pleasant little ceremony, only too short, Pippin thought. Seemed a pity folks didn't eat more. He would not hear of Mary's leaving the kitchen when Mr. Hadley came. The idea! He had nothing to say but he'd say it better for her bein' there; nor would he accept Mrs. Aymer's kindly proffer of the parlor. Full as much obliged to her, but—he looked appealingly at the chaplain, who laughed outright.

"We shall both be more comfortable in the kitchen, Lucy!" he said. "Come on, Pippin!"

So there they were, Pippin and his best friend, sitting by the table with its bright afternoon cloth of Turkey red, talking, listening, talking again; the elder man sitting with his head on his hand, his elbow on the table, in the attitude we all remember, the younger bending eagerly forward, hands on knees, face alight with happiness.

"No!" Pippin was saying. "You don't tell me Pete is pardoned out. Well, that does sound good to me. Old Pete! Green grass! Well, he's airned it, Pete has. And what's he goin' to do, Elder? Pete's no chicken by now!"

"Going back to lobstering. Some friends have bought back his boat for him"— some friends indeed! Lawrence Hadley, where is that new suit you were going to buy without fail this summer? You still have on the old one, white at the seams, threadbare at the cuffs!—"and he and Tom are going into partnership."

"Tom out too? Great! That surely is great, Elder."

"Yes, Tom is out, on parole; but we shall never see him back, I am sure. I took your advice, Pippin, gave him the money test, and he rose to it at once. You were right. He needed some one to trust him, and to show that he trusted him."

"You bet he did!" Pippin sprang up, and began pacing the room with light, eager steps. "You bet he did, and you done it! Green grass! I would say glory to God! And he found the Lord? Did Tom find the Lord, Elder? He couldn't help but, with you showin' him!"

"Why—" the chaplain paused, and a twinkle crept into his blue eyes, "I think he did, Pippin, but not just in the way you mean. The Lord has many ways, and everybody cannot be an evangelist, and go singing and praying about the country as I understand you do."

Pippin's eyes were very large and round.

"Sure I do! What else would I? The Lord give me the voice, didn't He? Behooves me praise Him with it; that's right, ain't it, Elder? Or ain't it? Have I took too much upon me? Say the word, and—"

"Perfectly right! Perfectly right, Pippin! Sing all you possibly can. But Tom cannot sing, and, if you ask me, I think he would make a very poor hand at praying; but he's a good fellow for all that. It's good honest work he's going to do, too; pleasant work. I'd like to go lobstering myself for a change!"

"You wouldn't! Not with all that mess of cold water heavin' up round you all the time—honest, Elder! I never was in a boat in my life, and I never hope to be."

The chaplain sighed and smiled. The sea had been his life dream. It came before him now, blue, alluring, mysterious—he brushed it away, and bade Pippin sit down.

"You've had your innings," he said, "and I've told you all I'm going to; now it's your turn to tell me, young man. How comes it that you are back in the city, Pippin? Didn't I warn you against it? Didn't I tell you you were sure to get into trouble if you came back?"

Pippin sat down and drew out his file.

"You sure did, Elder! and I never meant to set foot in the darned hole, honest I never! But look the way things come round! I had to, hadn't I? I just fair had to! I wrote you about that, didn't I?"

"No! You wrote me that you had found the dandyest place that ever was, and that you wanted to fill it plumb up with boys and bring them up clean and straight, and that you were going to do it soon as ever you had finished the job you had on hand, but you didn't say what the job was, and you didn't say that it would be bringing you back to the last place in the world where you ought to be."

"Is that so?" Pippin ran the file through his hair anxiously. "Now what a lunkhead I be! I sure thought I told you, Elder. Why—well, anyways, I'll tell you now. Why, 'twas at that place, Cyrus Poor Farm—it *is* a dandy place, now I want you should understand that; and the dandyest folks in it ever *I* see—almost!" His eye caught the flutter of blue ribbons as Mary entered after hanging out her dish towels. "And—why, 'twas there I found the Old Man, and made him the promise. He's on the blink, you see; in poor shape the Old Man is, and no mistake; and he wants to see his little gal before he goes—well, wherever he *is* goin'. His little gal, you understand, Elder; his kid, the only kid he ever had, I presume. Mother took her away from him—I'm sure no one can blame her for that—but—well, she's woman grown now, and he's never set eyes on her since she was a kid. Now wouldn't that give you a pain, Elder? He's a rip from Riptown, and he's never done a cent's worth of good that I know of; but there 'tis! And he plead with me, plead real pitiful, I'd find his little gal for him. What would you done, Elder? I looked for grace in him, honest I did, and I couldn't find one smitch, no sir! not one single, solitary smitch, till—what I mean—till—till I see how bad he wanted his little gal; and I thought mebbe that was the way it took him—you get me, Elder?"

"I get you, Pippin! Go on!"

"And—and mebbe if I could find the kid—I can't help but call her a kid, though she's a woman now, if she's alive—if I could take that kid to him, he might—get me?—might find the Lord through the lot he set by her. I ain't puttin' it the right way, but—"

Pippin paused, and his eyes finished the sentence.

"Perfectly clear, Pippin, perfectly clear; I haven't a word to say. You did right. But who is this old man? You speak as if it were some one I knew, yet you wrote me that Nipper Crewe died. What old man is this?"

Pippin stared.

"Ain't I tellin' you? Old Man Blossom! It's him, and it's his little May—"

Crash! Both men sprang to their feet. Mary-in-the-kitchen had dropped a plate, the first thing she had broken since she entered the Aymers' service. She stooped hastily to gather up the fragments. Pippin ran to help her, but she motioned him away, hastily, almost rudely. No, she thanked him—she was just as much obliged—she thought she could fit the pieces together. She didn't know what made her so careless— here she suddenly dropped the pieces again on the floor and ran out of the room and up the stairs.

"Green grass!" said Pippin. "Now wouldn't that give you a pain? Just one plate, and hurt her feelin's like that! They're so delicate in their feelin's, ladies is. Gee! 'Member when I fell downstairs with the whole of A corridor's dishes, Elder? Now *that* was some smash, it sure was!"

In her own room, standing at the window with wide eyes that staring out yet saw nothing, Mary Blossom wrestled through her dark hour alone. This, then, was what it all meant. This was what had brought him to Blankboro, the bright-eyed singer with his wheel. He was looking for her. That—that man—had sent him to hunt her down, to drag her from her safe, happy, respectable home, to drag her back to him where he lay, in a poorhouse, suffering a little—oh, a very, *very* little—of what her mother had suffered through him. After all these years, when she had all but—not forgotten mother; never! never! she broke into wild sobbing and crying—but forgotten him, and the shame, and misery, the cold, hunger, nakedness that he stood for. After all these years he had reached out that palsied, shaking hand and laid it on her. Or tried to! Mary stood still, and let the tide of feeling surge through and through her. Grief, resentment, resistance. Back and forth it flowed, till from its surge a thought was cast up. *No one knew.* He, Pippin, did not know; never would know, unless she told him. Why—should—she—tell him? No one—except Mrs. Appleby, of course; she knew, but she would keep it close. They never told a girl's past at the Home, unless there was reason; unless she was adopted, or—or married, or the like of that. Even Mrs. Aymer knew no more than that she came well recommended. (But here Mary was mistaken:

151

Lucy Aymer knew all about it.) She had had a note from Mrs. Appleby, asking her to come to the Home on her first afternoon out, and she would. She would tell that kind, motherly friend about—about—

The wild tides stopped racing. Her eyes dropped. What should she tell Mrs. Appleby about Pippin?

Straightway his figure rose before her. His eyes, dark, bright, glowing, looked into hers; she forgot Mrs. Appleby. What was it he was saying?

"He plead with me; plead real pitiful, I'd find his little gal for him. What would you done, Elder?"

She knew what he had done himself. He had left everything, he, a stranger—that is, one that had been a sinner—and come back where he knew there was danger for him, to look for the child of an old rascal who was nothing to him. That was what Pippin had done; and she, the old man's child—

New waves this time, Mary! Hot waves of shame and contrition, sweeping resistless through you, driving grief and anger and resistance away into the nothingness of past emotion.

Long she stood there motionless, still staring with unseeing eyes. At last she heaved a long, sobbing sigh. She would be good. God make her a good girl. She would try.

What was it he had said the other night, when he told her that strange thing about the Bible in his room, about the rules of some queer Society or other? She heard his laugh ring out clear and joyous, saw his head thrown back.

"Honest, Miss Mary, I'll never forget the Gideons. Why, since that night, if ever anything gets me riled up, I take and read th Corinthians. Then I'll say to myself, 'Have you give all your goods to feed the poor?' I'll say, 'Have you give your body to be burned? Well, then, dry up!'"

Mary laughed, a little broken laugh with tears in it.

"I certainly haven't given my body to be burned!" she said.

Half an hour later, a composed and cheerful Mary came quietly down the back stairs to the kitchen. The traces of tears were nearly gone; cold water can do much in that way. A Mary-in-the-parlor might have blotted them out with powder, but Mary-in-the-kitchen had never used powder in her clean, wholesome, scientific-general life. Her eyes merely looked rather larger than usual, and the long lashes were still curling from the water. She was not smiling yet, but she was ready to smile when she met the eyes of her friend. How they would flash when she told him, when he learned that his search was over, that she was Mary Blossom, that she would go back with him, to do what duty and kindness could do! How he would spring up—

So coming lightly down to the door, she paused a moment, not to listen, just to make sure she was not interrupting anything private. Pippin was still leaning forward, light, alert, as if even sitting he felt the wings on his ankles; he was looking at his friend, with a glance half timid, half whimsical.

"You see, Elder," he said, "I *ain't* exactly alone, like you think. You're right about it's bein' poor dope for a guy to live all by himself, but lemme tell you! I've got—what I would say is—well, I've got a family of my own a'ready—kind of! Not what you'd call a *reg'lar* family, but yet they're dandy, sir, they are so! Lemme tell you! I never told a soul about 'em, but—"

I have described the Mary who came down the stairs; it was a different Mary who confronted Pippin as, turning his head, he saw her and sprang to his feet. Marble white, with a blind dazed look, as if she had been struck in the face, the girl stood motionless.

"*My soul!*" cried Pippin. "What's the matter, Miss Mary?"

"What has happened, Mary?" Mr. Hadley had risen, too; both men stood looking at her in concern. Had she struck her head against something? the chaplain asked anxiously.

Mary was very well, she thanked Mr. Hadley; she had a little headache, that was all. She kept her eyes fixed on the chaplain, not even glancing at Pippin.

"I came," she said, "to tell you—Mr. Hadley, I heard what—what the young man was saying, and I came to tell you. I am Mary Blossom. It's me he is looking for."

"*You!*" Pippin sprang forward, with a shout that rang through the house. "You, Miss Flower!"

"My mother gave me the name of Flower when I went to the Home!" Mary spoke quickly and steadily, her eyes still fixed on those kind blue ones that always seemed to know what you were going to say before you said it. "She didn't want my father to find me; I didn't either. He was—he—never mind!" she hurried on. "But I am Mary Blossom, and I will go to see my—father, and try to do my duty by him." She paused. "That's all!" she said, and turned, still with that blind, stricken look, as if to leave the room.

"Stay, Mary!" Mr. Hadley took her hand gently. "No wonder you are bewildered, my child. Sit down, won't you? Let us talk it over. This is wonderful news, indeed!"

"I guess it is!" Pippin had found words at last. "Miss Mary—I—I am clean dumbfoundered, I guess. You! You, little May Blossom that I used to play with, back there in the lane? Well, if ever there was a dunderhead in this world it's me, it sure is. Green grass—I would say, Glory to God! Why, little May! Why, of course it is! Why, look at the color of her hair, will you? Just like he said it was, color of a yearlin' heifer! And—did ever you see a bonehead, Elder? 'Cause you see one now. May Blossom!" He moved nearer, and held out both hands with an appealing gesture. "Look at me, won't you? Look at Pippin! Don't you rec'lect how we'd play together? You couldn't say my name plain at first. 'Pittin!' you'd say. 'Pippin!' I'd say. 'Say Pippin, kiddy!' and you says—I can hear you now—'Pip-*pin!*' you says; and then— what—what's the matter, Miss—Miss Mary? You ain't mad with me, are you?" He faltered into silence.

Mary's eyes still clung to the chaplain's desperately.

"You must excuse me!" she said. Her voice trembled; she shook as if with cold. "I—my head aches; I must go back—"

"Yes, my dear!—go up and lie down!" said the kindly chaplain. "Take a good rest! I'll tell Mrs. Aymer you are not well."

He led her to the stairs, saw her totter up, feeling her way, watched till the door closed behind her, then turned to comfort as best he might a distracted Pippin who stood motionless, gazing with a stricken look at the door through which Mary had disappeared. As the chaplain advanced with outstretched hand, he turned bewildered eyes on him. "What—what's the matter?" he faltered. "What did I do? She wouldn't speak to me, Elder! she wouldn't look at me! She—gorry to 'Liza, she's mad with me!"

"No, no, Pippin!" The chaplain, puzzled himself, laid a kindly hand on the broad shoulder that was shaking like a frightened child's. "She has a headache, and she very likely didn't sleep last night. I don't believe you slept either; go home, now, like a good chap, and go to bed. But stay! First tell me about this family; what on earth do you mean—hey?"

But Pippin shook his head.

154

"Not now! I couldn't tell you about 'em now! To-morrow I will, Elder. I—I guess I'll go now, sir! I thank you—" He broke off suddenly, with something like a sob, wrung his friend's hand hard, then went out drooping, like a broken thing.

"Dear me, sirs!" said Lawrence Hadley.

Pippin did not go to bed. He had had little sleep for several nights; this last night he had had none. Excitement and emotion had run riot through him for twenty-four hours, and for the first time in his life he had turned from his food. These things, added to the lightning stroke of Mary's revelation and the strangeness of her manner in making it, brought about a condition which Pippin failed to recognize or to understand. His head seemed to whirl; his knees felt "like they was water in 'em"; black specks danced before his eyes. He was dead tired, and did not know it. Puzzled and bewildered, his simple mind fallen apart, as it were, into incongruous fragments; asking over and over again how and why, and again why and how. Deaf for once to the kindly voices of the creatures of his own brain, which had cheered and companioned him through these past months, he ranged the fields like a hunted animal; finally, long after nightfall, he sought his poor room and dropped exhausted on his bed. Here, as he sat with drooping head and hanging arms, sleep fell upon him like a mantle of lead, yet he struggled against it. He was all wrong inside, he now confided to "Ma" whom he seemed to feel once more beside him. "I'm all wrong!" he repeated. "It's like sin, or somethin', was gnawin' at me. I will—" Pippin struggled to his feet and made his little birch-tree bow, but very wearily, as if the tree had been beaten by tempests, "I will praise the Lord a spell before now I lay me down to sleep."

Why, even his voice was going back on him. At the strange, husky sound, his heart grew cold within him.

"My God!" he muttered. "What's this? Has Satan got a-holt of me?"

Clearing his throat violently, he summoned all his strength, and the great voice broke out like a silver trumpet:

"Throw out the life line across the dark wave,There is a brother whom someone should save;Somebody's brother! Oh, who, then, will dareTo throw out the life line, his peril to share?"

Thump! thump came the unmistakable sound of an angry boot on the wall.

"Shut up!" cried an exasperated voice. "Shut up, you darned gospel shark!"

Pippin stopped dead; his eyes blazed; molten flames coursed through his veins. He darted out of his own door and grasped the handle of the next one. It was locked, but that meant nothing to Pippin the Kid. One dexterous turn of Mrs. Baxter's hairpin (a dandy tool for light work, sure!) and the door flew open.

Mr. Joseph Johnson was a stonemason, and worked hard all day. He needed his sleep, and was not of mystic or dramatic temperament; it was, therefore, perhaps hardly strange that he was annoyed by vehement-tuneful demands for a life line at nine o'clock o' night. At all events, he was just bending forward to deliver another thump on the wall when, as has been said, the door flew open, and to him entered a lightly clad bronze statue, its arm outstretched, its eyes darting flames.

"Say!" cried the statue; "who are you that can't hear the Lord praised a spell? Who are you to stop a man in the middle of his song? Darn your hide! If you can't sing yourself, be thankful other folks can; you hear me? Have you said your prayers to-night? You never! Down you go!"

Mr. Johnson found himself suddenly on his knees, the statue, kneeling also, holding him tightly by the shirt collar. A short, sharp injunction was issued to Deity.

"O Lord, you make this man behave; he don't know how, no way, shape, or manner. Amen!

"*Now!*" Pippin rose, towering seven feet high, Mr. Johnson told the scandalized landlady next day. "Let me hear another word out of you!"

Mr. Johnson remaining discreetly silent, Pippin, after glaring at him a minute, dropped his fiery crest.

"Good-night, brother!" he said meekly. "I'm sorry if I spoke harsh. Pleasant dreams to you!"

156

CHAPTER XX
THE PERPLEXITIES OF PIPPIN

I DON'T know *what* to do with Mary!" said Mrs. Aymer. "I am really distracted about her, Larry. I don't think she's *fit* to go with you to-morrow, yet I don't believe anything can stop her."

"She certainly looks ill." The chaplain glanced thoughtfully toward the pantry door, as if he expected to see through it. "Have you had any talk with her, Lucy?"

"I've tried, but I had to do all the talking. She just pulls this little wooden smile— it's just that, Lawrence! it's as if she pulled a string and twitched the corners of her mouth up; there is no smile in her eyes. It's *tragic*! And all she will say is, 'It is my duty to go to my father; I must go, because it is my duty!' over and over; in fact—" with a petulant outburst—"I seem to have lost my Mary, and got a very beautiful talking doll in exchange—Only dolls *do* look cheerful," she added, "and they don't cry their eyes out all night."

"Have you heard her crying?" asked John Aymer.

"Heard her? No! But I see her in the morning, don't I? *I* am not an *owl*, my dear John!"

"No, my love, certainly not!"

The two men gazed meditatively at each other over their pipes. ("Since my husband must either smoke or fidget," Mrs. Aymer was wont to say, "I prefer to have him smoke; and there shall be no room in my house that he is obliged to fidget in.") But the pipes did not make for peace as usual; the atmosphere of the rose-shaded room was anxious and troubled, reflecting the mood of its little ruler. However things might be with Mary-in-the-kitchen, Lucy-in-the-parlor was not herself this evening. She would knit diligently for a few minutes, then spring up to turn down the lamp, to poke the fire, to straighten an already straight window blind, then plunge at her knitting again, and make the needles fly at a bewildering rate.

"It certainly is an extremely rum start!" said John Aymer thoughtfully. "Makes one feel as if one were living behind the scenes at the ——," he named a popular theatre.

"John Aymer!" The knitting was dropped, and two indignant sapphires burned on the guilty husband. "I don't *like* to think you are heartless, John," said Lucy; "but sometimes there seems nothing else *to* think. To *make game* of a poor girl's misery! Men are—"

"Not at all, my love, not at all! I am as sorry as sorry can be, and you know it. But none the less I cannot help feeling as if I were in a movie. Here are all the materials, black-hearted ruffian, lovely maiden, gallant youth—if that wasn't a movie scene the other night, I never saw one, that's all!— By the way, Larry, what of the gallant youth? How has pet-lamb Pippin been to-day? Or haven't you seen him?"

"Oh, yes, I have seen him. I don't believe he cried last night, but he doesn't look as if he'd slept much for several nights. The boy is as thoroughly upset as the girl." The chaplain stooped to pick up a coal from the hearth; then went on slowly. "On the one hand he is all joy at having found Mary; on the other he is all despair because he thinks he has offended her in some way. How about that, Lucy? They have been good friends up to yesterday, have they?" He looked inquiringly at his sister.

"*Good friends!*" Mrs. Aymer sprang up again and moved restlessly to the fire.

"*Hold on!*" her husband grasped her skirt and drew her resolutely back. "My child, if you put the Cape Cod fire-lighter *hot* into the kerosene, there will be an explosion, and we shall all be burned very painfully. This is the fourth time I have caught you on the point of doing it; the next time, I shall take the thing away and give it to your cousin Selina, who has never moved quickly in her life. Now, my dear girl, sit down, and *stay* down for ten minutes."

Mrs. Aymer subsided in temporary eclipse of meekness, and John Aymer turned to his brother-in-law, who also had sprung forward when he saw the glowing sponge approaching the brass pot.

"All right, Lar! She *will* do it, but I am generally on the lookout. You ask if Mary and Pippin have been good friends. Lawrence, I have been conscious for the last two weeks that while Lucy's body has had many occupations, her mind has done little except marry these two young people, establish them in a shed-apartment-elect (to be furnished, I gather, with all our belongings except those actually in use), and assist in bringing up their family. I feel quite the godfather already, I assure you!"

"Dear me, sirs!" the chaplain blew smoke rings and watched them with a critical eye. "I had no idea it had gone as far as that!"

"It hasn't, except in Lucy's fertile brain. Possibly neither of them has thought of it, though I admit the possibility to be highly improbable, at least on the boy's side. If I were in his place—"

Here Mrs. Aymer was discovered to be weeping quietly and drying her eyes with her knitting, to their imminent peril. Both men sprang to caress and comfort her. Her husband vowed that he would, if necessary, hale both the potentially contracting parties to the altar and make Larry marry them then and there. Anything, he declared, rather than have his wife blinded by knitting needles or destroyed by fire. Incidentally, he himself was a brute, and if his little girl cried any more, he would touch himself off with the Cape Cod fire-lighter and have done with it. Her brother said nothing, but took hold of her little finger and shook it in a particular way which had meant consolation ever since he was six and big, and Lucy was three and little. Finally, between them, they coaxed a smile from her, and a declaration that they were dear boys and she was a goose. Then it occurred to her that Mary might sleep better with a hot water bottle; this cleared up matters wonderfully, and she bustled off quite cheerfully, promising John that she would have one herself, and giving Larry a good-night hug as the best of brothers.

The brothers-in-law exchanged an affectionate nod as the door closed behind the little woman they both adored; a nod which said many things, all kind and patient and loving. They smoked in silence for ten minutes, then one asked the other where he got his boots; the other replied, and they talked boots with absent-minded ardor for ten minutes more, then fell silent again.

"*But*," John Aymer exploded suddenly, "it *is*, as I said, an extremely rum start. I suppose you feel perfectly sure of your pet lamb, Lar?"

"Perfectly—humanly speaking!"

"Then that's all right. The fellow is so infernally attractive—you understand! If I thought he would make Mary unhappy, or—or anything—I'd wring his neck for him, see?"

The chaplain nodded gravely. "I see! you won't have to wring his neck, Jack."

"Then that's all right," repeated John Aymer. "Glad of it! He certainly is as taking a scamp as ever I saw. Is he—has he any family? Nice comfortable mother or sister who would be good to Mary, eh?"

Lawrence Hadley shook his head; a slow, humorous smile curled the corners of his mouth. He heard Pippin's voice, eager, imploring. "You won't tell any one, will you, Elder? About Pa and Ma, I mean. Honest, sir, they've ben more help to me than lots of real folks I've seen. What I mean—well, I've seen folks act real ugly, you know, to their own flesh and blood; speak up real hateful, the way you wouldn't speak, no, nor I wouldn't, to a houn' dog! But these folks of mine, so good and—and so—well, kind of holy is what I mean, and yet ready to joke and laugh any time—gorry to 'Liza! Elder, I do wish you could *see* Ma and Pa, I do so!"

"No, John," said the chaplain, "I'm afraid—I have always understood that Pippin was an orphan."

The friendly silence fell again, and the chaplain's thoughts reverted to his conversation with Pippin that morning. What a child the boy was! How almost incredible—if the things of God could ever be incredible, mused the chaplain—that after such a bringing-up (say, rather, dragging, kicking, cuffing up) he should be what he was. Hadley's mind, always with a whimsical thread running through its earnestness, recalled a visit to an aquarium, and certain creatures of living crystal through which such organs as they had were visible as through glass. Pippin was like that, he thought. An Israelite without guile; the child of the slums, the young desperado; Pippin the Kid, alias Moonlighter, alias Jack-o'-lantern. Strange and true, and blessed! Out of the mouths of babes—gutter babes as well as those of Christian homes! But how absurd, how utterly unreasonable, this very crystalline quality made the boy! He had thought that once he found the girl, all would be plain sailing. He had actually expected Mary to start with him, hand in hand like two children, that very morning for Cyrus Poor Farm, thirty miles away. There was folks he knowed all along the road, dandy folks, would be tickled to death to take them in; what say? The chaplain vetoing this proposal decidedly, the eager light had died out of Pippin's eyes, the anxious cloud settled again on his brow.

"She's mad with me!" he lamented. "Green grass! She's mad with me, and I don't know no more than the dead what I done. Why, don't you rec'lect, Elder, she was puttyin' round there Pippin meant "puttering" while we was talkin', smilin' and—and lookin' pleasant, the way she does—why, you'd said I was welcome, wouldn't you? Sure you would! Why, sir, we was *friends*! There's things I've told that young lady— and she 'peared to understand, too, and to—what I mean—not be opposed to hearin' 'em—and then all of a sudden—I tell you, Elder, I don't know what I'll do if she stays mad with me, honest I don't." Pippin's voice broke, and he brushed his hand across his eyes. "Have you any *i*dea why she's mad with me, Elder?" he asked simply.

The chaplain patted his shoulder as he would a child's.

"No, Pippin, I have no idea. I don't even know that she is 'mad with you.' She has had a shock, and a great deal of excitement and—and emotion, and I don't think she is quite herself now. You must be patient, Pippin. A young woman's feelings are very sensitive, as you said yourself yesterday. Mary is very much upset, and she probably feels—she is a very sensible girl, and a very intelligent one"—"You bet she's all that!" Pippin murmured—"probably feels that as you are connected with all this excitement and emotion, it is better for her not to see you just now. Start along with your wheel, and Mary and I will follow by rail. Mr. Bailey can meet us at Cyrus Centre—it's a four-mile drive, you say? We'll be there as soon as you, Pippin, or before. Be off with you! And cheer up!" he added with his friendly hand on the broad shoulder that drooped as it had never drooped before since that hour among the buttercups. "Cheer up, Pippin! 'Praise the Lord with gladness,' you know, my son!"

"Amen, Elder! 'And come before His presence with a song.' I will, sir! Gimme a little start, and I will. So long, sir!"

It was not Pippin's own flashing smile that greeted the chaplain from the gate, as with Nipper on his back, the boy turned into the lane; but still it was a smile, and his chin was up, and his shoulders square once more. Yes, Pippin was all right again. But—the chaplain sank deep and deeper into reverie—what was to become of Pippin eventually? He could not go pirouetting across the stage of life as if it were—Hadley glanced at his brother-in-law, and saw him also deep in thought—a moving picture show. If he had only taken his, the chaplain's, advice in the beginning, and let him find an opening for him in some safe, steady business!

As if in answer to his thoughts, John Aymer looked up suddenly.

"How would Pet-Lamb fit into the hardware line?" he asked. "About as well as a salmon in a lobster pot, eh? Well, we must fit him in somewhere, Lar. I want Mary to stand by Lucy this winter, you understand!"

"Of course. And anyhow, Jack, the boy cannot expect to support a wife by scissor-grinding."

"All right!" John Aymer rose with an air of relief. "I was afraid that you might have some idea in your visionary old noddle. Come on! Let's have an apple and go to bed!"

When Pippin went his way that morning, with many a wistful backward glance at the friendly house and yard where now no blue shape of grace and youth smiled on him, he did not start at once for Cyrus Poor Farm. There was a visit to make first. He plodded along the streets, looking neither to right nor to left, his bell tinkling in vain (two or three housewives waved their aprons and called to him, but he did not hear them) until he came to the now familiar brick wall and the wrought-iron gate opening on the cheerful courtyard. He was a frequent visitor now at the Home; he knew every child intimately, and had won every adult heart, even that of Mrs. Faulkner, who declared that there was certainly no resisting him and that she had given up trying. Mrs. Appleby's heart had been his from the start, as we have seen, and it was she he had come to see, for the children, he knew, would be at school. Still, as a matter of habit he glanced at the upper windows, and was rewarded by the sight of a forlorn little freckled face which lighted into ecstasy at sight of him.

"Gee!" said Pippin. "Now wouldn't that—"

He waved his cap to the little prisoner, and a lively sign dialogue ensued. Had Jim, Pippin asked with expressive action of his hands, run away again and got behind the bars? Vehement denial, the red head shaken till it seemed in danger of coming off. Been cutting up, then, and got spanked good and hard and sent to quod? This also was rendered with dramatic effect, was also denied, with some show of indignation. Then what the didoes was the matter? Pippin spread his arms abroad with uplifted brows. For reply the window was pushed up behind the nursery bars, and a hoarse little voice croaked "Tonsilitis! Been abed—" Here the speaker was withdrawn swiftly from behind, and the window closed again. Mrs. Appleby looked down and nodded to Pippin, intimating that she would be down directly; then turned to the child, with admonition in every line of her firm, substantial figure.

Soon she came, with friendly hand extended; soon Pippin was sitting opposite her in the mission-furnished parlor, pouring out his artless tale of woe and bewilderment.

Mrs. Appleby had been expecting Mary for several days, had rather wondered at her non-appearance. She listened round-eyed to Pippin's account of the attempted burglary—his own part in the drama lightly dismissed with, "I knowed the guys, and I just put a spoke in their wheel. See?"

"Good gracious!" she ejaculated. "Why, they might have been murdered in their beds. Why, Pippin, your being there was simply providential."

Mrs. Appleby, like many another excellent person, had distinctly biassed views as to the part played by Providence in human affairs; not so Pippin, otherwise enlightened by his Elder.

"I view things generally in that light!" he said gravely. "All is, there's times when I can't understand 'em. Lemme tell you!"

He told her, with kindling eyes, of his discovery of the astonishing fact that Mary Flower was May Blossom. Yes, she knew that, Mrs. Appleby said demurely. She did? *She did?* Then why—Pippin stared at her a moment in blank bewilderment; then he smote his hand on his knee. That was right! He saw, he understood. That was why she wanted the letter from Elder Hadley; that was right! She couldn't have done no other way, she sure couldn't. And now, here was the Elder right in town here, and she could see him and make all the inquiries she—

But now the mobile face darkened, and the wail broke out.

"Mrs. Appleby, she's mad with me! Yes, ma'am, she is so! She won't look at me, nor yet hardly speak to me, excep' kind of cool and polite, like you'd speak to a stranger. Why—" he sprang up and paced the room, light-foot, absorbed, lifting his chin a little, unconsciously, as he reached either wall of the room, like a woodland creature in a cage. "Why, Mrs. Appleby, I respect that young lady more than anybody in the world. We was friends, I want you to understand, till this come up, real good friends!" cried Pippin, clutching at his file and stabbing the air with it as he paced. "Nor I don't know no more than the dead what it *was* come up! I never said anything anyways low to that young lady—my tongue would ha' withered in my mouth first. It makes me wild—"

Here he stopped, and, collecting himself with a great effort, sat down and begged Mrs. Appleby's pardon. He would ask the Lord to help him, he said gravely. 'Twasn't likely any one else could, and he'd no business to be bawlin' like he was a kid. He asked Mrs. Appleby's pardon again, and hoped she would overlook it. She, good lady, as much puzzled as he, tried to comfort him, as the chaplain had done, with hopes that all would come out right eventually. Mary was upset, and no wonder. This might make a great change in her life; Pippin must have patience.

"St. James!" Pippin's brow cleared, and he rose with his little bow which Mrs. Appleby privately considered the most graceful motion she had ever seen in her life. Talk of Russian dancers! "St. James! 'Let patience have her perfect work.' That's right! James, he's real good and searchin'; that takes holt of me. Well, ma'am, I'll wish you good day, and thank you kindly. You have helped me, too, you sure have."

At this moment a knock was heard, and the round-eyed pupil-teacher entered.

Please, ma'am, Jimmy Mather wanted to know could the—the gentleman Janey did not think "my Grindy Man" would be polite or proper to repeat come up to see him. He was flouncing about horfil, and she could not keep him quiet.

Mrs. Appleby hesitated. It was not usual, she said, but—the other children were at school, and Jimmy had been very poorly; if Pippin cared to go up for a few minutes—

"Sure I do! Tickled to death! Thank you, ma'am."

Mrs. Appleby led the way through cool, clean, stone-flagged halls and corridors to the pleasant infirmary with its yellow walls and snowy beds. Ten beds, and only one occupied, by a freckled, tousled quintessence of fractiousness in a blue wrapper.

"I *won't* behave! I *will* kick them off!" He did. "I want my grindy man, and I won't *ever* behave unless he comes. I won't, I won't, I *won't*!"

"Dry up!" Pippin stood in the doorway, erect, with eyes of authority. "What kind of way is this to act, I want to know? You lay down—" the boy obeyed instantly— "and you stay layin' down till I give you leave to set up. Now!" He nodded assurance to Mrs. Appleby, who withdrew, drawing a reluctant Janey after her. Janey admired Pippin as much as anybody did, and had her own thoughts about the foolishness of letting that kid have his own way like that.

But Mrs. Appleby did not go far, only into the sewing-room close by, where she sat down and motioned Janey to a seat beside her. The door was open—it would have been close with it shut—and she had left the infirmary door on the jar. Sitting at their sewing, the two women listened.

No sound at first except Pippin's voice in a low admonitory murmur. Then louder, in clear, crisp tones: "What say, kid? Goin' to try? Shake!" Two voices now, in brisk and cheerful dialogue; then gurgles and crows of childish delight. (What could Pippin be doing? As a matter of fact, he was giving an exhibition of the Wig Wags, his fingers impersonating these mystic creatures, and performing unheard-of acrobatic feats in connection with the bedposts.)

Then—and this was what Mrs. Appleby had been waiting and hoping for, came the injunction: "Now sing, Grindy Man!"

Pippin sang; and the mite of fractious quicksilver lay back on the pillow with a happy sigh. The matron dropped her sewing, and took out her handkerchief; she was easily moved to tears, good Mrs. Appleby. Downstairs from the housekeeper's room, upstairs from kitchen, dining-room, pantry, eager footsteps came stealing. Soon the whole household was sitting on the stairs, listening, and Mrs. Appleby was resolutely unaware of them, reflecting that some things were more important than others, and that nobody would die if dinner *was* a little late.

Sing, Pippin! Pour your heart out, and lift up the hearts of all that hear you, sad hearts and merry, dull hearts and quick, for with them you shall lift up your own also, till your eyes shine with their own glad light, and you go your way, once more joyful in the Lord:

"Fling out the life line with hand quick and strong:Why do you tarry, why linger so long?See! he is sinking; oh, hasten today—And out with the Life-Boat! Away, then, away!"

CHAPTER XXI
MARY BLOSSOM

TO Pippin the last month had passed like a watch in the night; say rather in the day, a watch on a hillside under a clear sky, with the sound of flutes in the air. But at Cyrus Poor Farm it had been a long month, and things had gone rather heavily. Brand, weaving baskets in his corner, thought it one of the longest months he had ever known. There had been many wet, cold days when the barn had been too chilly to work in, and though he loved the big kitchen, he preferred solitude for his work hours,—solitude, that is, enlivened by snatches of cheery talk as Jacob Bailey came and went about his own work, by whiffs of fragrant clover and hay, by the sunlight that lay warm upon him as he sat in the wide doorway, by the friendly whinnying of Molly, the pretty black mare, in her loose box close by.

Then Flora May would come drifting in, and would sit down beside him, and rub her smooth cheek against his, and coo and murmur like a white pigeon. They were intimate, the blind man and the simple girl. He was Uncle Brand, she was his little gal. They spoke little as they sat together, but now and then he would pat her fair head and say, "We knowed it, little gal!" and she would nestle closer and repeat, "We knowed it!" That was all the speech they needed.

But now Flora May seldom came to the barn; she seemed almost to avoid him, Brand thought. Maybe it was just the bad weather; she was apt to be moody in bad weather. But even in the house she was changed, somehow. She used always to give him a pat or a coo when she passed him; now—but he must not be demanding. Blind folks were apt to be demanding, he had once been told, and had resolved no one should have cause to say it of him.

There were other trials, too, that month. Some tramps came, asking shelter for the winter, pleading illness, promising work. Jacob Bailey had taken them in, not too willingly, but feeling it his duty to do so; and had thereby roused the indignation of all his other "boarders," except Brand. For three days the usually cheerful house had seethed like a witches' cauldron; then the tramps departed by night, carrying with them such small personal property as they could lay hands on, and peace reigned again.

Meantime Old Man Blossom was growing weaker day by day. The poor old body, sodden with drink and worse than drink, was nearly worn out. The machine worked feebly; at any moment it might run down and stop. One thing only, Mrs. Bailey thought as she watched beside the bed, kept him alive: the longing for his child. She spent every moment she could spare, good soul, sitting beside him, knitting in hand, ready to answer the inevitable question when it came. He would lie for hours

166

motionless, apparently sleeping. Then the lids would flutter open, the hands begin to wander and pluck at the bedclothes; the dim eyes, after rolling vacantly, would fix themselves on her, and recognition creep into them.

"Ain't he come yet?"

"Not yet, Mr. Blossom. He'll be here soon."

"You don't think—"

"Yes, Mr. Blossom?"

"You don't think he's slipped one over on me?"

"I think he will come as soon as he can; that is, as soon as he finds your daughter, you know. You don't want him to come without her, do you?"

"If he does—" the voice dies into a whisper, faint yet vehement. Bending to catch his words, Lucy Bailey listens a moment, then straightens herself with compressed lips. Mr. Blossom is consistent, and expresses himself in his usual manner.

Presently he finds his voice again, a whimper in it this time. "But ain't it hard luck, lady? I ask you, lady, if it ain't hard luck that I have to get a crook to fetch me my little gal. I ain't a con, lady! Booze was all my trouble—that an' not havin' the stren'th to work. I never got no longer jolt than a year. Now Pippin's a crook, born and bred. If he slips one over on me—" The voice sinks again into a hoarse mutter, and so lapses into silence. The face, puckered into sharp wrinkles of anxiety, seems to flatten and smooth itself till it lies like an old wax mask, ugly but peaceful. He will be quiet now for some time; Mrs. Bailey settles the bedclothes tidily and steals away.

Her faithful attendance on the dying vagrant has not been fortunate for the other inmates; her firm gentle hand is missed everywhere in the house. Her husband confides to her, in the quiet hour before bedtime, that things have been kind of cuterin'. Aunt Mandy was some fractious to-day; she made Miss Pudgkins cry at dinner, callin' her a greedy old haddick; no way to talk to Miss Pudgkins, Lucy knew.

Miss Pudgkins ought not to mind Aunt Mandy, Mrs. Bailey said; she knew full well what Aunt Mandy was. Pepper grass had to grow the way it grew; you couldn't expect it to be sweet gale, nor yet garden blooms. Yes, Mr. Bailey expected she knew that, but still, 'twas provoking, and in the face and eyes of the whole table. 'Twas true Miss Pudgkins had taken Brand's dish of prune sauce and put her empty one in its place.

"The mean old thing!" Mrs. Bailey spoke sharply, and a spark came into her kind eyes. She could not bear to see the blind man "put upon." "Now I am glad Aunt Mandy spoke out. I hope you took the dish right straight away from her, Jacob!"

Jacob looked troubled. "I couldn't do that, Lucy; women-folks, you know!"

"No, you couldn't. I wish I'd been there."

"But I give Brand another dish, and filled it plumb up, so he got more than she did after all." He looked up, and received a cheerful nod of approval.

"That's good. Brand likes prune sauce, and he has so few pleasures. Not that he's anyways greedy or lick-lappin'; far from it; but he tastes more than others do. Did he finish the two-bushel basket? He aimed to finish it to-day."

Jacob's brow clouded again. "He would have, but he couldn't lay his hand on his splints, and I was out of the way, so he had to wait a considerable time."

"Where was Flora May? Didn't she help him? I told her be sure to!"

"That was the trouble!" Jacob spoke reluctantly. "Flora May had an odd spell, and she—fact is, she took and carried the splints up chamber, and run out and hid in the haymow till dinner."

"She did! now, Jacob! Why didn't you call me? You can't cope with Flora May in her odd spells, nor it isn't right you should. Why didn't you call me?"

"I set out to, Lucy. I came to the door to speak to you, but I heard the Old Man mournin' and I—it didn't appear as if I could go in just then."

"No, you couldn't!" said his wife again. Then she sighed. "I don't hardly know what to do with Flora May," she said. "She's havin' those odd spells right along, sometimes two or three a week. She's been havin' 'em ever since—Jacob—" She looked around and lowered her voice. "I don't hardly know about his comin' back here—to stay any time, that's to say."

Jacob Bailey also glanced around apprehensively and spoke almost in a whisper. "You mean—Pippin?"

"Hush! Yes! She hasn't been the same girl since he was here. I'm scared for her, Jacob."

"Lucy, Pippin is as good as gold. There couldn't no father nor brother have handled her better than what he did that day."

"Hush! What was that?" She went quietly to the door that led to the back stairs, and opened it with a quick, noiseless motion. In the dusk of the stairway a board creaked, something white glimmered. "Who's there?" No answer. "Flora May, is that you? Answer when I speak to you!"

The voice was gentle, but compelling; the answer came, half sullen, half frightened. "I want a drink of water, Aunt Lucy."

"You go right back to bed, Flora May! I'll bring you a drink when I come up. Let me hear your door shut now!" She waited till a door closed upstairs; then latching the one she held in her hand, beckoned her husband, and stole to the other side of the room. "Like as not she'll be down again!" she whispered. "I've caught her listenin' here and there any time this past week. She thinks she'll hear when he's comin', or hear about him anyway. Jacob—whisper! I know Pippin's good; it isn't him I'm afraid of. It's her. It isn't a father that poor thing wants, nor yet a brother!"

"Flora May's a good girl!" Jacob spoke as if in defense of the girl who so short a time ago had been his little pet, his pretty kitten-like child plaything. "She's always been a good innocent girl, Lucy."

"Oh, good!" Lucy Bailey, sixty years old, New England born and bred, made an almost impatient gesture. "Who's to say good or bad, when folks haven't their reason? I tell you there's things workin' inside that poor child that knows nothing about good or bad, things that's stronger than her. I hate to say it, but she ought not to be here any longer, Jacob."

"Now, Lucy!"

"There ought to be places for such as her—there is, I b'lieve, if we but knew— places where they can be kep' and cared for and learned all they can learn. Yes, I know we've done our best—" in answer to a murmur of protest—"but our best ain't good enough, that's all. There! We must go to bed, father; 'tis late, and I promised that child a drink of water. Poor lamb! She was so happy till this come up! Let Rover in, will you? He's scratchin' all that nice new paint off the door. I'll put kitty down cellar. Here, kitty, kitty! The stove is all right, father; you lock up and come right up to bed, won't you? You've had a tirin' day with all them potatoes to dig."

She was tired too, good Lucy Bailey! Every part of her strong body seemed to ache; yet she lay awake long after Jacob's deep breathing gave her comfortable assurance of his sleeping. It did seem strange, how their quiet life was all jolted up, she thought, as she lay staring at the elm shadows that tossed in the moonlight. So long it had run on a level, as you might say, day by day, month by month, year by year. For her the years had been marked chiefly by the growth of the two young creatures, her nephew and the "simple" girl who had been a town charge from early childhood. Such a contrast! Myron so bright and quick; how his eyes would light up when he laughed! And poor Flora May; well! the Lord knew best! And now Myron was doing so well over at Kingdom, and so happy! Those nice Baxters! she must certainly ask them over to spend the day! If only they didn't spoil her boy, making of him so! But he was gone from Cyrus Poor Farm whose light he had been; and now came this old man whom Mrs. Bailey could not like, try as she might, sorry as she was for him; and then came Pippin, like a wandering flame, setting fire—so to say—where before was just straw or like that.

Sleep came at last, deep and sweet; from the quiet chamber it seemed to pass through the old house, laying a quiet hand on every living thing. The dog slept beside the stove, the cat in her cushioned basket in the cellar, the bird on his swinging perch; only in the attic chamber Flora May lay broad awake, staring through the dark, tossing to and fro on her narrow bed.

Mary Blossom started on her journey with a heavy heart. Duty might lead her by the hand, but could not lighten her burden. She had slept ill for the past few nights, had eaten little; her head ached, and even Mr. Hadley's cheerful talk could hardly bring a smile to her lips. Once in the train, however, the swift motion, the rushing panorama before her eyes, roused and interested her in spite of herself. The chaplain noted with delight her brightening eyes, and the faint color that crept into her pale cheek. Thank God, she was young, and joy was always tagging after youth, trying to keep hold of her hand, even when things pushed in between.

It was the first time she had ever gone far from the city. The yearly excursion of the Home children had been to a grove not ten miles off; since she grew up and went to work there had been no time to think about going "any place else," as Mary would have expressed it. She watched with delight as the swift miles sped by, and responded eagerly when the chaplain pointed out this or that object of interest. That was Tankard Mountain, was it? My! wasn't it high? Mary had never seen a real mountain before. (She called it "mounting," but then so did Pippin; some people will, strive as you may to teach them otherwise.) And that was Blue Lake? Mary wanted to know! Well, it surely *was* blue, wasn't it? Did Mr. Hadley know what *made* water blue like that? 'Twas the sky reflected in it? He didn't say so! Well, creation was curious, wasn't it?

Lawrence Hadley enjoyed the journey, too; the familiar landscape took on fresh beauty for him, and he began to recall bits of half-forgotten legend and tale to adorn it. "You see that steep rock, Mary, overhanging the lake? There, where the big pine is? They say an Indian maiden threw herself from that rock, long ago, into the lake, and was drowned. Her lover was false to her, I believe, poor thing!"

"Poor thing!" The shadow darkened again over the girl's face, and she looked earnestly at the dark cliff. "But I wouldn't have given him that satisfaction. I'd never have let on that I cared—that much!"

She spoke low, but with suppressed energy. Hadley glanced at her; seemed about to speak, but checked himself, and presently called her attention to another object. They were still skirting Blue Lake, a ten-mile stretch of dimpling, crinkling sapphire.

"That little pile of rocks is Lone Man Island. It got its name from a hermit who lived there twenty-five years and never spoke to a soul in all that time but just once."

"My! he was a caution! What did he say, sir, the time he did speak? It ought to be worth hearing."

The chaplain laughed. "The story is, Mary, that his wife talked so much he couldn't stand it, and ran away. His house—it's gone now—stood on the shore, just opposite the island. He took the boat so she couldn't come out after him, but every day, they say, for a long time, she would stand on the shore and scream to him, till her voice was gone, telling him to come back. He would sit on a stone by the water's edge, rocking back and forth, rubbing his knees and never saying a word. When this had gone on for a year, more or less, the minister in the village over yonder—" he pointed to where a white spire twinkled among the trees—"thought it was his duty to interfere; so he came with his boat, and took the woman over to the island."

He paused and his eyes twinkled.

"Well, sir?" Mary's face was bright with eager interest. "It was then that he spoke? He freed his mind, I suppose?"

"She spoke first, and then the minister spoke. They both had a good deal to say, I have been told. And while they were talking, Jotham Wildgoose—yes, that was his actual name—sat on his stone, rocking back and forth, rubbing his hands on his knees, saying never a word. At last, when both of them were out of breath and out of patience, the old man spoke. 'Get out!' he said; and never said another word as long as he lived."

"The *i*dea! Why, I never heard of such a thing, Mr. Hadley. Why, how did he live? How did he do his marketing?" The practical mind of the Scientific General pounced at once on the main issue. Man need not talk, but he must eat.

"He lived mostly on fish; he had his boat, you see, and he was a good fisherman. When he wanted other supplies, he took a string of fish to the nearest village and got what he wanted in exchange. He was very clever in making signs; he could write, too.

171

Yes, I believe Jotham Wildgoose lived to a good old age, and counted himself a fortunate man."

"And what became of his wife?"

"Poor thing! They say she scolded herself to death. She was a sad shrew, from all accounts. Of course, I am not excusing Jotham," he added hastily; "I am only explaining."

Mary pondered. "'Tis a queer story!" she said at last. "'Twas strange he wouldn't listen to the minister, though. You'd thought he would!"

The chaplain's eyes twinkled.

"They are taken that way sometimes!" he said.

"I'll bet he'd have minded if *you* had told him to go home!" Mary spoke with conviction, but the chaplain shook his head.

"Don't be too sure, Mary! Did you ever hear about Mr. Bourne and his wife? No, how should you! It was an old song when my father was a boy. Listen, now!

"Mr. Bourne and his wifeOne evening had a strife.He wanted bread and butter with his tea,But she swore she'd rule the roastAnd she'd have a piece of toast,So to loggerheads with him went she, she, she,So to loggerheads with him went she.

"Now there was a Mr. MooreLived on the second floor,A man very strong in the wrist.He overheard the splutterAbout toast and bread and butterAnd he knocked down Mr. Bourne with his fist, fist, fist,And he knocked down Mr. Bourne with his fist.

"Quoth Moore, 'By my life,You shall not beat your wife.It is both a sin and disgrace.''You fool,' said Mrs. Bourne,'Tis no business of yourn!'And she dashed a cup of tea in his face, face, face,And she dashed a cup of tea in his face.

"Quoth poor Mr. Moore,As he sneaked to the door,'I'm clearly an ass without brains.For, when married folks are flouting,If a stranger pokes his snout in.He is sure to get it tweaked for his pains, pains, pains,He is sure to get it tweaked for his pains.'"

"And that is a pretty accurate statement of the case, I believe!" said the chaplain. "But here we are at Cyrus, my dear, and there, from Pippin's description, is Jacob Bailey himself waiting for us."

Mary shrank, and drew in her breath with a sob. The journey, the cheery talk, had dulled for the time the pain at her heart, the suffocating dread of what was before her;

now both awoke and clutched at her. She clung to the chaplain's arm, trembling and sobbing, dry-eyed.

"I'm afraid!" she said. "I'm afraid!"

"Yes!" said Lawrence Hadley. "Yes, you are afraid, Mary, but that does not signify. What signifies is that you are bringing light into a dark place. Light, and warmth, and joy. Be thankful, my child; be thankful!"

He led her forward, and Jacob Bailey did the rest. His hearty, "Well! well! Here's the folks I'm downright glad to see," restored Mary's balance in an instant. "Elder Hadley, I presume?" he went on. "And this is Miss Blossom? Well, I *am* pleased to meet you! Step right this way, the team's waitin'."

It was dusk when they drove up to the door of Cyrus Poor Farm. Mary was stiff after the four-mile drive—she was not used to driving—and even a little chilly; at least, she was trembling, though the evening was mild. The cheerful rays that streamed from the opening door struck warm to her heart which was still throbbing painfully. She could not speak, could only return the warm pressure of Mr. Hadley's hand as he helped her to alight. Jacob Bailey held the other little cold hand and led her forward.

"This way!" he said heartily. "Here she is, Lucy. Make you 'quainted with m' wife, Miss Blossom. Reverend Mr. Hadley, make you 'quainted with Mis' Bailey. Walk in! walk in! I expect they're famished with hunger, Lucy; supper ready, hey?"

Ever since word had come that morning of the impending arrival, curiosity had run rampant through the house. Miss Mandy Whetstone's nose had been pressed against the window glass so often that Mr. Wisk (he was the fat old gentleman with the hoarse voice; his friends called him Whiskey, for reasons best known to themselves) asked her if she wasn't afraid of wearin' a hole in the glass. Miss Mandy, resenting this, replied that at least she hadn't been out the gate seventeen times—Mr. Wisk needn't say a word, she had counted!—to look down the road to see if they was any one coming. *She* had uses for her time, let it be with others as it might. Miss Lucilla Pudgkins, anxiously forecasting, presumed likely they would bring good appetites with them, traveling all the ways from the city. She took occasion, when the table was set for supper, to count the doughnuts on the plate, and with prudent forethought, Mrs. Bailey's back being turned, slipped two plump ones into a drawer of the table conveniently near her seat.

Now they were actually here, and the inmates took their fill of staring, open-eyed and unashamed; all except Brand in his corner, polishing a basket handle, and Flora May, rocking in her chair, crooning listlessly to the cat in her lap.

Pale and weary though she was, Mary's beauty shone in the doorway like a lamp, as Pippin would have said—poor Pippin, who was not there to see. Mr. Wisk rose to his feet and struck an attitude of respectful admiration; the two elderly women who had been plain all their lives uttered little whimpering moans of surprise. "What right has the daughter of that horrid old tramp to look like this?" they seemed to ask.

"I expect she's stuck-up!" whispered Aunt Mandy to Miss Pudgkins. "Look at that hat!"

It was the simplest possible hat, but it had an air, as all Mary's hats had. She trimmed them herself, and I believe the ribbons curved into pretty shapes for pure pleasure when she patted them.

Mrs. Bailey took no note of the hat; she looked straight into Mary's eyes, as clear and honest as her own, and answered hastily the unspoken question in them.

"Yes, he's livin', my dear, though feeble. I'm *real* glad you've come!"

"Thank you! Oh, thank you! So am I!"

The words came from her lips unbidden, and the girl marveled even as she spoke them. She *was* glad! What did it mean?

"She'd better have her supper before she goes in, Lucy," said hospitable Jacob, "seein' it's all ready, and she come so far!"

But his wife, still holding Mary's hand, shook her head, again in response to a mute appeal. "No, Jacob! She's goin' right in. I'll take her in a cup o' tea and a mite of something, and she can eat while she's sittin' there. This way, dearie!"

The door closed, and the inmates drew a long breath; it was as if the drop curtain had descended between the acts of a drama. It was cruel to shut them off from what was going on in that other room. Miss Whetstone even discovered that she had left her pocket handkerchief up chamber, and had her hand on the door when Mrs. Bailey, returning, intervened with the offer of a spandy clean one just ironed, and a bland but firm gesture toward the table.

"We'll set right down, if you please!" said the mistress of Cyrus Poor Farm. "Reverend Mr. Hadley, will you ask a blessin'?"

CHAPTER XXII
THE OLD MAN

THE chaplain was getting uneasy. His time was up, he ought to get back to Shoreham that night, and there was no sign of Pippin. Of course he could go back without seeing him, but—but he *wanted* to see the boy. Lawrence Hadley was at heart as romantic as his sister, and had built his own modest air castle for Pippin and Mary. There was a misunderstanding between them; he might be able to clear it up if he could have a good talk with them both. Well, there was an afternoon train; he would get back late, but still—

So the good man spent the morning at Cyrus Poor Farm, and enjoyed himself extremely. He had an interview with Mr. Blossom, a brief one. The old man was consistent; spiritual matters did not interest him in the least. All he cared for was the sight of Mary in her blue dress and white apron; he brushed the chaplain away with a feeble but definite, "Sky pilot? Nix! Lemme 'lone!" Hadley, wise and kind, said a few cheery words, nodded to Mary, and went away. But for the other inmates that morning was marked with a white stone. He talked with each one; better still, he listened to each one, not plucking out the heart of his mystery but recognizing it with a friendly and appreciative nod and leaving it where it was. He sympathized with every individual ache in Miss Pudgkins' j'ints, prescribed hot water and red pepper for her dyspepsy, and promised a bottle of his favorite liniment. He heard all about the Whetstones and the Flints (Aunt Mandy's mother was a Flint, and *her* mother was a Cattermole; he probably knew what the Cattermoles were), he heard the number of rooms in the Whetstone homestead, and the cost of the Brussels carpet laid down at the time of Aunt Mandy's Aunt Petunia's wedding. She married a traveling man, and had *everything*. All this with much bridling, and drawing down of an upper lip already sufficiently long. Hadley reflected that this poor soul could never have been anything but a fright, and his manner grew even kindlier.

He received the husky confidences of Mr. Wisk, who assured him, as between man and man, that this was no place for a gen'leman to stay any len'th of time. Good people in their way, good people, they meant well; but not, you understand, what a gen'leman was accustomed to. He, Mr. Wisk, was just waiting till his folks sent for him out West, that was all. Mr. Hadley didn't happen to have a drop of anything about him? A gen'leman was used to a drop after breakfast, and it came hard—all right! all right! No offense!

All this the chaplain took with cheerful friendliness; it was all in the day's work, all interesting; everything was interesting. But the talk he really enjoyed was one with Jacob Bailey and Brand, the blind man. They sat in the barn doorway, wide and sunny; Brand on his stool, finishing his two-bushel basket; Hadley on an upturned bucket beside him; Bailey leaning against the door jamb. They talked of stock and crops, of seeds and basketry and butter. Then some one said, "Pippin," and the other things ceased to exist. First, Jacob Bailey must tell his story, of how he had seen that young feller steppin' out along the road, who but he! steppin' out, sir, and talkin' nineteen to the dozen, all alone by himself; of their making acquaintance, and all it had led to. "Brand is like one of the fam'ly! I've but few secrets from Brand. Pippin saved my boy, sir; my wife's nevy, that's been a son to us both, and was goin' astray. Pippin saved him! Lemme tell you!" He told; the chaplain listened with kindling eyes, and then in his turn told of Pippin's life in the prison, of his influence over this man and that, of the help he had been as a trusty this past year, of how he had been missed.

"Why, actually, the place seems darker without him!"

The blind man, who had been listening intently, spoke for the first time.

"Yes!" he said slowly. "He is like light!"

The others turned to him.

"How's that, Brand?" asked Bailey, kindly.

"I have never seen light," said the man who was born blind, "but when this young man comes in, he brings something that seems to me like what light must be. 'Tis warm, but more than that; 'tis—" he shook his head. "I cannot put it into words!" he said. "I have never seen light!"

"You are right, sir!" the chaplain spoke with conviction. "You have described it exactly. Pippin is one of the light-bringers. They are a class by themselves, and—to judge by my own experience—Pippin is in a sub-class by himself. But, Mr. Bailey, this light must be focused; to do all it can do, all it is meant to do, it must burn steadily; must be a trimmed lamp, not a wandering flame. Do you take me?"

Bailey leaned forward, almost stammering in his eagerness.

"That's right! That's right!" he cried. "That's what I've been wantin' to say! That's what I want to go over with you, before he comes, Mr. Hadley. I've been itchin' to, ever since you come. Here's the way it looks to me!"

The other two men bent toward him; the talk went on in low, earnest tones. The sun poured in at the wide barn door; the hens and chickens clucked and scratched in the golden straw; from her loose box Polly, the black mare, whinnied a request for sugar. Past the farmyard gate went the road, a white, dusty ribbon stretching far into the distance; but look and listen as they might, the three men caught no glimpse of a gay figure swinging along, a wheel at its back, a song on its lips.

176

Mary was doing her duty, thoroughly and faithfully, as she did all things. The old man had been well taken care of before she came; the little room had been neat as wax, the old rag and tatter of humanity had been kept clean and wholesome as might be; but Mrs. Bailey had no time for the little touches, the scientific generalities, so to speak, that appeared wherever Mary went. The little trays, by whose daintiness gruel was made to appear a feast for sybarites; the tidy screen, fashioned from a clotheshorse and a piece of cheesecloth; the glass of flowers on the light-stand by the bed: all these said, "Mary-in-the-kitchen," as plain as things can speak; and Mary, sad and steadfast, found satisfaction in them. But Old Man Blossom cared for none of these things; dirt was good enough for him, he said, he was made of it, anyways; let Mary stop wieldin' that duster and set down by him, she'd been bustlin' the entire mornin'; he wanted to look at her. Mary sat down patiently, and took out her tatting— but the nerveless hand groped and groped till it touched hers, and clutched and held it. Then he lay quiet, gazing his fill, asking nothing more of earth or Heaven; and Mary sat patiently, seeing her duty plain, doing it thoroughly.

Loving it? No! She would not lie to herself. Her flesh would cringe and shrink at the touch of that other flesh, flaccid, lifeless, yet clinging so close it seemed to be sucking her clean young strength as a leech sucks blood. The visions would come, try as she might to banish them; visions of the old, dreadful days, of this face, now so peaceful on the pillow, purple and sodden, with glazed eyes and hanging mouth; of her mother, with the watchful terror in her eyes; mingled with these visions, inseparable from them, the smell of liquor and musty straw.

Then, as she fought with herself, striving to drive away the sight and the smell, lo! all would change. She would see a dark face glowing with a warmth of tenderness and compassion which—she told herself—her cold heart could never know.

"Poor old mutt!" said the voice that was like a golden bell. "He's on the blink, you see, and he wants his kid. Wouldn't that give you a pain? Honest, now!"

Then Mary would bend over the bed in an agony of self-reproach.

"Father, are you easier? Father, would you like a drink? Let me lift your head— so!"

And through it all, something at the back of her brain knew that along the white ribbon of road a figure was striding, lithe, alert, a wheel at its back and a song on its lips. Yes, a song! All would come right, it couldn't help but. The Lord was Pippin's shepherd, e'en as He was Mary's. He would make her see, make her understand. Glory be!

"Dinner's ready, Mary! Can you come?" Mrs. Bailey, opening the door softly, spoke under her breath, with a glance at the still figure in the bed, at the hand clutching Mary's with feeble, clinging grasp. Mary nodded and her lips shaped the words,

"Presently! He's dropping off asleep."

Five minutes passed; ten minutes. At last the fingers loosed their hold, the eyes closed, the lines faded, and the ugly old wax mask lay still on the pillow.

Quietly Mary rose, her soft dress making no sound. Quietly she stole to the door, quietly opened it, so quietly that no one saw or heard her, for at that moment another door was flung wide open from outside, and a gay "Hello! hello! hello!" brought every one to their feet. Pippin stood in the doorway, laughing, glowing, his wheel at his back; in his arms—a child—a little, dark, bright-eyed child, who clung to him and gazed wide-eyed at the strange faces, for all were clustering about him now with greetings and questions.

"Where have you been, Pippin? We've been looking for you all day. How are you? What you been doing? Whose child is that?"

"Easy, folks, easy!" laughed Pippin. "You're scaring the kiddy out of his boots— if he had any!" with a glance at the brown toes that were curling frantically round him. "Mis' Bailey, you come—"

"Whose child is it?" asked Lucy Bailey again, as she came forward.

"Well!" Pippin laughed again, as he tried to unwind the clinging brown arms from his neck. His face was alight, there was a ring of triumph in his voice. "He calls me Daddy. What do you know about that? I expect he's mine, ain't he?"

Mary! Mary! Stop! Wait and listen! This child is six years old, and Pippin two and twenty. Use the reason on which you pride yourself!

But Mary is gone, closing the door softly. Gone to fling herself on her knees beside the dying reprobate, to tell him—silently, be sure! His sleep must not be broken—tell him over and over that he is all she has in the world, that she is a wicked, wicked girl; that she will try to love him; she will, she will!

"Mother! mother! I will try!"

No one sees; no one hears.

Pippin, after a wistful glance round the room, sat down at the table and tucked the child comfortably away under his left arm.

"Set down, please, everybody!" he said. "I'm right sorry I disturbed you all. Seemed so good to get here! No, Mis' Bailey, full as much obliged, seein' he holds so to me, I'll keep him right here. If you'd pass me some bread and milk; he can eat by himself," proudly; "can't you, old sport? There now! Fall afoul of that, what say? Elder, I am proper glad to see you, I sure am. I was scared to death you'd got out of patience and gone. Mary—Miss Blossom—well? The Old Man—she got here in time?"

Reassured on this point, he drew a long sigh of relief. "That's good! That's good! I kep' on thinkin' and thinkin', what if she come too late? She comin' in soon?"

"Pretty soon, Pippin; he can't bear to have her out of his sight, so she's waiting till he drops asleep. If you don't tell us about that child, Mrs. Bailey won't give you a morsel to eat, will you, Mrs. Bailey? And it's the best corned beef hash you ever tasted."

Pippin threw back his head and laughed again, the gay, triumphant laugh that rang through the kitchen.

"Got you all guessin', ain't I? Now I'll tell you all about it. Yesterday I was slammin' along the ro'd—it's been a long trip, twice as long as gettin' there, 'cause I didn't stop any place excep' I had to—slammin' along to beat the band, when I heard a kid hollerin', hollerin' like he was hurt. Come round the corner, and there—green grass! there was a big Dago guy with an organ, and he was layin' into this kid. Layin' into him, you understand, with a stick—little kid like this! Wouldn't that give—Well! I guess I went sort of dotty. I—well, you'll excuse me, ladies! I done what appeared the right dope—in that case, you understand. I give him his, in good shape! And then I dumped his organ atop of him, and took the kid and e-loped. That's all there is to it, really." He swept the table with a smile as confident as it was appealing. "Guess you'd all done the same, wouldn't you? The gents, I would say."

There was a doubtful murmur, which might mean assent or dissent; the chaplain alone spoke out.

"I don't know, Pippin! Of course you were right to stop the man's beating the child; but if he was his father—"

"Father nothin'! He was one of them Pat Rooneys."

"Pat Rooneys? What do you mean?"

179

"That's what they call 'em!" with an assured nod. "Never knew why they give 'em an Irish name, for they're I-talian dagoes, every man Jack of 'em. *Buy* kids, they do, or as good as buy 'em, and learn 'em—"

A light broke on the chaplain. "Oh! *padrone*, you mean!"

"That's what I say. Pat Roney or Rooney: Rooney's a more common name. There's Rooneys every place, I guess, but they're mostly Irish. Well! Now you see, Elder, this kiddo—lemme tell you! Say, kiddo! Where's Puppa?"

"Papagondaiddo!" replied the child, burrowing his head into Pippin's shoulder.

"Where's Mamma?"

"Mammagondaiddo!"

"Want to go back to Pat Rooney?"

The boy screamed, and clung frantically round Pippin's neck, half choking him.

"There! You see, Elder, and folks! And you see this!" he added gravely, pulling the ragged shirt from the little shoulders. The women cried out in pity and horror; the men grew red and muttered. Pippin pulled the shirt up again, gently as a woman. "I know the way that feels!" he said simply. "I've been there!"

There was a moment's silence, while he stroked the curly head absently. Then Lucy Bailey, the tears running down her cheeks, held out her arms. "Come to me, little lamb!" she said. "Come and have a nice warm bath and some clean dry clothes! Then we'll go out and see the chickabiddies and the ducks! Come to Auntie!"

The child resisted at first, but after a long look at her, put his hand in hers and trotted off obediently. Pippin drew a breath of relief, and turned eagerly to the chaplain.

"Glory!" he cried. "Glory to God! Wa'n't that a leadin', Elder? Honest, now, did ever you see a leadin' made clearer? I set out to find that little gal, allowin' soon as I'd found her, to do thus and so—You know, to get some boys and give 'em the glad hand, help 'em up. And the very day after I find that gal—" again that wistful glance round the room; she was long in coming—"the *very day*, sir, the Lord sends this kid right in my road. And—" Pippin's eyes brightened; he brought his hand down with a resounding smack on the table—"green grass! *before* that, Elder!—there's another kid, all ready to come and start right in, waitin' up there to the Orphan joint till I tip him the signal, and then just watch him make tracks for Cyrus! I—I guess I'll have to sing, Elder; I feel like I was bustin'. Shall we praise the Lord a spell in song?"

180

He was springing to his feet, but the chaplain, exchanging a glance with Jacob Bailey, laid a quiet hand on his shoulder.

"Not just yet, Pippin!" he said. "You are going too fast; we must talk this over. Come out with me—why, you foolish fellow, you haven't eaten any dinner!"

"That's right! I haven't. And I'm holler as a pail, too. Trouble you for a mite of that hash, Mr. Bailey? Gee! it *is* good, no two ways about that!"

Absurd that they should all sit and watch Pippin eating his dinner, but they did. He drew them like a magnet. Some of them lingered because it put off a little longer the return to work; this was the case of Mr. Wisk, who did not like to dig potatoes. Others, like Brand and Miss Whetstone, pricked eager ears for the scraps of gay talk that alternated with Pippin's mouthfuls; while Miss Pudgkins watched the mouthfuls themselves with mournful interest, and while admiring the skill with which Pippin handled his knife (his formative years had not known forks), saw with dismay the dwindling pile of savory hash. She had counted on a portion for her supper; she must say he was a master hand at eating. The chaplain for his part watched the meal with mingled amusement and impatience. It was pleasant to see a perfectly healthy creature enjoying his food, but, with a third mountain of hash just begun upon, and kindling glances thrown toward the custard pie and doughnuts, what was to become of the "heart-to-hearter" which he must have with his "wandering flame"? The moments were passing, the afternoon train looming larger and larger.

But the chaplain was not to take the train that afternoon. Just as Pippin had flung himself joyously on the pie, the inner door opened, and Mary, pale and grave, appeared.

"Mr. Hadley," she said, "will you come? Father isn't so well!"

CHAPTER XXIII
THE CHAPLAIN SPEAKS HIS MIND

WHEN it was over; when the spirit—gladly, one must think, with never a backward glance—left the broken shell on the pillow and went its way, there came to Old Man Blossom his hour of dignity and importance. This shell, after all, was what had borne his name, spoken with his voice, thought such thoughts as were his. Washed and combed, dressed in clean white clothes that smelt of lavender, covered with spotless drapery that hung in as comely laps and folds as for any bishop at St. Praxed's, the old man lay in state, and Cyrus Poor Farm, individually and collectively, came to do him honor, and to pronounce him a "beautiful remains." By and by this was over, too, and Mary sat alone in the little room, her capable hands folded in her lap, with a strange, numb feeling that was part thankfulness, part relief, and all desolation.

To her, thus sitting, appeared Pippin in the doorway, the little Italian boy clinging to his hand. The child (his name was Peppino, a diminutive of Giuseppe, but Pippin thought it was Pippino and another finger post in the path of his "leading") would hardly leave his adopted daddy for an instant. Through the funeral service he had clung to his knees; and when Pippin sang "Abide with me" (sang it like a surrup, Miss Whetstone said; she like to bawled right out), the child's eyes glowed with the delight of a Latin, and he murmured an unconscious alto.

"Miss Mary—" Pippin spoke timidly; "I thought maybe—won't you come outdoors a spell? It's a nice day!"

Mary looked up with cold sweet eyes. "No, thank you!" she said. "I am tired."

"Is that so? Well, of course you are, all you've ben through. Would you like me to bring Pippino in to set with you? He'd admire to, wouldn't you, Pippino?"

Mary's white brow contracted. "You must excuse me!" she said. "My head aches. I don't feel like seeing company."

And her arms were aching for the child! She wanted to hold him close, close, to fret him with sallies of her kisses, to twine his curls round her finger. From the tail of her eye she absorbed his beauty, the roundness of his cheek, the deliciousness of his chin, the dark stars that were his eyes. But she set her lips, and turned away toward the window, and Pippin, with a murmured, "Come, kiddo! Best we go along!" went his sad way out into the sunshine.

Instinctively he turned his steps toward the barn, and there the chaplain found him soon after. He was sitting on the upturned bucket, leaning listlessly against the door jamb. Peppino was playing beside him with a box of red and white beans, very wonderful. Now and then he held up a handful of the pretty things with a gleeful shout; and Pippin would nod and smile and say, "Some beans, kiddo! They sure are!" His whole air and attitude were so wholly unlike himself that Mr. Hadley said involuntarily,

"What's the matter, Pippin?"

Pippin rose and bowed, with the ghost of his own smile.

"That you, Elder? Well, now! That was a nice funeral, wasn't it? He couldn't ask for no nicer, not if he was the President!" He spoke with obvious effort; his eyes, meeting the chaplain's keen glance, dropped.

"What's the matter?" repeated Hadley.

Pippin sat down again, the other beside him. There was a pause; then—

"I've lost my grip!" he said heavily. Hadley waited. The father in him, the son in Pippin, must meet in silence, if they were to meet at all.

Presently the words came in a rush. "I've lost my grip; things has got away from me. I don't know what I done—" his eyes, dark with pain and trouble, roved hither and thither, as if seeking enlightenment—"but I done something I hadn't ought to. She has no use for me any more!"

Still Hadley waited. The voice rose into a cry. "I thought," Pippin mourned, "I thought when she come to see her Pa, and—and knew how he sent me, and I looked for her—looked for her—I thought she'd feel different, but she doesn't, sir; no, she doesn't. She never give me one look to-day, just passed me by same as if I was a chair, or like that. And—just now—I see her sittin' all alone there, and I thought—I tried—but 'twas no good. I don't cut no ice with her, that's all there is to it. I don't know what I'll do, Elder; I don't—know—what I'll do! Nor that ain't all! I've lost my folks!"

"What do you mean, Pippin?"

"My folks: my movie folks, that I made up like I told you: Pa and Ma, and the rest. They've gone back on me, Elder."

"Tell me!"

The kind hand on his shoulder, Pippin poured out his tale; how since he first saw Mary things had begun to change, little by little, so gradually that it was a long time before he realized it. Then it came over him, suddenly, that all was not right, that the beloved figures were less clear, less sharply defined than they had been.

"They'll come when I speak to 'em, yes, and they'll answer, but it's like I had to make up what I want 'em to say, 'stead of them wantin' to say it themselves. I know—Elder, I expect you'll think I'm wantin' in my mind, but—I *know* they wa'n't real folks, but yet they was real to me. They acted so live, and so good and lovin' and all—why, Ma—why—what'll I do without Ma?" He broke off and stared into vacancy. "I see her now, but she's different: more like a shadow, and when I look at her, she changes into—you know what she changes into, Elder?"

"Yes, Pippin, I think I do!"

"She changes into Mary!" Pippin sprang up, and paced the barn with eager steps, throwing up his chin at every turn. "And Pa similar. And the little gal—but I never see her so plain, some ways, I never—what I mean—she always appeared like she was some person else, and now I know it was little May, little May Blossom!" He choked. The child, dropping his beans, came and pulled at him with eager hands.

"Daddi Pippin, what a matter, Daddi?"

Pippin looked down, and patted the brown head tenderly. "Say, kiddo, you run in and ask Mis' Bailey for a cooky and a mug of milk; what say? It's time you had a bite!"

The child hesitated. "And bring-a Daddi piece?" he inquired.

"Daddy'll come in directly and get his piece. You cut along now and wait for me in the kitchen. You can play with the kitty till I come."

The child obeyed, only half willingly.

"Say, isn't he a dandy kid?" Pippin turned to the chaplain with a wistful look. "I've got him!" he said. "I've got the kiddo, and I've got my work to do. Maybe the Lord didn't intend for me to be happy; everybody can't be, it stands to reason."

Mary's own phrase! The chaplain looked at his watch, and stood a moment as if irresolute. Then—"Pippin, wait here for ten minutes, will you?" he said. "I have to see about something. Just wait, will you?"

"Sure!" said Pippin, wondering.

Hadley nodded, and walked back to the house with a quick decided step, his watch still in his hand. Glancing toward the pasture gate, he saw Jacob Bailey approaching it, leading the Pilot colt which was, he knew, to take him to the station. He quickened his pace still more, and, entering the house, made his way to the room where Mary Blossom was still sitting, her capable hands idle in her lap, her eyes turned toward the window, seeing nothing.

"Mary!" At the sharp, decided tone, the girl looked up with a start. The chaplain shut the door, and stood with his back against it, watch in hand. "Mary, you are behaving badly! Yes!"—as the color rushed over the girl's astonished face. "I mean it! Listen to me, for I have only a few minutes. Pippin has done you an incalculable service, incalculable! He has shown you your duty and has made it possible for you to do it. No!" as Mary made a movement. "You must hear me; I haven't time to hear you. This boy, brought up in a slum cellar, trained for crime and steeped in it, has shown himself your master and mine, in practical Christianity. Knowing the danger, knowing that he might meet the ruffians who so nearly killed him, as you know—" Mary winced—"he went back to the city, because an old dying vagrant asked him to find his child. He found that child, you know at what cost; through him, your father died happy, the desire of his heart fulfilled. In return, you treat him like a dog! Instead of gratitude, you give him the cold shoulder. Shame on you, Mary Blossom! your conduct is heartless and wicked. You know Pippin loves you. You know there is no one in the world but you—"

He paused involuntarily, for Mary had risen and faced him, white as marble.

"No one but me?" she cried in a voice that shook with the cold passion of a sword. "I don't know what you mean, Mr. Hadley. Hasn't he got his family?"

"His family?" repeated the chaplain.

"His family, that I heard him tell you about; the family that wasn't just exactly regular, but yet was as dandy as any—I haven't forgot!" cried Mary with a sob. "Where do I come in, I should like to know? Why doesn't he go to his dandy family?"

The chaplain's face, that had been set as steel, broke into lines of exquisite kindness.

"My soul!" he said. "And I've only five minutes. Listen, my dear child! I'm sorry I scolded you!"

Briefly he told her of the family, of Ma and Pa, Little Gal and the baby; how the lonely boy had fashioned them out of his great longing heart, had warmed himself at the shadow fire of their affection.

"Till you came!" cried the chaplain. "Till love came! Then—he has just been telling me, poor boy!—his shadows grew cold and dim. He has lost them; he gets nothing in return. Mary!"

"But—" Mary pressed her hands to her head, bewildered—"the child! I saw the child; he calls him—Daddy. I heard him say so; I heard him say, 'He is mine!'"

"My soul!" cried Hadley again. "Where were you when he told us? The child? A waif like himself, a lost baby whom he found on the road being cruelly beaten by a brute of an Italian *padrone*. Pippin thrashed the brute and took the child. What else would he do, being Pippin? Mary!" he opened the door and spoke over his shoulder. "He is out in the barn now. I told him to wait ten minutes. Good-by! Remember, *opportunity comes once!*"

But even as he left the room, there was a swift movement behind him; he heard a sob; his hand was caught and a swift, shy kiss dropped on it.

"Ain't got any too much time to spare!" said anxious Jacob, gathering up the reins.

"Thank the Lord! I mean—we'll fetch it!" said the chaplain. The first words broke unconsciously from him, for he had seen from the gate a light figure emerge from the house and hasten toward the barn.

"Well," said Bailey, "what d'he say when you put it to him? Saw reason, didn't he? He would! He's real reasonable, Pippin is."

The chaplain hung his head. "I—I forgot!" he said. "I'll come over again next week!"

Panting, sobbing, so blinded with tears that she could hardly see her way, Mary fled out of the house, across the wide barnyard. The turkey cock, her terror and abomination, ruffled his feathers, spread his tail, and advanced upon her with swelling gobbles of wrath, but she neither saw nor heard him. There never was such a barnyard; there seemed no end to it, and she kept stumbling, now over the puppy, gamboling to meet her, now over the Muscovy duck that *would* waddle directly in front of her. At last she reached the barn, but only to pause, for she heard voices. No! one voice, Pippin's, loud and angry, as she had never heard it before!

"I tell you, *beat it while your shoes are new*! I've got no use for you, and don't you forget it. I know all you're tellin' me, and I tell *you* I don't care!"

Wondering much, Mary peeped round the corner of the barn, and saw Pippin standing in the middle of the doorway. No one else was in sight, but his eyes, shining with angry light, were bent forward on something that he saw plain enough. Mary, this is a matter too hard for you. Were the chaplain here, he would know all about it.

He might even smile, and murmur to himself, "Dominic!" or "Francis!" as the notion took him; for he knows that the mystic did not pass with the Middle Ages, but is to be found in the twentieth century as in the twelfth. Mary, of temperament wholly non-mystical, could only look and listen in terror as the voice rang out again.

"I know all you've got to say. I know I've lost 'em, Pa and Ma and all. I know I'll never get 'em back. And I know I'll never get my girl; never! never!" His voice broke, but next moment it rang clear again: "And I say to you what I said before, what I'll say while I have a tongue to speak. You, Satan, *beat it!* you hear me!"

Now, Mary! Oh, now, run forward! Clasp his hand, your own true lover; cry to him:

"You can have your girl! She is yours, yours, yours, every inch of her, now and always!"

Her feet were starting forward; her lips were opening to speak, when she heard something beside her, a breath drawn sharply in with a hissing sound. She turned, and met the eyes of the imbecile girl, gazing at her with strange and deadly looks.

CHAPTER XXIV
PRIMAL FORCES

COMIN' in to supper, Brand? The horn has blew!" Mr. Wisk paused, one foot uplifted for the next step.

To realize what a tribute to the blind man's personality lay in this pause, one must have known Mr. Wisk. As his internal clock pointed the approach of supper time he had been standing, poised for flight, an elderly and ramshackle Mercury on a half-dug potato hill. At sound of the horn he started, head bent forward, nose pointing as straight for the kitchen as ever porker's for the trough. He would not have stopped to put away his spade, because the corner behind the right-hand door jamb of the barn had been long since appropriated by him for this purpose; he could reach it without breaking step or slackening his pace. Probably nothing on earth would have checked him except the very sight that now met his eyes: the blind man standing just inside the door, feeling over various things on a shelf so high that he (a very tall man) could but just reach it. Mr. Wisk hesitated; it was his happy boast never to have been late to a meal since he came to manhood.

"Want—want I should help you?" he quavered.

"No, thank you, Wisk! I'll be in presently, tell Mrs. Bailey. I have to look for something just a minute, tell her."

He smiled at the sigh of conscious heroism which drifted back from the departing Wisk; but the smile faded quickly, and his face was anxious enough as his fingers closed round one object and another on the shelf; a bottle, a jar, a row of paper bags neatly tied with twine. To the casual eye these bags were all alike; one must read the label, see the skull and crossbones, to distinguish them; the blind man needed no labels.

"Lime, Paris green, Bordeaux mixture, arsenate of lead—one, two, three, four—there should be five. Lime, Paris green, Bordeaux mixture—*where is the hellebore?*"

He paused, his hand resting in an empty space between two bags. The hellebore should be there; it was always there. He had used it himself yesterday. He had counted these objects every night for the past ten years, and never before had one been missing. No one but he could reach the shelf; even Jacob Bailey had to stand on the bucket to get at it, and the rule was strict that none but one of these two was ever to touch any object on it. Brand stood pondering, with bent head, his hand still on the shelf. Who had been in the barn this afternoon? He himself, Jacob, Pippin, and the child. No one else—except the little girl; Brand always called Flora May the little girl.

She had been there, not half an hour ago; he had heard her step, had spoken to her, but she did not answer. In one of her odd spells, probably, poor child! But she could not reach the shelf, even if—

The supper table was less gay than usual that evening; silence prevailed instead of the usual cheerful chatter. A stranger, glancing round the table, would have seen for the most part faces absent or absorbed. Jacob was thinking about Pippin, regretting that the chaplain had failed to have that talk with him, wondering how he should himself make the matter clear to the boy. His wife was disturbed about Flora May who was evidently on the verge of one of her odd spells, for she had acted strangely all day, and she looked wrong to-night. When she crumbled her bread and didn't seem to know the way to her mouth, look out for trouble!

In the minds of Miss Pudgkins and Mr. Wisk the same thought reigned supreme. The pie looked to be smaller than common; would she cut it in six and fetch in another, or would she make it go round? Miss Whetstone was inwardly lamenting that she had not told Mr. Hadley of Jonas Cattermole's having been two years in the legislature. He'd see plain enough then that folks was folks, even if they found it convenient to board a spell with relations that happened to hold a town office. Miss Whetstone raised her nose loftily, and told Mr. Wisk with a grand air that she would trouble him for just a mite of them pickles if he could spare any.

And Mary?

Mary had changed her seat, with a murmured excuse about a draft on her back. She had usually sat between Jacob Bailey and Flora May, sat there with an inward protest. She shrank from contact with the imbecile girl: the instinctive shrinking of the healthy from the sick, the unconscious cruelty of the normal toward the abnormal. Hitherto she had given no sign of this, ashamed of an instinct that was yet too strong for her; conscious, too, under the skin of her mind, of the warmth of compassion, the tenderness of courtesy, with which Pippin always treated the poor girl. If she had been the First Lady of the Land, he could have shown her no more attention, Mary thought.

But to-night there was something more; Mary was afraid. The look she had met, out there by the barn, the dreadful look which seemed to strike like a sword at her springing hope and lay it cold and dead—she shuddered now at thought of it; she would not meet it again. If she had turned her eyes toward Flora May, she would have seen the beautiful face sombre but quiet, the eyes cast down, the girl's whole air listless and brooding; only—if she had looked longer—she might have seen now and then the heavy white lids tremble, lift a little way, and a glance dart from under the long lashes toward Pippin where he sat opposite her.

Mary dared not look at Pippin either, for she felt his eyes upon her. Not yet, not before all these people, could she give him back look for look, tell him silently all that was crying out within her; but soon, soon, Pippin! Meantime she had drawn the child Peppino into the seat next her, and was lavishing on him all the innocent wiles of the child-hungry woman; and the child nestled close to her, and looked up at her with adoring eyes. Pippin would see, would understand. All would be well.

Pippin saw, but did not understand. He had wrestled and overcome, but the stress of conflict was still upon him, the air was still full of the clash of arms, the sound of great wings. His shadow world was gone, swept away into nothingness; and of the actual flesh-and-blood realities he saw nothing except Mary Blossom. There she sat opposite him, in all her loveliness; surely he might look at her now, might for once take his fill of gazing on the lovely head with its clustering hair ("The color of a yearlin' heifer—Poor old mutt! What a way to speak of it! Wouldn't that give you a pain?"), on the long dark lashes against the exquisite curve of the rose-white cheek, on the perfect mouth—

Pippin's eyes grew misty; the world fell away from him—say, rather, it narrowed to a point, and life and death and every other creature were merged in that fair head of the love he thought he had lost.

"Flora May!" Mrs. Bailey spoke abruptly, almost sharply; every one started. "Wake up, Flora, and set up straight; you're all slid down in your chair. Here! Take this cup o' tea to Miss Blossom, dear!"

The brooding face lightened, sharpened, in a strange way; the girl rose with a swift, sudden movement, and went obediently to the end of the table to take the cup. If Mrs. Bailey had looked up then—but she was busy over her tea things.

"You put the sugar in, dearie—she likes two lumps—and cream! Mr. Brand, you ready for another cup?"

Pippin had started with the rest, when Mrs. Bailey spoke. Now his eyes followed Flora May for a moment; she had turned her back to the table, and was—what was she doing?

An old-fashioned mirror hung against the wall, dim with age, yet not so dim but that Pippin saw in it the graceful figure of the girl reflected. She paused, the cup in her left hand, drew from her bosom a folded paper, shook into the cup what looked like a white powder, replaced the paper carefully. Now what was that poor thing doing? Putting salt in Mary's tea for a joke like? Lacking reason, they were like monkeys, some way—

Then the girl lifted her head, and Pippin saw her eyes. In a flash he was beside her, and had taken the cup from her hand; now he lifted it, smiling, as if to drink.

"I guess that's my cup, ain't it, Miss Flora May? I guess Mis' Bailey made a mistake for once!"

It all happened in a moment, in the twinkling of an eye. Before the cup touched his lips, the girl struck it out of his hand. It fell with a sharp crash on the floor. She threw up her arms with a cry which rang through the house, and darted out into the night.

"She's got a spell on her!" said Jacob Bailey, rising quickly. "It's been coming on this week past, m' wife says. Come, Pippin; come, Wisk! We'll have to find the poor child and bring her home."

He spoke sadly, but without surprise, as of a thing well known.

"You come too, Brand! Oftentimes she'll answer your voice when she won't another. The barn first!"

"She was there this afternoon," said the blind man, following. "Likely she's gone to put back something she—borrowed!"

Not in the barn; not in the corncrib, where she used to sit by the hour, crooning her wordless songs; not in the kennel with old Rover, where they had found her more than once, poor thing, her arms around the dumb creature who perhaps—who knows?—was nearer her dumb mind than the human beings around her.

"This way!" said Brand. "Here's a thread of her dress on the gatepost. She's gone to the wood lot."

Not in the wood lot; no answer to the calls of friendly, tender voices.

"Flora! Flora May! Where be you, little gal? Speak up, won't you?"

Further on, through the meadows, guided by the blind man's unerring fingers which found here a broken twig, there a shred of cotton, here again a knot of ribbon caught in a bramble wreath; searching, calling, searching, through weary hours.

So at last to the distant pasture where the lily pond gleamed under the moon.

There they found her, poor Flora May. Lying among the lily pads, her lovely hair twined about the brown stems, her fair face turned upwards, the clear shallow water dimpling and wavering above her, so that she seemed to smile at them in faint, disdainful mockery; so they found her, lying quietly in the place of her rest.

"Don't cry, mother! don't ye! the Lord has took His poor lamb home. Don't take on so, Lucy!"

Thus Jacob, patting his wife's shoulder with clumsy, tender hand. He had never seen her so overcome; the calm, self-contained woman was crying and sobbing like a child.

But now she collected herself with an effort, and dried her eyes.

"I know, Jacob! I know I hadn't ought; I know she's better off; but—'tis so pitiful! Oh, 'tis so pitiful! She couldn't help it, my poor girl; she couldn't help it. 'Twas stronger than her. And, oh, Jacob, I can't but think—if her father had been— different—"

"There, Lucy! There! Such things is beyond us."

"They hadn't ought to be!" cried Lucy Bailey, and her tears broke out afresh. "They hadn't ought to be beyond us. The Lord intended we should live clean and decent, and made us accordin'; and them as don't, it's their children must pay, like the Bible says. But what keeps comin' back and back on my mind is—she was so innocent and so pretty! Full as pretty as what Mary is, to my thinkin'. Seein' her lyin' there, so pretty—oh, so pretty! I couldn't but think—I couldn't but think—if she had had a fair chance—"

If she had had a fair chance! So Pippin thought, as he stood by the little white bed in the narrow room. He had carried her home in his young strong arms, had laid her here—reverently, as he would have laid a royal princess—on the bed where she had tossed and moaned her heart out for him; now she had no thought for him, she was all for sleep. He had left her to the women, and gone to join the older men, a sorrowful little group about the kitchen fire; but now, when all the house was still, there could be no harm in his entering the quiet room once more, humbly, with bowed head, to say a word of farewell to the poor sweet pretty creatur'; to say a little prayer, too, and maybe—whisperin' like, not to wake a soul—to sing a little hymn, seeing she used to set by his singing. He looked round the room, neat and bare, yet a girl's room, with pretty touches here and there: a bird's nest on a mossy twig, a bunch of feathery grasses in a graceful jug, bright Christmas cards framing the little mirror, drooping over them a necklace of wooden beads carved by Brand for his little girl. Beside these things, on a stand by the bedside, some pond lilies in a glass bowl, drooping with folded petals. Pippin shivered, and his eyes turned to the still figure, the white lovely face.

Kneeling humbly by the humble bed, he said his prayer; then raised his head, and softly, softly, a golden thread of sound—sure no one could hear!—his voice stole out in the hymn she had loved best:

"There is rest for the weary,There is rest for the weary,There is rest for the weary,There is rest for you!

"On the other side of Jordan,In the green fields of Eden,Where the tree of life is blooming,There is rest for your soul!"

Pippin rose and stood for some moments looking down on the quiet face; then he made his reverence—bowing lower than usual, with a gesture of his hands as if taking leave of something high and noble—and turned away.

Closing the door softly, he paused, looking into the darkness of the passage with wistful eyes. He was very, very lonely; his heart was sad as death. Could he—might he not, once more, call up to comfort him the shadow faces he had loved so well? Now? Just this once! He bent forward, his eyes fixed intently.

"Ma!" he said softly. "You there?"

A moment's pause; then a sob broke from him and he turned to go.

But then—oh, then!—came a rustle of something soft, came a flash of something white. Two arms were flung round his neck, pressing him close, close; a radiant head lay on his shoulder.

"Will I do?" cried Mary Blossom. "Oh, Pippin, Pippin! Will I do instead?"

CHAPTER XXV
PIPPIN OVERCOMES

WELL, how about it?" said John Aymer.

A council was being held in the pleasant parlor with the rose-colored shades. John Aymer, Lucy his wife, and Lawrence Hadley, his wife's brother, were sitting together, talking of things with which we have some concern.

"How about it?" repeated the hardware merchant. He planted both elbows on his knees, rested his chin on his hands, and, as he would have said, squared away for action. The others looked up inquiringly. "Pippin is your hunt, Larry, and from your point of view—and his—he is on the right track, and it's all highcockolorum Erin go Bragh. But Mary is our hunt, Lucy's and mine, and we don't feel so sure about all this."

"I do part of the time, John!" Mrs. Aymer spoke with a certain timidity, unlike her usual gay decisiveness. "When I talk with Larry, or see Pippin—even just look at him—it seems all as right as right; but then—"

"But then you look at Mary, and it doesn't. See here, Lar!" John Aymer laid down his pipe, a token of strong interest with him. "Pippin is what you call a mystic and I call a glorified crank. All he wants in the world—beside Mary—is a chance to help, as he says; and it's great. I know it is, and I'm proud to know the chap, and all that. But that *isn't* all Mary wants!"

The chaplain looked up with a grave nod of comprehension.

"Mary Blossom," John Aymer went on, "is a fine girl, and she's an ambitious girl. She has done well herself, got a first-rate education of its kind, made herself a first-rate all-round young woman, capable of doing—within limits—anything she sets her hand to. Now—she's as dead stuck on Pippin as he is on her—"

"John! What language! She adores him, if that is what you mean."

"Well, she adores him, then—doesn't sound half as real—but she doesn't adore the line of life he is laying out for himself and her. I don't believe she takes any more stock in it than—than I should. She would like to see her husband a church member in regular standing: a vestryman; doing no end of pious work, you know—he has to do *that* or bust; even I can see that—but doing it in a regular respectable kind of way: chairman of Boards—what? Frock coat, handsome rooms, subcommittees, secretaries, that kind of thing. She wants to see him a leader, and she believes he can be. This picking up a boy here and a tramp there, singing and praying, hurrah boys and God bless you, doesn't cut much ice with Mary. Poor little soul, she cried an hour on Lucy's shoulder the other night. Lucy cried, too, of course; water works all over the house, almost drowned me out."

"John!"

"Well, sir, that kind of thing—the chairman, frock coat, committee-room thing, is what Mary wants for her husband; and who can say but she's right? I don't say she is, mind! I'm not a spiritual kind of man, and I know it; but I do say that Pippin ought to realize how she feels and the kind of life she would choose. Then he can face it, squarely, and make his own decision, knowing what it means to her. You say—" he turned to his wife, who was listening intently—"he's had no education. Granted—in a way! But you can't keep Pippin from education any more than you can keep a dog from water when he's thirsty. (Nip's bowl is empty, by the way, Lucy; might cry into that next time, what?) I don't say it will be book education; much good my books have done me, and as you say, Lucy, my English resembles a tinker's—well, thought it, if you didn't say it—well—what do you say, Reverend?"

Lawrence Hadley threw his head back with a little reversed nod that was all his own.

"Give me a minute, Jack! I'm assimilating! Give me a minute!"

He took a minute, whistling "Am I a soldier of the Cross?" through slowly and carefully. Then he took three more in silence, walking slowly up and down the room, the others watching him anxiously.

All true—so far as it went. Pippin ought to see, ought to realize, what Mary wanted. Ought to realize, too, what power he would have in that way, the frock coat, roast-turkey, mahogany-and-brass-rail way. Popularity? He might become the idol of a day—of many days. Men's hearts would open to him like flowers to the sun. Mass meetings; hospitals; his voice floating through the wards; "the bright seraphim in burning row!" Yes! Mary beside him, glorified in him, shining with his light and her own—Yes!—On the other hand—what? A dying tramp comforted; a weak boy saved from ruin; a poor old sinner made happy. Not much, perhaps? And yet—had the Master founded hospitals there in Judea? Had He healed all the lepers? He healed one, and the world changed. The hospitals have been building ever since.

At last he spoke.

"Every word you say is true, Jack! Hold on!" as the other reached for his pipe with an air of relief. "Don't light up yet; you won't be so pleased in a minute. Every word is true, I say, but it's only half the truth, and the less important half!"

Hadley's eyes kindled, and he began to beat time with his fist on the arm of his chair. He was getting up steam.

"What do you mean?" said Aymer, rather shortly.

"You are right about Pippin's realizing Mary's point of view. He ought, and he shall; you shall put it to him yourself, as strongly as you like; but—here comes in my half—she must also realize his, and that is what she doesn't do."

"That is true, John!" Mrs. Aymer started forward, clasping her pretty hands in an adorable little way she had when strongly moved. "She *doesn't* realize, any more than you do; any more than I do, except just the least little bit. But, oh, I know Lawrence is right! I feel it in every bone I have. John dear, do as Lar says; put your side—*our* side, for, oh, I *am* such a worldly little animal!—before Pippin plainly, and then let Lar show Mary the other!"

"Agreed!" said John Aymer.

"No!" said Lawrence Hadley. "Pippin shall show her the other himself."

At this moment came a knock at the door.

"Come in!" said John Aymer impatiently.

The door flew open, and Mary entered, a Mary at sight of whom Mrs. Aymer sprang forward with inarticulate murmurs, while the two men rose to their feet in confusion. A wholly unfamiliar Mary; one would have said an impossible one. Crying, laughing, clasping and unclasping her hands wildly, she ran to the other woman, and melted into her arms as if there were no such things as class distinctions in the world.

"Oh! Mrs. Aymer!" she sobbed. "Oh, Mr. Aymer and Mr. Hadley! If you please! I have been a wicked, wicked girl!"

Sorely puzzled, the three friendly conspirators looked past the bright head, now resting on Mrs. Aymer's agitated shoulder, to the doorway, where stood Pippin, silent, motionless, but radiating light and joy and pride, "Like a torch!" "Like a blooming lighthouse!" said the two men, each to himself, in his own speech.

"I wouldn't cry, Mary!" Pippin spoke quietly, as he would to a child.

"You would!" Mary flashed round upon him. "You'd cry your eyes out, and wish you had more to cry out! I've been a wicked, wicked girl! Oh, Mrs. Aymer! Oh, dear! Oh, dear! No, my kind lady, don't stop me, for it has to come out. He took me—my

Pippin took me—down—down to those dreadful places where he used to live. I went into a cellar, dark and cold—oh! and there was a little child, all thin and cold and dirty, not clothes enough to cover him; and bruises on his little flesh! Oh, my heart! And Pippin said—Pippin said—'That might be me, Mary!' Oh, Mrs. Aymer! Oh, Mr. Hadley! *It might have been me, too!* It all came back. I remember—I remember—"

The sobs choked her, but she fought them back fiercely, and went on, struggling for utterance, still clasping and unclasping those eager hands. "He showed me more, but that was enough. I says to myself, 'Who am I, to turn him from his own work? Who am I, to come between him and the Lord? No! no!" She turned, and held out her hands with a passionate gesture. Pippin stepped forward and clasped the hands in his.

"We're going to work together!" said Mary Blossom. She spoke quietly now, though the sobs still tried to break out. "I'm going to follow him, help him, serve with him, every minute of my life from now on. He will do all the real work, everything that counts; but I can cook, and mend, and—oh, Mrs. Aymer, I can wa-wa-wash for them!"

She caught Pippin's hand to her lips, then flung it away and ran out. A silken flutter, and Lucy Aymer was after her like a flash. There was a tempestuous rustle of petticoats, and the sound of sobs and cooing; then silence.

The three men looked at one another. Presently John Aymer drew a long breath. "So *that's* all right!" he said. "One to you, Parson!"

The chaplain laughed, a contented little laugh. "Very handsome of you, Jack!" he said. "What do you say, Pippin? Is it all right?"

"It is, sir!" Pippin raised his head, which had been bent for a moment. "Yes, Elder, and Boss—I would say Mr. Aymer, sir; it is all right. I knew it would be; I never had no fears. I knew as soon as Mary sensed it she'd realize how 'twas. Yes, sir, I took her down—" he named a certain quarter of the city—"and showed her. I didn't need to say a word, hardly. She saw; Mary saw! And now, Elder—" he turned to Lawrence Hadley, and his eyes kindled. "Lemme tell you! It's like you said. I've got to get edication. I'm not fit to take holt of kids yet—not yet—but I will be! I'd like to start right away, if agreeable to you. You say where to go, and I'll go, if I have to wheel myself in a barrer!"

CHAPTER XXVI
PIPPIN PRAISES THE LORD

TWO years have passed, as yesterday, as a watch in the night. Once more the chaplain sits in his office, the bare, unlovely little room where we first saw him. Once more he is opening, sorting, reading his morning mail, his brow saddening, lightening, saddening again. Finally, once more the cloud rolls away entirely, and he settles himself in his chair with a comfortable sigh.

"Pippin!" he says, and composes himself to read. Let us look over his shoulder and read with him!

HONORED AND RESPECTED SIR,

I take up my pen with pleasure, to express the hope that the present seasonable weather may find you in good health and the enjoyment of every blessing. Well, Elder, I haven't written this good while past, because I wanted to wait and see would I be able to tell you what I *wanted* to tell you. Well, Elder, I want you should know it's *all right*, I have got that degree! I had a talk with the Old Man last winter, and he surely is great. He said I was all right on chemistry and crops and soils and like that, and similar on social economics, and mathematics, but where I fell down was on rhetoric and English literature. I said did he think that cut any great amount of ice when all I wanted was know how to run a farm and bring up boys straight and white. He said he didn't know as it did, but yet I didn't want those boys to grow up speaking ignorant. You bet I don't says I, but what's to hinder me learning 'em? I says, and learning myself at the same time? Have the books, and study right along with 'em I says, and there would be others could teach me, I says. Then I told him how it was about me and Mary, and how it didn't seem as if I *could wait any longer*. He laughed real pleasant, and said he guessed I wouldn't be called upon to wait very long, and I should have the degree all right first minute he could give it to me. Then he explained just how it was, and of course I saw in a minute; he couldn't give a degree to a guy for knowing a thing when he didn't know it. He knew how 'twas with me, and that I was doing chores and odd jobs to pay my way. And grinding! Elder, I was thankful to Nipper for that wheel. I sure was. I kept the whole show sharpened up good, now I tell you.

Well, Elder, now I want to tell you. When you first said, and Mr. Bailey upheld you, that it behooved me wait two years, and go to State Agricultural, and do thus and so, before I'd be fit to handle boys and be trusted by them as had 'em in charge—I tell you, sir, it seemed as if I *couldn't*, no way in the world. It appeared like I couldn't do it. It was like as if I was in Heaven, and you took me by my scruff and pants and hove me out. "It's more than reason," I says to myself. "It's more than flesh and blood can stand; it's like I was white-hot metal, and they took and threw cold water over me!" Well, Elder! You see where that was leading me? I bet you do! But I didn't, not at first. I went out to the barn, you rec'lect, and just set there by myself, humped up on the meal bucket, sayin' over and over, "I was all white hot to do the Lord's work, and they've took and threw cold water over me!"

And then, all of a sudden, it come to me, and I laughed right out. You must have heard me over to the house, I expect. Mary did, and she come running—bless her! "You lunkhead!" I says. "You lunkhead from way back everlasting, how do they temper metal *but* with cold water? Nice kind of steel you'd get without it, what say? Like to shave with soft iron, what say? And when you put it in the water it hisses," I says, "and so does the old gander hiss, and I know which you are most like!" I says.

I was laughing, you rec'lect, when I come back to tell you 'twas all right; I expect you knew pretty well how twas. You were whistling "Soldier of the Cross," and that showed me.

Well, Elder, I have had a *great time* over to State Agricultural, I sure have. The folks have been dandy, sir, simply dandy. Folks couldn't *be* no dandier than what they have to me. I used to think college folks and like that was *wanting* somehow, but I found the boot was on the other leg, it was me that was a nut to think so. I've made friends—why, they are *all* friends, I do believe. I'll tell you all about it first chance I get, but what I want to say *now* is, Elder, *my time is up*! I've got my degree, and Mr. Bailey is satisfied, and the cottage is ready (I've put in all my vacations on it, you know, and Mr. Bailey and the selectmen have been more than kind, the neighbors too), and Mary is ready; bless her heart! and Mrs. Aymer can spare her all right, or at least she says she *can't*, but she *will*, the kiddo learning to walk and like that; and she's got Mary the dandiest outfit ever you saw, Elder! If she was the President's wife, it couldn't be no dandier. And I've been to see all those gentlemen you said, the Boards and like that, and they was all dandy too, and said "Go ahead," and *I'm going*! So name the day you can come over, Elder, and *Mary and I will be there*. The Lord is so good to me—I don't know why He is so good, except that He *is* good. And all my life long, sir, I'll try my best to make other folks happy, I sure will. So no more but thanking you Elder, because under the Lord you really done it all sir. With a grateful heart though faltering pen I beg to convey to you, reverend and highly respected Sir, the assurance of my being

Your most obedient humble servant
PIPPIN.

P.S. I could have written and spelled it better if I had have taken time and followed this book, the "Polite Letter Writer"; a guy loaned it to me over to State Agricultural. I began this letter with it, but it balled me up so I couldn't keep on and I'm in hopes you will excuse bad writing and spelling. But I aim at a correct and elegant style, dear Sir, in epistolary communication—green grass! maybe when I have *more time*, Elder, I can do it, but it's no use, I cannot now.

The chaplain read this letter through twice. Then, after docketing and filing it carefully, he rose, and tucking his coat tails under his arm, proceeded to dance gravely up and down the little bare room, singing the song that was his high water mark of joy and triumph:

"Green is for Ireland, Ireland, Ireland,Green is for Ireland, fiddle dal day!"

The day was named; the day was here. Boards, councils and committees sent each a kindly delegate to the opening of the new Boys' Cottage at Cyrus Poor Farm. The opening was to take place in the afternoon; eight of the ten boys were to be brought over from the city by the president of a certain institution; there were to be addresses and formalities. But a few delegates had been asked to come early, to attend the wedding of the young couple who were to take charge of the new cottage. These delegates came smiling, full of cheerful expectation. This, they told one another, was Lawrence Hadley's venture. Good fellow, Hadley, excellent fellow! Yes, he vouched for this young chap, absolutely. Seemed to be an extraordinary chap; State Agricultural College gone wild over him. Kind of athletic evangelist, it appeared; led 'em all by the nose, they say. This cottage was his idea; yes. And there it was; pretty cottage!

A pretty cottage indeed; red brick, like the mother building which smiles friendly upon it across the green yard; its creepers already started, its flower beds already in bloom; its brass knocker defying the sun. Inside, all fresh and bright, homelike and— full! Full to overflowing, so that the kindly delegates pause astonished, and wonder whence all these people have found their way to so remote a district as North Cyrus. Who are all these people? Come and see!

First, in the shining kitchen, which has walked bodily over, it would appear, from Mr. Aymer's home in the city suburb, who are these two busy, rosy, white-capped and aproned people, man and woman? Why, these are Mr. and Mrs. Baxter, who are preparing the wedding breakfast. Who else should prepare it, they would like to know? Weren't they the first to welcome Pippin when he came to Kingdom? Wasn't he like their own, a son to them, a brother to Buster? Buster is in the shed now, "spelling" Myron at the ice cream freezer, both so eager that they are making five-minute shifts at the handle. Glancing through the open shed door, you may see Jacob Bailey in his Sunday suit, deep in talk with Father O'Brien and Elder Stebbins— pleasant talk, to judge from their faces. From the barn comes Brand, he too in his decent best, threadbare but spotless, carrying in careful hands the wonderful nest of baskets on which his spare hours for the past year have been spent: his wedding present for Pippin and Mary. Look at him! He has never seen light, but we see it in his face.

Who is in the dining-room of the cottage? Mrs. Bailey, of course, with Aunt Mandy Whetstone and Miss Pudgkins. Miss Whetstone opines that if there was need of city folks to do their table settin' for them, it was time they give up! With trembling hands she is laying out on the table the four silver teaspoons and the gravy ladle which commonly repose with her burial money at the bottom of her trunk. The trunk is kept locked, strapped and corded, the key hangs round Miss Whetstone's neck on a string; you never know, and in case of fire, there you are! Miss Pudgkins has no teaspoons, but she has "loaned" for the occasion the chief ornament of her bedroom, a magnificent wreath of "preserved" funeral flowers in a glass case. The cloud on her brow at this moment comes from Mrs. Bailey's kindly but firm refusal to use the wreath for a centrepiece.

"Fresh flowers is rill common!" Miss Pudgkins thinks.

One cannot say that Mr. Wisk is in any special room, because he is in them all, following his unerring nose from dining-room to kitchen, from kitchen to pantry, wherever the smell of food leads him; pointing industriously, and whispering in any willing ear that that ham, sir, is the "pick and peer of swine p'dooce the country over, let the others be who they will." Mr. Wisk has unearthed from some mouldering portmanteau an enormous red velvet waistcoat with glass buttons, reaching halfway to his knees. He is proud of every inch of it, and struts gloriously when glances are cast toward it.

Who is in the parlor? Why, who but Mrs. Appleby and Mrs. Faulkner, both in holiday guise; both beaming with the same effulgence of joy that lights every face in this astonishing cottage? Here in the parlor also is the chaplain, holding in either hand Peppino and Jimmy Mather, who are straining like puppies on a leash.

"Keep still, youngsters!" commands the chaplain. "You nearly had me over that time. I'll tell you as soon as I see—ah! there they are!"

The mellow note of a Gabriel horn is heard; an automobile comes dashing down the road. It is John Aymer's new car, the "Son and Heir," and John Aymer is driving it. Beside him sits Mrs. Aymer, all smiles and roses and pink muslin, as becomes a matron of honor, in her arms the son and heir himself, *almost* big enough, she thinks, for a page, (but not quite, since every third step still brings his nose to the earth). And in the tonneau—are these two glorified spirits from another world, radiating light and joy and triumph? No! These are Pippin and Mary; she in white, with white roses in her pretty hat, he—but no one could ever tell what Pippin had on.

At sight of him the chaplain looses his hold of the two boys. They make one bolt for the door, fall out of it together, wriggle up again, and rush like a double whirlwind to the gate, rolling under the wheels of the car, which has fortunately come to a standstill.

Pippin and Mary spring down. Seeing them, the cottage becomes all eyes, guests, helpers, delegates, crowding to the windows. Most of the women begin to cry. Foolish creatures! What is the matter with them? And why, on the other hand, do most of the men suddenly develop head colds, and flourish handkerchiefs violently? Is it just because it is the common way at weddings? Or is it because these two young people have been patient, valiant, and steadfast, and now, after the long days of their waiting, there is something in their faces that brings the tear as well as the smile to all that see?

Here they are, hand in hand. Everybody is shouting, "Pippin! Pippin!" and crowding round him and Mary. The delegates rather think everybody has gone suddenly mad, but they don't feel quite sane themselves somehow. Something in the air, something in Pippin's face and voice, goes to their heads too, and they find themselves shaking hands with everybody, and echoing the chaplain's shout,

"Glorious! Glorious! Great guns, this is glorious!"

The time has come. The workers hurry in, breathless but demure, the guests smooth their dresses and settle with a solemn gesture.

"Dearly beloved—"

Then, the seven minutes over that have made Pippin and Mary man and wife, what a rush of kisses, slaps on the back, handshakings, good wishes, congratulations! Amid all which Mrs. Baxter and Mrs. Bailey nod to each other and steal out, beckoning to their aids. "Dish up!" the word passes round, low and emphatic. The Baxters fly, the Baileys flutter, Mr. Wisk and his pointing nose get in everybody's way and narrowly escape upsetting Mr. Baxter as he comes proudly into the dining-room, carrying his life's masterpiece, the wedding cake. Such a cake! Frosting as many inches deep as frosting can be; citron and angelica, plums and comfits—even Solomon in all his glory had no cake like this. Mr. Baxter, in his rapture hinting at this, is promptly rebuked by Mrs. Baxter, and told not to be profane, father; before the boy, too!

"Breakfast is served!" says Mr. Baxter, as if he were reading the Declaration of Independence.

In they all come, Pippin and Mary leading off, the guests following in a joyous mob, the delegates bringing up the rear, smiling twice as hard as when they came. Most extraordinary occasion! Must remember all this to tell the wife. Most extraordinary people!

They have all got round the table, no one knows how. Pippin and Mary are standing, still hand in hand, all heaven in their faces. Pippin looks round, and his eyes fill with tears like all the rest. He bows his head for a moment, his lips moving silently; then he looks up, and his smile lightens the room.

Once more his eyes make the circuit of the table, every face kindling from his glance. He lifts his hand, and makes his reverence like a young birch tree in the wind.

"Mary and folks," says Pippin; "seein' the Lord has dealt with us not accordin' to—I would say *my* sins, Mary not havin' any, nor I wouldn't presume likely any of you dandy folks—what I would say—shall we praise Him in song?"

He lifts his head; his voice breaks out, solemn, jubilant, triumphant.

"Praise God, from Whom all blessings flow!"